"What about the car?"

"I just told you, stolen."

"No," she said, patting his chest, "I mean really. How do we get rid of it?"

"The only thing I came up with is the ravine. Anything else meant someone new would have to know. The blanket was to cover the car after we pushed it over the edge."

Her head rocked side to side. "I don't know."

"Exactly. That's why we're not doing it. It can't work. I'm sorry." He stepped around her.

"Do it anyway," she said, hooking his elbow. "How can it hurt?"

"For one thing, it's another crime. Several, in fact."

Sneering, she flapped the back of her hand. "Maybe they won't look, and if they do, that's when we say I did it. The boys helped me. You never knew a thing."

"Diane, forget it."

"No." She pressed her fingers to his lips. "Jordan, we're screwed. I get it. I also know the consequences would be much worse for you. That's why you're the one who's staying out of it. Now, tell me what to do here, then *you* take the bottles to the river." Eyes wide, she leaned closer. "I'm saving my sons. If I have to kill people, I will."

He pulled her hand from his mouth. "Are you threatening *me*?"

"Get going. You can't be here if the police show up while this is going on."

A softening in her expression confused him. First time in years she'd wanted them to be a team, and it could land both of them in prison.

Praise for Rick Maloy

Evenings and Mournings

by

Rick Maloy

Evenings and Mournings

Cover Art by *Kristian Norris*

The Wild Rose Press, Inc.
PO Box 708
Adams Basin, NY 14410-0708
Visit us at www.thewildrosepress.com

Publishing History
First Mainstream General Edition, 2017
Print ISBN 978-1-5092-1726-7
Digital ISBN 978-1-5092-1727-4

Published in the United States of America

Dedication

To my four siblings,
protectors and fellow adventurers on some stormy seas

Acknowledgements

My biggest debt is to Steve Lipsitz who encouraged me to pursue the writing life. He was friend enough to trash the inaugural efforts and supportive enough to point me in valuable directions.

Workshop gurus Lynn Skapyak Harlin and Frank Green deserve credit for any "craft" that's found its way into my books. Each emphasized short fiction as the path to disciplined writing, and both turned weak efforts into learning opportunities.

My wife, Ann Marie, and published author, David Laird, were my test labs. Each plodded through the stream of chapters, unearthing bright spots and flaws. If this book is a pleasant reading experience, it's because of their countless hours and invaluable feedback.

A special bow to Ms. RJ Morris, co-founder of The Wild Rose Press, for accepting Evenings and Mournings, and for assigning Laura Kelly as editor. Their combined professionalism, timely engagement, and spot-on recommendations helped smooth this challenging process.

Finally, a salute to authors Sohrab Fracis and Parker Francis for offering publishable praise of my work.

Sincere apologies to all those I've missed.

Chapter 1

Jordan was innocent. He'd only received the kiss, but his aide's lips-to-lips greeting in front of Diane flipped her switch. Nostrils flared, lips pressed flat, his wife herded their two sons from the cocktail reception to the dais. Seated between the boys, she stared into nothing, the expression of a serial killer awaiting sentence. She had no right.

Prior to her overreaction, the event had been his. Months invested in conceiving and bankrolling the scheme, and this evening, the payoff. Honorable Jordan and Diane Carpenter, center stage at the Trenton banquet, feted as *The Arc*'s first-ever "Special Patrons of the Year."

Following his shortened speech, Jordan sidled toward Diane after each handshake, air kiss, or backslap. Every step found her unchanged: seated, gazing forward, and ignoring another perplexed well-wisher. At her chair, he gathered their sons in a standing semicircle behind her. This permitted some damage control, but if the prize were to retain any luster, he had no choice. She had to be removed.

****

Driving the family home, he exploited Diane's silence to prep for the blowup. She and eleven-year-old Kevin always used the house elevator from the garage, so he would take the stairs and waylay her when they

1

exited on the first floor. The prime complication would be keeping voices temperate enough that Kevin didn't unravel.

He pulled his Mercedes McLaren into the third bay and led their older son, Wyatt, through the finished basement. "Sorry, Dad. Late," Wyatt said, bumping him off balance as his son rushed past. Their lanky seventeen-year-old pounded up the steps, through the kitchen, and up the back staircase to the bedrooms.

Jordan arrived on the first floor well ahead of the lethargic elevator. He hurried down the hallway leading to the butler's pantry, wine room, and elevator. Ducking inside the wine room, one hand still on the doorknob, he listened until the mechanical droning stopped.

"Wyatt?" Kevin called as he thumped past and followed his brother's trail up the back staircase.

Relieved that Kevin wouldn't be there for the dustup, he waited a surprising number of seconds before Diane's high heels clicked an irregular beat in the hallway. With neither son in earshot, he slipped through the doorway and blocked her path. "We have a deal," he said, glowering down at her.

"Move." One hand shielding her eyes, she stopped after a single wobbly step.

He knew she'd had nothing to drink. "Are you ill?"

Eyes averted, she pressed her back against the wall and slid sideways past his offer of a hand.

"Diane, *you* are losing your goddamned mind."

She spun and stabbed a long fingernail into his chest. "Discretion," hissed through her clenched teeth. "That's our deal."

At least now he had confirmation why she'd

reneged on her promise to play the devoted spouse in public.

"Rutting pigs," she said in a hoarse whisper, her fists trembling near his face. "You and that...that cotillion cretin, Amanda. You're the one who's insane."

"What did you say?" In the eleven years since Diane had given him permission to "bed anyone you like," Amanda was the first she'd acknowledged by name, rather than refer to her as one of his "evenings."

Pain displaced passion on her face. "Get out of my way."

Ready for the catch, he followed her unsteady steps into the kitchen until she parked in a chair at the wide-plank farm table.

"Is it already too late?" she said, elbows on the table, fingertips of both hands stroking her forehead. "Are you two intimate, as they say?"

He pointed to the back staircase. "Voices carry."

"And at the office." The massaging fingers crawled to her temples. "How stupid can you be?"

He continued to point toward the stairs. "Shall I ask the boys to join us for this? Is it time they learned?"

"The longer you wait," she said, dropping her voice, "the worse it will be. End it now."

She'd waived her right to this opinion years ago, and discussing Amanda had the awkwardness of a sex talk with his grandmother. "Good chat, even though you don't know what you're talking about. I'll be in the wine room if you need anything."

"Haven't you had enough?" she said to his back.

He froze. Her question dangled like blundered testimony in his courtroom. Words he'd honed to perfection for just such a moment pushed against his lips but found no way out. His muscles relaxed enough to resume a casual gait into the wine room. "Tonight," he called through the door he'd left ajar, "we're Special Patrons, and I, for one, am going to celebrate."

Drifting along the racks, he stopped now and then to finger the neck of a dusty bottle. Each evoked a different aroma and flavor. Some, an occasion. All good until the day Kevin was born. "The Patroness is welcome to join me." He slid a Cabernet from its cradle, wiped the label, and studied it. Hawaii. His first million-dollar contingency fee. After years of failed attempts, Wyatt was conceived on that trip. The perfect choice if she had any interest. "How about a Chateau Montelena?"

Silence.

So clever. Now he'd have to chase down her rejection. "Yes or no?"

A side wall of the wine room followed the slant of the back staircase. It creaked as she climbed. Shortly afterward, three pairs of teenage feet thundered down the same steps. "Mom, Dad, we're going."

"Not so fast, Wyatt." He flicked off the wine room light, closed the door, and headed toward his son's voice. "To where?" he said, slapping the bottle of Chateau Montelena into his palm.

Dressed in a baseball hat, t-shirt, jeans, and sandals, Wyatt curved his lean frame backward in front of the open refrigerator and drank from a plastic jug of orange juice. "Graduation party," he said, swiping a forearm across his mouth. His friends, Tanner and Billy, who'd waited at the house during the award dinner, waved off his offer of the container.

"Use a glass," he barked at Wyatt. "And who's still

having graduation parties in the middle of July?"

"This girl I know," Billy said.

Tanner and Billy spent enough time at the Carpenters to qualify as legal squatters, but those four words were more than Jordan had heard from Billy in months.

"Dude?" Tanner said to Wyatt. Eyes wide, he tapped his watch and started the threesome toward the basement stairs. "Later, Judge C," he said over his shoulder.

"Hold it, men." Jordan pointed toward a bank of windows overlooking the deep ravine behind their house. Twitters of lightning backlit distant clouds. "Wyatt, we're supposed to get some nasty stuff tonight. Three weeks doesn't make you an expert. Pull over if it gets heavy, and use the flashers."

"Driver's Ed 1.0, Dad. Let's go, guys." Wyatt tugged the door shut and added to the rumble on the steps.

Chapter 2

Diane had waited outside Kevin's room, bristling as Jordan pontificated to the three teenagers. As soon as the boys left, she knocked softly on Kevin's door and entered. Dressed in his pajamas, he must have heard her and Jordan bickering because he paced beside the bed wringing his hands. "There's my good boy," she said, relaxing him with a smile. She flipped back the bedcovers. "In you go, honey. And what would you like tonight? *Goodnight, My Someone*?"

A grin popped onto his face. "Yeah." He scrambled to the far side of the bed, arms reaching for her.

Overnight it seemed, dark hairs had infiltrated the blond fuzz on his lip. With Nature's confusion already looming, she decided to end their nightly embrace while she sang him to sleep. Kneeling next to the bed, she took his hand in both of hers. "We're going to do it this way from now on, sweetie. Move closer to me. Head on the pillow. Now, close your eyes."

He did as she said, but his face didn't uncoil until she'd finished nearly the whole song. Before the end of a second chorus, he was asleep.

Tiptoeing toward the master bedroom, she glanced down the back staircase to the kitchen. Jordan stood motionless, facing her, arms at his side, the neck of a wine bottle in his grip. If his stance was a threat, it was toothless. He would never risk notoriety. And if he was trying to appear abject, a man deserving of gentle attention, that was even more absurd. She continued to their room and clicked the door shut.

Dressed for bed, she stepped slowly into the master bathroom and toward the mirror at her sink. Arms crossed in front, she hooked fingers under the spaghetti straps of the nightgown and slipped it over her head. Pointing an armpit at the glass, she walked fingertips around the edge of her right breast, stopping on a Band-Aid over the biopsy. Gentle pushes bumped a sore nugget side-to-side. Her frown leaned closer to the glass. "It begins?" she whispered to the reflection.

Chapter 3

Jordan stayed immobile in the kitchen until the master bedroom fell quiet. Too much evening still remained, so he dragged himself to the wine room. At a granite countertop he uncorked the Cabernet and emptied it into a long-necked decanter. Crystal gonged as he slid a deep-bowled glass from the hangers. "I'll be in my office," echoed during his pass through the two-story foyer. "As if anyone gives a shit," he added under his breath.

He shuffled past the carved alabaster mantel in the great room, to the mahogany door on the far wall. Inside the office, a leather desk chair sighed under his mass. Seat tipped back, he swirled the decanter and sniffed at the opening. Cherries, cinnamon, a hint of black currant. His mood softened as he poured. Pitching forward, he set the decanter and full glass next to a laptop and powered it up. In the search box, he typed *Judge Jordan Carpenter*.

Second item on the first page showed *Judge Jordan Carpenter and wife, Diane, named...* He clicked and leaned toward the screen.

The Arc, *formerly the Association for Retarded Citizens, announced today that Federal District Court Judge, Jordan Carpenter, and his wife, Diane, of Tewksbury, NJ, are its inaugural Special Patrons of the Year. Judge Carpenter, former senior partner of*

Wheaton, Weiss & Carpenter, was appointed to the Federal bench in 2009. The Carpenters have a son with Down syndrome and have given generous support to The Arc *for many years.*

"God almighty," he muttered, head shaking slowly, "million bucks a line." He lifted his feet onto the desk and dipped his nose into the bouquet of the wine. Despite tonight's cost, he congratulated himself for once again recognizing a sliver of daylight and charging through. Without question "Special Patrons of the Year" was a plastic honor, but it applied another sanitizing layer over his fortune and career.

His personal life needed a similar, single-stroke repair. He sipped the Cabernet. Superb. As often happened in these solitary moments, the wine's spreading warmth invited Diane into his reverie. Not the glaring zombie of recent times, but the Diane who once treasured him, who hooked a hand onto his elbow whenever they walked or stood together, who fell asleep in his lap after five minutes of TV.

Losing her had de-magnetized the compass of his life. Eleven years gone. Days had turned into months, into habits, into years, into tonight: celebrating alone in their mansion after arguing about the suitability of a mistress. Not just depressing, but debilitating. Fifty-eight was too old for a tomcat's life, and even with a permission slip from the wife, philandering never improved a biography. Devoted commitment did, like his first thirteen years with her, but tonight she seemed more irretrievable than ever.

She, too, may have sensed they'd arrived at a fork. Her first-ever objection, and by name. Jealousy would have been satisfying, but unlikely, not after so many years, so many others. But neither had she ever witnessed any of the women kiss him so affectionately. None were as young or had been Miss South Carolina.

Perhaps she saw Amanda as the first legitimate contender for second wife. If so, she was wrong. Marriage to her would soon devolve into an older man consuming a younger woman, eventually saddling her with the untidiness of his decline. He could admit to black marks in his life, but that would not be one of them.

Eleven years in Diane's exile, a longer sentence than if he had been guilty of "inviting death into their lives," which he had not. He'd done nothing more than suggest they were past the time for babies. Perhaps he'd floated that opinion more than once during the pregnancy before Kevin, but he'd never insisted on anything. Never a demand.

His fingers tightened around the glass. The "Special Patrons of the Year" should have been in their bedroom now, changing out of their evening clothes, chatting and laughing. The man's crooked smile would acknowledge the woman's unspoken, sparkle-eyed invitation. Each gaze would telegraph her desire to please, to reward, to claim. Skills he found more native to a mistress than a wife. He sipped the Chateau Montelena, swirled it around his mouth, and sorted options.

Chapter 4

Rain slapped the windshield of Wyatt's Volvo like a carwash. Chin hanging above the wheel, his head tick-tocked in sync with the wipers. "Brutal," he said to his two friends. Around them, light skittered and exploded, flashing quick-cut images of the few houses they passed. "How can it get like this so fast? Check it out, Tanner. No center line. Like driving on a lake." He glanced to his right and forced a smile. "Like Jesus."

"Jesus from Guatemala, maybe," Tanner said. "The real one wouldn't be caught dead in this four-door piece of shit. Might as well be tracking beaver in my mother's minivan."

"You're crazy," Wyatt said. "Car's awesome. Powerful. Lots of speakers." He bounced his butt in the seat. "Pretty comfortable. And since it's all they'd buy me, I love it."

"Pussy car," Tanner said.

"He's right, Wyatt," Billy said from the back seat. "Your family's got more money than Bill Gates. Could've at least sprung for a Beemer or something. Feel like I should have on shorts and shin guards."

"You could always get out and walk, Billy," Wyatt said to the rearview. When the back seat stayed quiet, he squinted through the windshield again. "Thought so. And what's wrong with them wanting me safe?"

"Dude," Tanner said, "you are *so* lame, and you,

11

shit-for-brains, where the hell's this party?"

"Stupid bitch, Jessica," Billy said, "she's not answering my texts, but I remember she said it's in a development next to Solberg airport. We gotta be close. Look for a bunch of cars along the street."

"Dude," Tanner said, "that airport has four exposures." He shoved Wyatt's shoulder. "Poor little guy's still struggling with spatial relationships."

"Suck it, Tanner," Billy said.

"Play nice, children." Wyatt flicked his gaze from Tanner to the mirror. "We'll be at the party soon. Maybe there'll be cake."

"Cake?" Tanner said. "Was hoping for pie."

Wyatt heard a fizzy pop in the back seat. A hand holding a can of beer appeared next to his face.

"Here you go, shithead," Billy said. "Maybe this'll give you some personality. How about you, Wyatt? Ready for one?"

"Toss that, you idiot. I could lose my license."

"Man, quit being an old woman," Billy said.

Wyatt's thumb pumped at the can hovering next to his head. "Either that goes or you do." He clicked the wipers to max speed. "Can't see a friggin' thing." Slurps and a long, breathy belch floated from behind him. Inside the car, the storm got loud. A can clunked onto the street before the car got quiet again.

"If you didn't like that," Tanner said, "you're *really* gonna hate this." He shifted in his seat. "Brought something special tonight. I'll share if you ask nice."

Crinkling sounds drew Wyatt's attention to a yawning zip-lock bag on Tanner's leg. "No way," he said. "Is that what I think it is?"

"Not being clairvoyant," Tanner said, "I'm going

to say, probably." He fished a cocktail straw from the bag and hunched forward. "Don't hit any bumps. This cost me a shitload."

"When the heck did you start with that?" Wyatt said.

A seatbelt unclicked behind him, and Billy's face poked between the bucket seats. "I'll try it."

Air sucked through Tanner's teeth. "Ooo, I don't know, Billy. The warning label said anyone who got less than a thousand on the SAT's could suffer permanent brain damage. Oh, and an oily discharge."

"Quit being a douche. Can I?"

"Let's see," Tanner said. "I got fifteen eighty-eight. Wyatt got fifteen thirty. And you—"

"Go fuck yourself. Where'd you get it?"

"Shut up. Gotta concentrate." Tanner pinched a small amount into the groove he'd made with his index finger and thumb. "Watch and learn." The cocaine disappeared in a sniffing sweep of the straw and lick of his fingers.

Wyatt followed everything, both horrified and impressed. He waited for Tanner to change somehow. "Do you feel it already?"

"Hey!" Hands pushing forward, Tanner braced his legs and slammed backward into the seat.

"Shit!" Hand on the horn, Wyatt stomped the brakes and jerked the wheel to the left. The blaring car began a slow spin. Girls' screams joined the jumble of noises. A wall of water wumped against the passenger side, up the windows, and across the windshield.

"No!" Tanner shouted. The baggie of cocaine spiraled a whiteout across the front seat.

Billy tumbled across the back seat and banged into

the door.

Outside the car, thuds.

The spinout ended with the Volvo still on the street, facing where they'd just come from.

Wyatt shoved the shift lever to *Park*. He popped his seat belt, opened the door, and stepped one leg out. Summer downpour clattered on the bill of his hat. "Aw, Jesus," he whispered. Along the edge of the lane they'd just left, three bodies sprawled on the road. Two squirmed near a churning stream of runoff. The third wasn't moving.

"Take off," Tanner hollered.

Wyatt stepped farther out of the car, dazed about what to do first.

Tanner stomped a foot onto the brake pedal and banged the shift lever into *Drive*. "Take off!" His hand latched onto Wyatt's belt.

Tires rolled.

"What are you doing?" Wyatt stretched his foot onto the brakes.

"Go!" Tanner tugged on the belt. Hunched over the lever, he yanked Wyatt's foot off the pedal.

Porch lights flicked on in two nearby houses.

"Quit it!" Wyatt hopped on one foot alongside the moving car and backhanded punches into Tanner's arm.

Tanner held fast. "Get in!"

He managed to press a foot onto the brake pedal. Battling to keep it there, his gaze bounced between Tanner, the downed bodies, and the houses.

Silhouettes charged through the doorway of one home. An umbrella wobbled down the front steps of the other.

"He said go!" Billy shouted.

Tanner yanked harder on the belt. "Not getting arrested! Go!"

Flash-bang lightning filled his eyes and ears. Up the road, headlights crested a rise and grew larger in the murk. "Go!" boomed at him from the front and back seats. Faster. Louder. The pressure on his belt dragged him back into the car. Voices and storm merged into a steady roar. Without him knowing how, the Volvo wiggled, steadied, and sped away.

Chapter 5

Frank Califano's boots pounded holes in the water sheeting down their driveway. "Hey," he shouted at the sedan speeding away.

His wife, Angie, trailed behind, panting "omigod" every few steps.

Through the windblown rain, he could make out three mounds on the street. One of the lumps rose to its hands and knees. "Aw, no," he said. A second bump rolled into a sitting position. The third stayed motionless. He'd gotten close enough to lose any hope. Their youngest daughter, Monica, was on her hands and knees. Her sisters, Beth and Torrie, had to be the other two.

Middle daughter, Beth, the girl sitting up, was the closest. "Daddy," she screeched when their eyes met. Hands on top of her head, jaw hanging slack, she tipped her face into the downpour. Her body shook, but she made no sound. When he dropped beside her onto one knee, she started to wail.

"What hurts?" His gaze darted to the other daughters. Monica was still on her hands and knees, but Torrie hadn't moved. "Beth, point if something hurts."

Eyes closed, she shook her head but continued howling into the storm.

"Omigod." Angie had caught up.

He stood and met his wife's rush by gripping her

shoulders. One hand let go, the other guided her toward the daughter getting to her feet. "Check Monica. I'll get Torrie. I think Beth's okay."

"God bless, honey." Angie kissed her fingertips and tapped them on Beth's cheek on the way past.

An approaching car slowed, swung wide of the activity, and stopped near Frank. The driver lowered the passenger window. "Need help?" he said, holding a phone in his free hand.

Frank cupped hands around his mouth and shuffled backward toward Torrie. "Call 911. Three people hurt. Address is six-one-one-nine Pulaski Road."

The man nodded. He tripped the emergency flashers, backed the car across both lanes, and trained his headlights on the scene.

Shielding his eyes from the high beams, Frank caught sight of a tilted umbrella approaching from the house across the street. His father's skinny legs hopped through the roiling runoff along the roadside.

"Frankie," his father said, panting as he hurried after him, "I was at the window, watching. Car came. How bad?"

"I don't know yet." He dropped to his knees beside Torrie.

Facedown on the road, her legs rocked in the gushing runoff. Like a sleeping newborn, loose fists rested on either side of her head. Droplets splashed on her face, dripped from her nose and chin. "Torrie?" He wiggled her wrist.

Nothing.

"Honey, can you hear me?"

Nothing.

He hesitated before laying a hand on her back.

His father's feet stopped next to him. "Frankie," he yelled over the rain drumming on his umbrella, "I said I'd drive them." Moaning with each labored breath, the old man stooped over Torrie. "They said no. Oh God, she's dead."

"She's not!" Frank snatched his father's shirt. "And don't let Angie hear you say that. If you can't help, go home."

"Sorry, Frankie. Sorry. Whatever you need."

Angie's voice drew close. "They're more scared than hurt, I think. How's my Torrie?"

"She's knocked out," Frank said. Angie's hands weighed on his shoulders as she peeked over.

"Dear God," she said, her voice trembling. Wedging between him and Pop, she dropped prone onto the street and inched her face close to Torrie's. Cradling her daughter's hand in both of hers, she pressed it to her lips. "Please, God, no."

"Be careful with her." He pushed to his feet, still hunched against the pelting rain. "Pop, keep the umbrella over them. I'm gonna check the others again, see what's keeping that ambulance."

The old man pressed his lips tight and nodded.

Hugging in the glare of the stranger's headlights, Beth and Monica stood in the middle of the road.

"Girls," Frank shouted as he approached, "can you walk?"

First Monica, then Beth, raised her head and nodded.

"Daddy," Monica said, her voice cracking, "is Torrie dead?"

"No. She's breathing. I don't know what's wrong, but she's not dead."

"She hasn't moved. Beth says she's dead."

"Well, she's not!" He checked both directions. "C'mon, get out of the road, onto the driveway. I'll bring some blankets down in the truck. You can sit in that until the ambulance comes." He held out his elbows. "Grab on. If anything hurts, we'll stop." Halting steps got the three of them off the street. "One second," he said. Bent at the waist, he lumbered to the stranger's car. The driver's window lowered as he neared.

"They're on their way," the man yelled, phone still held to his ear. The other hand shielded his face from sweeping rain. "They said I should stay on the line."

"They say how long?"

"Just said 'on their way'. Everybody okay?"

Frank shrugged and shook his head. Up the road, flashing lights and sirens joined the lightning and thunder. "This must be them." He backed away from the car. "Hey, thanks, buddy."

"I'll keep the headlights on you until they get here."

Frank trotted toward the driveway but detoured to Torrie. "Ambulance is almost here," he said, bending low enough to squeeze Angie's shoulder. "How's she doing?"

His father shook his head.

Angie's lips quivered. "She's cold."

"It's the rain," he said. "We're all cold. They'll have blankets in the ambulance. It's coming now. Hear it? Everything's gonna be all right."

Chapter 6

Wyatt's gaze seldom left the rearview. Hips raised off the seat, he dug into the front pocket of his jeans. "I'm calling 911." The phone glowed at the first tap of his thumb.

Tanner snatched it. "Mistake."

"Gimme that."

Billy gripped the top of the seats and pulled his face between them. "What just happened?"

"Dude, use your head," Tanner said. He twisted away and elbowed at Wyatt's grasping hand. "They'll see your number. Why would you call 911, say you saw girls hit, but not stop? Cops would be at your house before we are."

"Goddamn you!" He slammed a backhanded fist into Tanner's shoulder.

"Where's my coke?" Arm raised as a shield, Tanner pointed to the driver's side. "Went over by you somewhere."

Wyatt groped between the door and seat and found the empty baggie. He threw it at Tanner. "Oughta kill you." His foot eased off the gas. "I'm going back."

"With coke all over the car?" Tanner held the bag to the light. "Shit," he whispered. "And it's too late," he said, tossing the empty bag out the window. "People saw you leave. You're as fucked as you can get." He pointed forward. "Keep going, and stay off the big roads. We have to get back to your house before the cops put the word out."

"Someone tell me what happened?" Billy said, pitching the beers out the back window.

The car regained speed. Panting and rocking, Wyatt flicked his gaze between the road and the mirrors. "We hit some girls."

"I know that," Billy said. "I mean how?"

Wyatt licked his lips, swallowed hard. "The rain. I couldn't see. Then there they were. Right there. Three of them."

"They had to see your headlights," Billy said. "Don't you think?"

"Had their backs to us," Wyatt said. "Idiots were dancing, right in the middle of the road. When I turned the wheel, the tail went like this." His right elbow swung forward. "We must've slapped them with the side. Not real hard, I think. Kicking up all that water felt like it slowed us a lot." He shot a glance at each friend. "Think so?"

"Hell yeah," Billy said. "Had to, man. Flung me across the seat."

Tanner craned his face around Billy and squinted out the rear window. "Hard enough to flush half my graduation money down the toilet," he said, sounding distracted. "They're probably fine." He faced front, heel tapping on the floor, fingers snapping. "Dude, lights behind us. C'mon, fire this bitch up. Let's go."

"If they're fine, why were they all down?" Wyatt said, head shaking.

"Faster, goddammit." Tanner's fist beat on his bouncing knee.

"Even in all that noise, I heard crying. They're

hurt," he said, voice breaking.

"Hit the fucking gas!"

"Shoulda stayed." Wyatt rubbed his forehead, pounded the wheel. "How could I let—"

"Shut up! It's done." Tanner checked the rear window again. "And we're covered in coke. You'd test positive just from breathing. You had no choice. Maybe you'd like being cuffed in the back of a cruiser right now. Not me." He pointed to a side street. "Turn there."

"I don't think they're fine," Wyatt said, tears blurring the road. "Two of them were rolling around like, I dunno, cut worms or something."

"You missed it, asshole." Tanner slapped Wyatt's shoulder. "Pull over. Shaking like you're having a fucking seizure."

"Stop telling me what to do."

"Dude, you're dangerous. Pull over. I'm driving."

Wyatt swiped a wrist across each eye. "We have to go back."

"Maybe Tanner should drive," Billy said. "You're all over the place."

"Right there." Tanner pointed to a wide stretch of shoulder. "And easy on the brakes this time."

Soon as the car stopped, the driver's door flew open. Wyatt pitched to the pavement on hands and knees and threw up.

****

Headlights off, the Volvo snaked through the storm's tapering drizzle, up the long driveway to the Carpenter's house. Tanner braked to a stop in front of the garage doors. He fished out his phone and checked the face. "Not even 10:00 yet. I'm gonna call home, tell them I'm staying here tonight. You, too, Billy," he said to the rearview. "We can't drive this thing around anymore."

"Down a little more," Wyatt said. "Second one." He reached for the door-opener button.

"No." Tanner smacked his hand away. "Dude, pull your head out of your ass. There has to be dents in this thing. When The Judge goes to his car tomorrow, he could see them. It has to stay outside. Somewhere they won't show. And there's coke everywhere. Gotta clean it first."

At the far end of the garages, a slat-rail fence ran along the rim of the ravine. Wyatt pointed to it. "Against that?"

"Yeah. That'll work."

Tanner and Billy made their calls. The threesome climbed out of the car, entered the garage through a side door, and filed into the finished basement.

"I'll be right back," Wyatt said, shuffling toward the stairs.

Tanner trotted in front of him, palms raised. "Where are you going?"

"Gotta see Kevin. I'm busting."

"Kevin? Dude, did you whack your head? No, you are *not* going up there. Not tonight. What if your parents are up?" His hand fanned between the two of them. "What's all this white powder? Were we baking? Don't you think they'll ask? The Judge would crack you in ten seconds." He draped an arm around Wyatt's shoulder and guided him to a long wet-bar. "First we clean up, then we need a good story."

Wyatt flopped onto a bar stool and buried his face in his hands. "Should've stayed."

"I know this is bad," Billy said from beside him,

"but Jesus Christ, man. You sound like a bigger retard than your brother. Repeating the same—"

They crashed to the floor, Wyatt on top. He squeezed Billy's face with one hand and drew back a fist.

"Hey!" Tanner hooked Wyatt under the armpits and hoisted him before he could land a shot. "Assholes," he said in a strained whisper, "both of you." He shoved Wyatt backward as Billy scrambled to his feet. "That's it," he said, arms extended against each of them.

Wyatt paced a tight line, loud breaths whooshing through his nose, finger jabbing at Billy. "Once more and I'll beat your brains in."

Tanner's face pivoted between the two. When neither pursued the fight, he lowered his arms and shook his head at Billy. "Pretty stupid, dude." He faced Wyatt. "We done?"

Hands on his hips, he nodded but continued to glare.

"Sorry, man." Billy smoothed his long, brown hair behind his ears. He leaned around Tanner and held out an open hand. "Sorry."

Wyatt's slow slap ticked Billy's fingertips. He tottered back to the bar, sat on a stool, and covered his face. A hand touched his shoulder.

"What Billy meant was you're wrong about us staying there, and you better start believing it. Otherwise, you might do or say something stupid, and it could get us caught. Tonight wasn't your fault. Those girls shouldn't have been there. No way you could have missed them."

"If I was watching the road instead of you, maybe I

could've."

"I saw them the same time you did. Nothing you could do. They were lucky you didn't bust them with the grill. And those people in the houses? One of them had to call an ambulance. Help wasn't going to get there any faster if we stayed. Dude, c'mon."

A hand shook him by the shoulder, kept doing it until he uncovered his face. He caught a glimpse of Tanner and dropped his gaze back to the bar top.

"Think about it," Tanner said. "Was it going to do those girls any good if we got arrested? No. And it's too late anyway. Let it go. It's done."

A light slap on his cheek got Wyatt to look up.

"Are you a criminal?" Tanner said.

He shook his head.

"Course not. Eagle Scout. Key Club president. Started a volunteer program at the ARC. One of the finest kids this town's ever produced. And how about this? Did you want to hurt those girls?"

Another head shake.

"That's right. Will any of that matter to the cops? No. Are you gonna be a better person after getting butt-fucked in prison for ten years? No. But your life will be over, and that's what you have to be thinking about." Tanner eased onto the next stool and laid his forearms on the bar. Head down, he watched his fingernail click at a seam in the oak countertop. Without looking up, he pointed toward Billy. "You have to think about us, too, y'know."

"You? What about you?"

"Dude, I'm only seven weeks from Princeton." Tanner swiveled the stool toward Wyatt and tipped his head closer. "Nothing's messing that up." His nostrils widened. "Understand?"

"You're some piece of work," he said, shoving Tanner away. "Tell me how either one of you is in trouble. Whose car was it? Mine. Who was driving? Me. Who even knows you guys were in the car? Nobody. Once you take a shower and wash your clothes, you're clear. And who had the coke?" He stabbed a finger in Tanner's face. "*You.* Who used it in my car? *You.* Who was I stupid enough to protect? *You.* And you know what? I still don't know why."

Tanner's gaze darted to Billy and then off into the distance. Pushing the stool back onto two legs, he stroked fingers across his chin. "Yeah, you do know," he said, pitching the seat forward. "It's because the three of us have been best friends since first grade, and the only way Billy and I are really clean is if we turn you in. I wouldn't do that, and neither would he. Right?"

Billy shook his head. "NFW, man."

"So we're sticking together, and you're not getting caught." Tanner's fist floated in front of Wyatt's chest. "Friends forever."

After a short pause, he knocked a soft punch into the fist. "I guess."

Billy stretched across the bar and batted knuckles with each of them. "Yeah. That's what I'm talking about." He headed for a laptop near the video game setup. "Let's go online. Maybe there's something about the accident already."

"Hey, walnut brain," Tanner said, "searches can be traced. Why the hell would we be *googling* from this computer twenty minutes after the accident? Hangs a bulls-eye right on Wyatt. Don't do or say anything without asking first."

"Suck it, Tanner."

"Billy," Wyatt said, "he's right." Elbows on the bar, eyes closed, he massaged his neck. "I've heard The Judge talk about stuff like this. People catch themselves all the time. Conscience gets them, or they can't stay away from the investigation. Something the cops always look for. If we're really gonna do this, we all have to act like tonight never happened."

"More than that," Tanner said, making his way to the other side of the bar. "There's still the car. Even after we clean it, where'd the dents come from? You can't just ignore it." He peeled off his shirt, slapped it on the bar a few times, and turned on the water at the sink. "You still need a good story," he said, scrubbing his arms and face. "Something easy to remember. Where were you tonight? What'd you do? Who'd you see? Stuff like that, and it can't wait until morning."

"...best friends since first grade..." Waiting for his turn at the sink, Wyatt wondered how anyone could ask a best friend to go to jail for him.

Chapter 7

Dressed in a blue shirt and white boxers, Jordan whistled while he knotted his tie and wandered the master bedroom. He'd slept on his post-midnight decision to resuscitate life with Diane, and it still felt right. Treating this new marriage reclamation project like preparation for a trial put him in the zone. He'd rarely lost in court and wouldn't now. He even had the presence of mind to delay the campaign until morning. Last night she would have credited alcohol for any overtures.

Unhappy with the lengths, he stripped the necktie and started over. At a set of windows overlooking the bottom of the driveway, he paused his stroll, puzzled by Wyatt's Volvo being parked along the ravine fence instead of in the garage. A news reader on TV, his usual morning companion, redirected his attention by mentioning Readington Township, New Jersey and a family name he recognized, Califano. He quit whistling and ambled closer to the screen.

"Diane," he called to the bathroom, "something's happened to the Califanos. It's on TV."

Wearing a silk, mid-thigh nightgown, she hurried from the bathroom and joined him in front of the TV, toothbrush rolling in her mouth.

A peek at all of her dried his mouth. Without starvation or surgery, the years had matured her beauty from starlet to classic. Slender but decidedly female. Fine chestnut hair that swept her long neck after the slightest move.

"Around 9:30 last night in rural Whitehouse, New Jersey," the reporter said, "a hit-and-run driver mowed down Frank and Angela Califano's three teenage daughters, only steps from the safety of their home. That terrible moment, on the normally quiet country lane pictured behind me, has left the oldest of the girls, sixteen-year-old Torrie, fighting for her life in Overlook Hospital. Police are asking anyone with information to call the number shown at the bottom of the screen."

"You think it's the people from the farm stand?" he said.

She nodded and resumed pumping the toothbrush. That slight motion swayed her body enough to fire up memories of what he wanted back: mischievous laughter, snatched hugs, half-hearted refusals, and electric surrenders. During her stroll back toward the sink, bathroom brightness silhouetted her body under the creamy silk. The glossy fabric hitched with each glide of her long legs.

Absurd, he knew, but today had a bursting-from-the-chrysalis feel. He'd seen it in court after acquittals. Glum faces suddenly radiant. Peril replaced by prospects. If he could just make her enter that world. "Diane."

She faced him and stared.

"Would you?" Her face offered him a cryptic nothing. After so many years he needed at least a glimmer of understanding if not encouragement. "What's Wyatt's car doing in the driveway?"

She slid the toothbrush from her mouth, squinted,

and shrugged.

"No. I don't suppose you've been out yet." He'd made love to this magnificent woman countless times. All he wanted now was to touch her, even if only through words, but he was bumbling.

Head shaking, she started for the bathroom again.

"Wait." The words he intended held power only when whispered. He needed a venue demanding soft speech. Smiling bought time, but nothing clever filled the void. "Any chance?" he said, tilting his head toward the bed. "Special Patron of the Year and all?" *A life built on words, and I come up with that?*

She cupped a hand under her chin to catch a burst of white foam and disappeared toward the sinks. Swooshing tap water followed the sound of spitting. Her toothbrush dinked against the edge of the granite.

"Idiot," he whispered. Still, she did laugh. He couldn't remember the last time he'd made her do that. Unsure whether to be hopeful, he followed but hesitated in the doorway.

In front of the mirror, both hands brushed and shaped her hair. Frowning, she rested the hairbrush on the counter. Her left hand reached toward her right underarm.

The only way to begin was to begin. He strode in. "You—"

She flinched and clutched her chest. "God, Jordan, don't *do* that."

"Sorry. Thought you heard me."

Brush in hand again, she returned to primping. Her raised arms lifted the nightgown hem to an even more enticing height. "What do you want?" she said, pivoting to check her reflection from several angles.

He circled behind, locked eyes with the stare in the mirror, and reached for her shoulders.

"Don't be stupid." She pressed forward against the sink.

His hands fell away but stayed ready. "Diane, last night in the office. The Chateau Montelena. It made me remember Hawaii. Don't you miss that, too? All of it?" His fingertips touched her ribs. "Any of it?"

She clamped her elbows above his hands and pushed down. "Stop it."

Calmness in her tone encouraged him. "Please," he said, "we don't have forever. Things can change."

The expression in the mirror remained stony.

"Let's start over." He pulled one of her shoulders, pushed the other. "Today. Now."

Her hairbrush clattered in the sink. She spun and shoved him onto his heels. "Don't *touch* me!" she said, teeth bared. "You're diseased!"

Heat rushed to his face. Physical? Was she insane? His fingers curled into fists. He could have ended her. Right there. One hammering hand, non-stop into that harpy snarl. Swell those raging eyes shut. Batter her acid mouth into hamburger. No more rejections. No groundless condemnations. Ever. The abortion. The women. All her fault. And she knew it.

Chin high, she stood unblinking, offering no defense.

His size alone should have made her cower. Another possibility stunned him. She might truly be insane. Wanting him to do it. To hurt her. Kill her. Sacrifice herself to destroy the life he'd made for all of them. How long, he wondered, could such a plot have been incubating? Years of torture whirled in his head.

31

Sharing the bed. Always the alluring nightwear. Timing her showers when he could watch through the glass. Naked or lacey indecision in closets and at open dresser drawers. Dangled and denied sex as a suicide weapon. The mad, patient genius of it terrified him, but if that was her plan, he would disappoint. Open hands raised high, he tottered from the room.

In the bedroom, trembling fingers couldn't master a shirt button. A hurled cufflink gouged plaster from above their headboard.

"Jordan?"

His imagination probably, but her tone hinted of remorse and drew him back to the bathroom.

Facing the mirror, she flipped at her bangs with the brush and her fingers. "Jor—Ah, there you are. Now that we're finished with that—forever, I hope—I need you to do something for me."

"Drop dead," he said, turning back to the bedroom.

"How lovely. It's for Kevin, actually," she said, her voice close behind him. "I'm very late, and he's probably frantic for his Froot Loops by now. Thank you, and please shut our door."

The pocket door between the hallway and bathroom grumbled in its track.

"Does he take milk on it?" he said, facing the closed door.

She rolled it open enough that her face filled the gap. "He's eleven," she said, lips pulled into a tiny smile. "You don't know by now?"

"Answer the goddamn question."

"A little," echoed from behind the closed door.

Jordan knocked on Kevin's door. He opened it and peeked around the edge.

Already dressed, Kevin stood in the middle of the room. The smile he'd readied for someone else collapsed.

His son's guileless disappointment deflated Jordan's hopes for the day even lower. He dropped to one knee and stretched his arms wide. "G'morning, big shot. Ready for some breakfast?"

Almond eyes sparkled in Kevin's smiling face, an expression that said, *"Hey, maybe I was wrong about you."*

He wasn't. Kevin's birth marked the day Diane ended their marriage, and unfair as Jordan knew it was, the blameless boy lived every day under that shadow.

Stumpy legs pounding in place, Kevin leaned forward and rushed into the waiting hug. "Froot Loops?"

"Don't strangle me for heaven sake." He pried out of Kevin's powerful grip and struggled to his feet in stages. Groaning, he massaged his knees and back. "I'm afraid fifty-eight's a little too old for floor time, Kev. I think we'll do these 'good mornings' standing up from now on."

"Don't be old," he said, head shaking. "You'll die."

"Well, not *that* old yet. Just too old for floor time."

Kevin's face pulled tight with concentration, then broke into delight. "Froot Loops!"

"Froot Loops it is, my good man." He smiled and held out a hand. "This way, please." Together, they hopped down the back staircase to the kitchen, one tread at a time. "Alley," from him, "Oop," from Kevin, who added a croaking giggle with each landing. For the first time, he noticed a change in Kevin's voice. Eleven

33

for a boy seemed young, but if puberty was afoot, that could have been another reason Diane was behaving more stressed than usual lately.

In the kitchen, Kevin dashed to a low cupboard and hauled out colored craft paper and a plastic bag of thick crayons. Kneeling on a chair at the table, he organized everything and began scribbling.

Slow feet scuffed on the basement steps and paused at the top. The door cracked open before swinging wide. Rubbing a hand across his eyes, Wyatt eased into the kitchen. "Morning, Dad. Hey, Kevin."

"Wyatt." Kevin waved a yellow paper with blue squiggles. "Trees."

"Wow. A whole forest. Good job."

"G'morning, son." Jordan's attention flipped between Wyatt and the bowl while he poured milk on the cereal. "You look like you just woke up. Did you sleep down there?"

"Froot Loops, Wyatt." Kevin held out a spoon and pumped his legs so hard his backside bounced off the seat.

"That's great, buddy. Gonna have your favorite." Wyatt mussed his brother's close-cropped hair on the way to the refrigerator. "Tanner and Billy stayed over. Didn't want to mess up any rooms. We were fine down there. Newspaper here yet?"

Jordan laughed. "Newspaper? Going retro in your old age?"

"Billy wants it. He likes the comics."

"It's still in the driveway if it's here. Why don't you go look?" He set the bowl in front of Kevin. "And speaking of the driveway, why's your car out there? Had to be teeming when you got home."

"Pretty much stopped by then." Wyatt sipped from a glass of juice and carried the container toward the basement door.

"Wyatt, the newspaper?"

"I'm in bare feet."

"Put some shoes on."

"Why can't I do it later?"

"First, because I asked you to do it now. Second, because there was a hit-and-run in Readington last night, and I'd like to read about it. Your mom thinks it's the Califanos from the farm stand.

"It is," Wyatt said, staring into his juice. "We saw it last night on, y'know, TV."

"Do you know the girl?"

"Torrie. Yeah." Wyatt shifted his feet, glanced down both hallways and up the stairs. "She's a junior."

"The newscaster said it's pretty serious. Amazing, huh? Some guy hits three girls and just drives away."

"Really stinks." Wyatt sipped his drink and walked past the breakfast table to the bank of windows overlooking the ravine. Topping off his glass, he took another small swallow. "How do they know it was a guy? Someone see him?"

"Busted."

"What?" Wyatt's face snapped toward him.

"Caught me. Presenting a fact not in evidence. No, all they said was her injuries are life threatening. Nothing about the driver or the other two girls. Knowing how TV focuses on gore, that has to mean they're fine."

First one, then two sets of footsteps clomped up the basement stairs.

"Yeah, probably," Wyatt said, gazing at the

basement door.

A duet of "G'morning, Judge C," floated through the open doorway from the basement.

"Well, well, if it isn't Hunterdon High's gift to Princeton and Raritan Community College. Good morning, men." One eye lowered, his gaze swung from Tanner, to Billy, and settled on Wyatt. "Hard night last night, fellas?"

"Nah." Wyatt flapped a hand. "We blew off the party. Got back here by 9:30 and played a bunch of video games. Guys," he said, bobbing his head toward his father, "my dad heard about Torrie."

"Couldn't have been 9:30," Jordan said. "Aw, Kevin." He picked Froot Loops from the floor on his way to the breakfast table and blew on the pastel bits before dropping them back in the bowl. "Can't you be a little neater? And we use napkins, not sleeves. Remember?"

Kevin swiped his mouth with a paper napkin and grinned up at him.

"Good man." He strolled back toward the teenagers, now spaced in a semi-circle around the far end of the center island. "As I said, it had to be later than 9:30. The basement was dark when I put my briefcase in the car at 9:33. I remember seeing that on the dash clock."

Faces blank, the boys' gazes flicked from one to another. Jordan had seen that deflection too often to mistake the meaning.

"That's probably my fault, Judge C," Tanner said. "I'm too lazy to change for *Daylight Savings.* Must have given one of these guys the wrong time." His fingers beeped buttons along the edge of his watch.

"There. That won't happen again, at least not until November." He slapped Wyatt's arm. "So, what about Torrie Califano?"

"Oh, yeah. It was on TV again this morning. They said she's in pretty bad shape. Didn't say about the sisters. And nothing about the car or the driver. We'll google it after breakfast." Wyatt swept his arm around the kitchen. "Help yourselves."

Jordan checked the oven clock. "Forget the paper, Wyatt. I have to go. Maybe I'll catch more on the radio." Returning to his bedroom, he glanced at the closed bathroom door and grabbed his suit jacket from the bed. "Running late, my ass," he muttered on his way into the hall. His first foot strike on the back staircase hushed three whispers in the kitchen. The only clear snippet he'd caught was, "First thing, genius. Messed up on the first thing."

"Dissension among the ranks, men?" Jordan said, stepping off the bottom tread.

"No way," they said in unison.

"Don't do anything I wouldn't do, boys." He scooped his keys from the built-in desk and smiled at them from the door to the basement. Something was afoot with those three.

Chapter 8

Hands pumped and shook Frank's shoulders. "Honey, wake up." It was Angie's voice, the one she used at 3:00 AM when he was asleep in front of an infomercial. Eyelids blinking, he rubbed fingers across his face and left them hanging on his cheeks. His shoulders slumped when his gaze found Torrie. Tubes and wires poked from her arms, bandaged head, and hospital nightgown

Angie pressed a soft kiss onto his hair. "Doctor's here, honey. He wants to talk to us."

"How is she?"

"He's gonna tell us."

Frank peeked around Angie to see a doctor and nurse busying themselves with Torrie. He gripped the chair, pulled his knees up as far as his paunch permitted, and rocked onto his feet. Arms hooked around each other, he and Angie approached the bed.

The doctor's thumb stretched Torrie's lid upward. An instrument held next to his nose shined light into her eye. "Be with you folks in juuuuust a second." He clicked off the light, gave the nurse some instructions, and extended a hand for them to shake. "Dr. David Michelson, resident in Neuroscience." He tilted his head toward the bed. "I'm very sorry about your daughter, but rest assured we're doing everything we can for her. And if you want some backhanded good news, you're lucky this happened so near to us. This facility is probably the best in the country."

"She gonna be okay?" Frank said.

The doctor wrinkled his nose and rocked his head. "Not out of the woods yet," he said like sharing a secret, "but she is stable. That's a start."

"Why doesn't she move, or blink, or anything," Angie said. She patted the bed. "I been here every second since they let me in. Talked to her all night. Rubbed her hand. Brushed her cheek. Nothing. She's—"

Dr. Michelson raised his palm. "Someone should have explained. She's in what's called an induced coma. It's a precaution we often take in cases like this. That lets the body have nothing to do but heal. It also keeps the patient from moving in a harmful way, or accidentally removing the IV's or monitor wires."

"We're strong people," Frank said. "Be straight. When she's better, will she be, y'know?" He tapped the side of his head.

"I can't answer that yet. What I can tell you, though, is that it was a pretty nasty whack, in a lucky sort of way, if that makes any sense." He side-stepped to the top of the bed. "There's bruising on her left hip and shoulder," he said, pointing to each spot, "so she must have been sideways. Her torso took the brunt of the impact, but her head struck something. My guess would be a car window. There's only a small break in the skin, and hitting the pavement would have torn it badly, so we think she must have landed in the water. That's the lucky part." He pointed to a tube disappearing behind Torrie's neck. "The bad part is that the blow was traumatic enough to cause swelling inside

39

the skull. First thing we did last night was install a shunt to relieve pressure and prevent further damage to the brain."

Angie's fingernails gripped into the soft flesh over Frank's belt. "There's brain damage?"

"We've been taking readings, but they don't always give a clear picture. We'll have to see how she is after the coma. I'm sorry. I wish I could be more specific."

"How long?" Frank said.

"A week. Probably less." The doctor tapped his watch. "I'm sorry, folks, but I have to get on with my rounds. The nurses can probably answer any questions, but if not, I'll see you either tonight or tomorrow. In the meantime, there's not much for you to do except hold her hand and be positive." He patted each on the shoulder as he left the room.

Not five seconds later, daughters Beth and Monica walked in dressed and ready to be discharged.

"We were listening," Monica said, her gaze fixed on Torrie. Legs stiff, she walked into Angie's open arms but didn't complete the hug. Both bandaged hands stuck straight out behind her mother.

"Aw, your poor hands, and your chin," Angie said, planting kisses on her youngest daughter's cheek. She yanked Beth into the huddle. "And Beth, honey, you were so lucky. You have the best guardian angel. Hope you said a nice prayer to thank her."

Beth ducked in for a kiss and short hug before rushing to Frank. She wrapped her arms around most of his middle. "Daddy, he said brain damage." Her squeeze tightened.

Monica nudged Beth aside. "Daddy, *please* make

her shut up." She stood on tiptoes, and pulled him down for a kiss on his cheek. "She's been like all doom and stuff since last night. Torrie's going to be fine. Tell her."

"You heard the doctor," he said. "For now? We hope." He lowered one eyelid and nodded. "But y'know, you may have a good idea."

"I *only* have good ideas," Monica said, "but, um, which one are you talking about?"

"Telling Torrie she's gonna be okay."

Monica pointed to Beth. "I meant you should tell the drama queen."

"It's okay, honey," he said to Beth, his thumb bobbing at Monica. "She's just trying to look tough. We're all afraid, but I kinda like telling Torrie she's gonna be okay. C'mere." He herded the girls to the side of the bed across from Angie, who was in constant motion, fussing with bed linens, brushing her fingers on the girl's arms, legs, and cheek, all the while mumbling or moaning.

He leaned over the bedrail and kissed Torrie on the forehead. "G'morning, honey. Beth and Monica are here."

"Hey, big sister."

"Hi, Torrie."

Seconds passed while the three of them stood silent, staring at the peaceful face in the bonnet of bandages. He rubbed a hand over his nose and mouth. "You girls start. I gotta get some coffee. Still half asleep. Want some, Angie?"

"I'll go." Angie picked her purse off the nightstand, clicked her wallet open, and pinched through some paper money. "Girls, anything?"

"No, thanks," each said in a small voice.

"Cheer up your father while I'm gone. This has been very hard for him." She squeezed and patted Torrie's toes on the way out.

He turned his back to the bed and laid a thick hand on each daughter's shoulder. "I know it's pretty scary seeing her like this," he whispered, "but we gotta deal with it. You were all in the accident last night, so let's do this. Beth, you tell Torrie how you're doing today. Then you go, Monica. Might make everyone feel, y'know, more normal. Whadaya say?"

Beth backed away. "You first, Mon."

"Really?" Monica wrinkled her nose. "So I should just, like, talk to her?" Her eyebrows rose. "Okay, I guess." She took a big breath and inched to the edge of the bed. "Hi, Torrie. It's Monica. I'd ask how you are, but I already know. Doctor says it's gonna be like a week before you're better. Just wanted to let you know I'm okay." After a long pause, she sneaked a bandaged hand under each eye and cleared her throat. "Well, actually, I'm not *totally* okay. My butt's killing me, and my palms are like all shredded and stuff. Oh, and I have a chin like Jay Leno. But everything'll be good in a couple days. Like you, I hope." Teary-eyed, she turned to Frank, shook her head, and shrugged.

He nodded and mouthed, "Keep going."

Facing Torrie again, Monica patted the bedrail. She giggled and leaned forward. "Omigod, Torrie, you should see what Beth and I have on. The cops took our clothes for tests. Gonna check for like paint and stuff. Just like a CSI episode. Could anything be more awesome? Anyway, so get this, Daddy called PopPop and told him to go into our rooms and bring stuff here."

She bent closer. "Torrie," she said in a hush, "he had to bring like bras and panties. Did you hear me? PopPop handled our underwear. How totally sick is that?"

Frank glanced down at Beth, who'd tented a hand over her smile.

"He brought me jeans," Monica said, "which would be okay most of the time, but they're too tight. I can barely move without like totally screaming. Know how you're always saying I have the biggest thirteen-year-old butt in the history of the world? Well, it came in handy last night. I musta been doing like this…" She crouched and covered her head. "Because that's the only place the car hit me. I checked it in the mirror this morning. *Gross*. All blue and green and yellow and stuff. Can't even think about sitting down. I actually peed in the shower this morning."

"Monica! I was in there right after you." Beth buried her face in Frank's side.

The three of them were laughing when Angie showed up holding two capped cups. Face blank, she shoved a cup at him and returned to her bedside station. Her unopened coffee banged onto a rolling tray table. Bed covers got a fresh snapping and smoothing as her gaze swept the three of them. "Wouldn't it be nice if she could be in on your jokes?" Eyes full of tears, she bent forward until her hands and lips touched Torrie's fingers

"Aw, Angie, don't." He circled the foot of the bed. "It may even be good for her to hear some laughs. Doctor said be positive, right?" He slid his arms under hers, eased her up from the bed and into a twisting hug. "C'mon. No more of this. You'll make the girls think they did something wrong. They didn't." He kissed her on top of the head and leaned back. "Let's agree," he whispered, "no more crying in front of her." When Angie didn't look at him, he gave her shoulders a little shake. "C'mon, Babe, probably better for all of us. Whadaya say?"

She nodded, but he knew she wouldn't be able to do it. Bad as the moment was, he understood this was only the beginning.

Chapter 9

Jordan clicked his seat belt, started the engine of his Mercedes McLaren, and grasped the shift lever. The ring of an incoming call popped *Office* onto the dash display. "Can't even get out of the damn garage." He poked the answer button on the steering wheel. "Judge Carpenter speaking."

"Well, good morning, Your Honor."

Amanda's Charleston accent poured into his ear like a warm whisper, conjured the taste of her lipstick and scent of her hair, her hypnotic beauty in candlelight, head deep in a pillow, crooked smile, green eyes glittering, inviting, insisting. "And good morning to you," he said.

"You asked me to call and remind—"

"Thank you, I have it." He patted the briefcase sitting on the passenger seat. "But you continue to be a treasure."

She answered with a soft laugh.

The rearview camera displayed nothing unusual on the dashboard screen, so he dropped the car into reverse and glided backward. Grit on the driveway crackled as he spun the wheel and accelerated into the expansive turnaround. "I should be there in about—" Sensor beeps raced from calm to manic. He'd already bashed into something before his foot found the brakes.

"Jesus *Christ*!" he said, seeing Wyatt's Volvo in

the rearview.

"Jordan, are you all right?"

The heel of his hand bounced off the steering wheel. "Idiot!"

"Jordan, answer me."

"Fine." He squeezed his forehead so hard it hurt. "Amanda, I'm gonna be late. Get postponements for everything this morning. I'll speak with you later." He ended the call and pulled the car forward a few feet. Standing on the driveway, he used two hands to slam the car door. Eyes closed, hands clasped behind his neck, he wandered away from the damage, grumbling non-words. On one of his pivots, he caught sight of Wyatt in the doorway between the garage and basement. He crooked a finger at his son.

Chin on his chest, Wyatt stepped barefooted onto the garage floor.

"Why did we give you a space in the garage?"

Wyatt trudged toward him but didn't answer.

"So something like this wouldn't happen!"

"Sorry. Is it bad?"

"Haven't looked yet, but whatever it is, I should make you pay." He pantomimed a strangling. "Why didn't you use the damn garage?" His arm swung back to the Volvo. "And why there? Look at it. No one could even get out the passenger side the way you parked it. Did one of you nitwits have to climb over the console?"

Dressed in a tennis outfit, Diane appeared from the garage. She circled toward the rear of the Mercedes, fingers pressed to her lips. "Yikes. So this is what I heard."

He faced her, but jabbed a finger in Wyatt's direction. "I was on an important phone call. There's never anything back here, but today, because he's irresponsible, thousands of dollars and my valuable time are shot to hell."

A corner of her mouth curled up. "He didn't do anything. You're just embarrassed. And it's only money."

She never missed a chance to leave him on the outside, or turn him into the villain. "And you say 'only money' like you have a clue as to how it's made." In angry moments like this, he often credited money as the reason she stayed. Except half would still be more than she could ever spend. The real reason still mystified.

Her face reddened and tightened. "Are you home this evening? I may have to discuss something with you."

"Spare me the dramatics. Just say it." He caught Wyatt eyeing them.

Her gaze also found their son before sliding back to him. "Are you home tonight or not?"

Amanda's voice had already lit the burner for his evening. Excellent food and wine, mutual admiration, laughter, and great sex. "Probably not."

"Stupid me," she said, opening the driver's door of her Range Rover. "Wyatt, don't forget you have Kevin until Blanche gets here." Her SUV backed out of the garage, sped over the stone bridge, and down the driveway.

"Dammit," Jordan said, kicking in the direction of her escape, "should've taken her car. I can't drive mine looking like this." He plodded to the rear of the Mercedes. On the way, he pointed to the dented Volvo. "Try your door. Better yet, get your keys. I want that moved. Now." He bent over the Mercedes' crumpled trunk lid and ran fingers across splintered light covers. "Son of a *bitch*. Five thousand if it's a penny."

"Dad?" Wyatt's toes hung over the edge of the concrete. "I was going to drive Tanner and Billy home after breakfast. No point moving it now."

"Y'know, you spend more time telling me why you can't do something than it would take to do it. Get your goddamn keys."

Soon after his son disappeared, the door for the Volvo's garage rolled up. Wyatt jogged to his car and started it. He shifted into reverse, pulled around the Mercedes, but had to abort trying to back the car into the garage.

"Hold it," Jordan hollered. "One accident this morning's enough. What are you doing? Pull it in forward, for God's sake." As soon as Wyatt jockeyed the car into the proper position, Jordan noticed the dents on the passenger side. He pumped a finger at the three depressions. "Hoho. So that's it. Stop!"

Wyatt slid from the car and dragged both hands into his hair. Short, tottering strides brought him closer to Jordan.

"All this so you could hide a dinky accident from me?" He pointed to the shallow dents in the rear door and fender. "Are you kidding? You have to know I wouldn't care about something like this. Your mother's right. As long as nobody's hurt, it's only money."

Wyatt's eyelids closed. His lips compressed, chin trembled.

"What the hell? You're going to cry now?"

A trickle leaked from each of his son's eyes.

"What's up with you? I haven't seen you cry since tee-ball." He rested one hand on his son's shoulder, the other rubbed the boy's hair. "Hey, forget it," he said, stroking a bit harder. "It's nothing. I overreacted."

"Dad, last night." Wyatt's voice broke. "Those girls. It was me."

The hand on Wyatt's head tightened around a clump of hair. "What? Wait." His son's words replayed but made no sense. "Say again. You what?"

"It was me. I hit the Califano girls. What am I gonna do?" Tears flowed faster.

He dropped both arms from his son, stepped away, and revisited the dents in the Volvo. Each was a young girl, slammed into the darkness, stunned, in pain, terrified. And abandoned. His All-American son, a coward, a felon. "Why didn't you stop?"

"I don't know."

"Were you drunk?"

"No."

"Drugs?"

"No," he said after a pause.

That incriminating hesitation. Thoughts swimming, he rushed at Wyatt, snatched two fistfuls of shirt, and hiked him onto tiptoes. "Tell me the truth!"

"Dad, I swear." He hung limp, unresisting, eyes closed.

"How could you not stop? Look at me!"

Watery eyes met his. "I panicked. I just panicked, okay?"

"Not okay." A solid shove banged Wyatt against the Volvo. He stalked after his son, finger stabbing. "One more time. Why did you leave?"

"Judge Carpenter," Tanner called from the garage, "it's my fault." First he, then Billy, approached from the shadows. "Wyatt's protecting me."

The prospect of a substitute perpetrator introduced a rush of hope. "Were you driving?"

Tanner shook his head. "I was texting someone and stuck the phone in front of Wyatt's face so he could read it. He kept pushing it away, but I thought it was funny, so I kept pushing it back. He couldn't see the girls on the road because of what I was doing. It was my fault."

"Dad, that's not true."

"Wyatt." Tanner's gaze darted to Jordan. "I already said it was my fault."

"Dad, there was cocaine in the car. And beer."

Focus became a challenge. If Saint Wyatt had secrets, no life could be understood. "Jesus Christ," he whispered at the sight of Blanche's ancient Dodge Dart billowing exhaust on its way up the driveway. Last thing they needed was for anyone else getting involved. "Inside, all of you." He led them through the basement and up the stairs.

Still at the breakfast table and kneeling on his chair, Kevin waved a new drawing. "Dad, a bear." He held the blue paper with red swirls in front of his face. From behind the picture, his growl mixed with a laugh.

"Not now, Kevin."

"Wyatt, a bear."

Jordan took a long stride toward Kevin. "I said not now!"

The boy's chair tipped sideways onto two legs. Slapping and grasping at the table's edge, Kevin fixed his startled gaze on Jordan during a slow motion topple that landed him on his rump.

"Dad, he didn't do anything." Wyatt raced to his brother and helped him to his feet. "You're fine."

The elevator motor engaged, mixing the housekeeper's ceaseless singing with the electric hum.

Wyatt righted Kevin's chair and patted the seat. "C'mon back up here. You're fine." He smiled and rubbed his brother's hair. "Lucky you landed on that big backside, huh?"

Mouth small, Kevin nodded, his teary gaze still locked on his father.

"Take everyone into my office, Wyatt. I'll be right there." He dropped to one knee and watched over his shoulder as the three boys trooped down the long hallway. "I'm sorry," he said to Kevin. "I'm not mad at you."

"You yelled," he said, new tears forming.

"That was a mistake, and I'm sorry. You're a good boy." *And one without a hidden life.*

"Mad at Wyatt?" Kevin said, wiping hands across his wet cheeks.

"Yes." Hearing the elevator drone to a stop meant this chat was over.

"Why?"

"You wouldn't understand."

Blanche's songless singing approached the kitchen. Lugging a canvas tote bag, she tottered into the room. "I thought that was you in the driveway. G'morning, Judge. Don't get to see much of you."

"Hello, Blanche." He puffed and groaned as he struggled to his feet.

"Too old for floor time, Dad."

He studied Kevin's face and wondered how much capacity existed behind it.

"If you're leaving soon, Judge, be careful of my car. Had to park kinda funny today because of your

51

cars." She walked into the pantry next to the refrigerator and stowed her bag on a shelf. "Whoee. Wasn't that some storm last night?"

"Huh? Yes. Terrible night," he said, backing out of the kitchen, his gaze still on Kevin. "Blanche, I'll be in my office. If the phone rings, unless it's Mrs. Carpenter, please take a message."

"Dad, no yelling at Wyatt," Kevin said, shaking his head. "No yelling."

"Right," he said, knowing there was little chance of that.

Chapter 10

Long, slow strides carried Detective Sergeant Len Moseley through the precinct. Today's scenic drive to work, coupled with thoughts of his impending retirement, had blunted his 24/7 grouchiness. Wary faces and delayed smiles met his waves and nods as he ambled toward his desk. His good mood dropped a notch when he noticed a female leaning a shoulder against the doorjamb of Captain Garner's office.

Only the back half of the tall woman showed from his angle, but he recognized Connie Dalton. Sandy hair clamped into a shaggy bundle at the back of her head, shoulders back, poking out those melons, laughing inside because the captain had to pretend he didn't notice them. Polished fingernails scratched the wood trim while she ran her mouth at Garner. A bent knee tightened cream slacks around her hips. No panty line.

Cops in thongs. Get me out of here. He shook his head and continued to shake it even after she pushed away from the frame and glanced his way.

"He's here now," she said into the office. "Yes sir, I'll tell him." She dipped her head and smiled as she hurried by. "Captain wants to see you."

He slowed to a stop and watched her leave. Down the corridor. Past the elevator doors. Around a corner. She was still in his head when he stuck his face into the captain's open doorway. "Morning, Captain. I'm not on for twenty minutes. Okay if I get some coffee first?"

"Ain't a clubhouse, Moseley. You're here, you're working." He spun his hand in a tight circle. "Let's go. Chop chop."

"Do I need something to write on," he said, middle finger scratching his chin, "or is this a friendly chat?"

"Just get in here."

Inside the office, he stood in front of the desk, feet wide, hands clasped behind his back.

The captain scowled and flapped a hand toward a nearby chair. "Cut the crap. Sit down."

He dropped into a molded plastic chair, slid into a slouch, and crossed his ankles. "Ever notice how beautiful it is the day after a big storm, Captain? Came in today along the Rockaway River. That little puddle was roaring. Air still smelled like poplar and pine from all the snapped limbs." His fingers danced across the air. "Sun sparkling on the wet leaves. All the colors—"

"Enough." The captain shoved an open palm at him. "Gonna be a poet in retirement, Moseley, or just being a jackass who's trying to waste twenty of my minutes?"

He smiled, twisting deeper into the chair. "No clue what I'm gonna do when I retire, Captain. Probably should work on it, though. Forty-seven more days."

"Well, do it on your own time." He spun a skinny manila folder across the desk. "I'm giving you the Califano hit-and-run. You and Dalton."

Moseley stretched for the file. "And that would be?"

"The three teenage girls?" Captain Garner's eyes widened. "The sisters?"

Moseley shook his head and closed the file.

"Got hit last night on Pulaski Road?"

He continued to shake his head.

"Do you watch TV, Moseley? Listen to the radio?"

"Little as possible, and you can forget Dalton. I'm not working with her."

"That's not your call."

"We don't need her, Captain. Hit-and-run? Piece of cake. I'll do this solo until Karcher comes back."

"We work in pairs, Moseley. You know that. And Karcher's disability has been extended for at least—"

"What?" Moseley snapped upright in the chair.

Garner's brow creased. "You didn't know? You've been partners for six years, for God's sake. Don't you talk?"

"No."

The captain lowered one eyelid. "Something I should know?"

"Nope." He eased against the backrest. "The job's the job. My life is mine."

"Sure there's nothing you want to tell me?"

With forty-seven days left? "Hundred percent."

"Okay," the captain said, ending their brief staring contest, "for your remaining time, Dalton's your partner." He leaned back in his chair, fingers knitted together on his stomach. "She asked special for you, soon as she heard about Karcher being out. I thought this would be a good case to try it. She learns something, and you coast out of here on an easy one."

"Get someone else, Captain."

"What the hell's your problem?"

"She's not right for the job. Something happens out there, she'd be useless."

The captain busted out a laugh. "This is a hit-and-

55

run, for crissake. What the hell can happen? And I already told her, so deal with it."

He scraped a finger at an itch on the edge of his eye. "Why isn't she here for this briefing?"

"You're over fifty," the captain said, lurching forward in his chair, "and you still think that's funny? That's the second time."

His hand froze mid-scratch. "What?"

"You know what." The captain's fingers fluttered next to his face. "That high school, flipping me off thing."

Moseley inspected his scratching hand, gaze flicking from the still-extended middle finger to the captain's glare. "Sorry," he said, "this one was purely accidental." He slid the hand under his leg. "So, why isn't she here now?"

"Don't smartass me, Lenny. I don't care how far we go back."

"Thousand pardons," he said, bowing his head. "So, why isn't she here?"

The captain eased back in his chair. "I sent her to see what C.S.I. has so far."

"C'mon, Captain, feet instead of phone?" He shook his head. "What's really on your mind?"

Garner smiled. "All right. Lenny, I'm still gonna need good people after you're gone. I have to know if Dalton could be one. The more time she spends with you, the faster she might get there." His expression morphed from benign to angry. He leaned over the desk and shook a finger. "But we both know how you can be. Keep. Your mouth. Shut. Do you understand?"

"Yeah, yeah," he said, his head and open hand bobbing in tandem. He held up the folder. "I assume this is the report from the uniforms?"

"Doesn't help much. We got no car, no driver info, nothing from C.S.I. yet, and the witnesses are weak. One's in a coma, so only two of the three girls could be interviewed. Both said headlights came up behind them. Driver hit the horn. Headlights turned to the left. They heard a rumble. Water smacked them, and then the car."

"We know it's a car?"

"They confirmed it was a dark sedan. That's all they could give us. It was only there for a few seconds, then took off back where it came from."

"So the damage, if there is any, will be on the passenger side."

"Obviously."

"Jersey tag?"

"They didn't see anything, at least anything helpful."

"Hear anything?"

"One says she heard two male voices, maybe three. Sounded like an argument. She thought they might be young, possibly teenagers."

"Yeah, and it could've been the radio." Moseley stood and fanned the air with the folder. "Guess we better find some paint on the clothes."

"Lenny," the captain's voice softened, "you're sure there's nothing you want to tell me about Karcher?"

"What's going on? Sounds like maybe there's something you want to tell me."

The captain wiggled a finger at the door. "G'won, get outta here. And I'm serious about Dalton. The world's moved past your sense of humor. Only forty-seven more days. Keep a sock in it."

Forty-seven days with her. Nightmare.

Chapter 11

The phone in Jordan's home office rang. Caller ID displayed *Diane Cell*. He snatched at the receiver and fumbled it. "Shit!" The handset clattered onto the polished cherry desk. "Still there?" he said, pressing it to his ear.

"There's a charming greeting. So, three missed calls from you in twenty minutes. Must be—"

"Where the hell are you?" Heavy breathing on the other end told him he'd started poorly. "Diane, we can't do this now. Something's happened. We need to talk."

"Who's being dramatic now?"

It took a second for him to remember he'd said the same to her when she asked if he'd be home tonight. Masterful. She filed away every dig, then flung them back like a *jai alai* player. "You want it straight? All right. Wyatt hit the Califano girls."

"You're lying," she said after a short pause.

"Wrong. Wyatt's the driver."

"How do you know this?" Her voice had gone soft, trancelike.

"He told me. Right after you left. I saw some dents in his car. When I pointed to them, he confessed. Just like that. I never even asked how they got there. He started to cry and confessed."

"How could he just leave? Was he drunk?"

"Cocaine, but—"

"Impossible."

"Wyatt and Billy say that only Tanner used it. It was in a bag on his lap. When they had the accident, it flew all over the car. Everyone panicked, and Wyatt took off."

"What's going on?" a woman asked Diane.

He jolted upright in the chair. "Who's with you?"

"Where is he?" Diane said. "I mean," her voice cracked, "has he been arrested?"

"Who's been arrested?" the other woman said.

"Diane, shut up. Who's with you? Stop talking about this."

She broke down. "Don't let him go to jail. Not even for five minutes. You know people. Call someone."

"Shut up! I mean, please stop talking and just listen," he said, trying to drain the anger from his tone. "No one's been arrested. At least not yet. The police obviously don't know, or they'd have been here already."

"Put him on."

"No. He's in his room, calming Kevin down."

"What did you do?"

"I was in the office with the three boys and things got a little heated. Kevin must have heard because he was very upset when we came out. After Tanner and Billy left, I told Wyatt to keep him occupied until you and I took care of this. I wasn't going to do anything until you knew."

"What does 'take care of this' mean? 'Take care' how, exactly?"

"He has to turn himself in."

"No!"

"Diane, I'm an officer of the court. Unless I want the next cell, I can't ignore this."

"You filthy bas—" She hung up.

Pacing the center design of the Oriental carpet in his office, he alternated the phone between his hand and ear, depending on whether he was hitting *redial* or getting her voicemail greeting. Blanche's singing had arrived in the great room, only feet from the office door. She may have already heard too much. No more calls from the house. He replaced the handset in the cradle and headed for his car.

Behind the wheel, he powered up just enough to activate the systems and pressed the *Phone* button. "Call tennis," he said to the simulated female. Diane had been dressed for tennis.

"Tennis Center, Chrissy speaking."

"Chrissy, this is Judge Carpenter. If my wife is still there, please tell her to call me on my cell. It's rather important."

"Is she *still* here? Judge, I haven't seen Mrs. Carpenter all day." Papers rustled. "I'm checking the sheets. Nope. She's not even on the schedule today. Sorry. Anything else I can help you with?"

He ended the call and drummed fingers on the leather-wrapped wheel. "Dammit," he whispered. His thumb popped the phone back on. "Call office."

"Judge Carpenter's office. Ms. Longstreet speaking."

"Good, you're there. Amanda, I'm not going to be in at all today. That problem this morning is more complicated than I thought. In fact, you better clear my calendar completely for today and tomorrow. Oh, and let Chief Justice Lansky know I'll call him later today."

"Oh my. That bad, huh?"

"I'm afraid so."

She cleared her throat. "Will this involve your evening plans as well, Your Honor?"

He closed his eyes and flopped back against the headrest. Even before today's disasters, time with her was time outside the cauldron. If she was in the passenger seat right then, they'd disappear forever. "Yes. I'm sorry."

"Well, that's a pure shame. I know how much you were looking forward to it. Well, maybe, y'know, you could just swing by for dessert."

"None of that's going to happen for a while. I can't go into it right now. Soon as I get a handle on things, I'll call. It won't be today, though. I'm sure of that."

"Sounds serious. Is it?"

"Yes, but not the way you might—" An incoming call beeped into the conversation. "I have to take this, Amanda. We'll talk later." He pressed the button. "Diane?"

"Please, Jordan," she said, her voice hoarse and stuffy, "tell me you haven't done anything yet."

"I haven't. Are you all right?"

"I'm with my sister. We're about five minutes from the house. She's dropping me off. Jordan, we have some things to talk about. Promise you'll wait. You won't call anyone."

"I won't. But Roberta's dropping you? Where's your car?"

"Promise me."

"Okay." He hurried back into the house and found Blanche still tidying the great room. Winded from his stumbling charge up the steps, he rested his hands on his hips and bent forward. "That'll be all for today," he said through heavy breaths. "You can go home now."

"Y'all right, Judge?"

"Not as young as I used to be."

"Amen to that." She smiled and leaned around him to check the grandfather clock in the foyer. Her brow creased. "Still got almost two hours left. Mrs. Carpenter would be pretty unhappy with me if I left now.

He pulled the dust cloth from her fingers and placed a hand in the middle of her back. "I'll explain everything."

"But I haven't even touched the kitchen. I always do that after Kevin and I have lunch."

His hand nudged a little harder. "You keep your things in the pantry, don't you?"

"Why you pushing me?" Her face held a deep frown.

"I'm sorry. See, we need the house to ourselves this afternoon, starting in about two minutes. My wife must have forgotten to mention it. I'll see she pays you for the two hours."

"I get paid?" she said over her shoulder on her way to the pantry.

"Of course." He stayed in the hallway, between the kitchen and the foyer.

She hiked the tote bag onto her shoulder. "Say goodbye to the boys for me." A big smile livened her face. "A two hour paid vacation. Jackpot." She disappeared down the hallway to the elevator. Her soft singing succumbed to distance and the hum of the motor.

He leaned against a wall in the foyer and trained his gaze on the front door, dreading the battle to come.

Chapter 12

Detective Dalton strode toward Moseley's desk, each foot landing in front of the other, reminding him of a Victoria's Secret model strutting down the runway. He slumped against the seat back and flipped his pen onto the desk. "Like you don't know," he said, softly enough that she was still smiling when she dropped into his side chair, a yellow sticky-note plastered to her finger.

"I didn't catch that, Moseley. Happy to be working with you, Dalton? Was that it?"

He slid his butt forward on the cushion, leaned toward her, and rested his forearms on the desk. "Here's the deal, so pay attention. We're not going to be friends. I'll take a bullet for you out there, but only because that's the job, not because of some bullshit partner kind of thing. Capeesh?"

Her face screwed up as she laughed. "Man, get over yourself." She shook her head and laughed again. "So, Rambo, are you interested in what the lab found?"

Fighting off a smile, he sat back in the chair. His chin bobbed at the paper stuck to her finger. "Is it on that official looking document?"

She peeled the note off and stuck it to the dark screen of his computer. "The report will be in the system later today, but this is all we really need. One of the girls had a good scrape of paint on a rivet of her jeans. I hung around while they ran it through the spectrometer. Got the impression they thought I was in the way, but screw 'em." She tapped a finger on the sticky. "We're looking for a Volvo, Pacific Blue Metallic, either an S40 or a V40, any year since 2004."

"Put out a bulletin yet?"

"Yup. State Troopers, too."

"Pretty good." Her initiative surprised him.

"So," she said, "who does the body shops and who does Motor Vehicles?" She picked a cardboard coaster from his desk and balanced it over a cocked thumb. "Stained side gets Motor Vehicles. Call it."

He shook his head. "You're doing both. I'm going to talk to the girls. Maybe they'll remember something new today."

"Bullshit. I'll take the ride, and you do the dial-around."

Knuckles resting on the desk, he stood and zoomed his face forward as she retreated. "I'm running this investigation. You'll do what I tell you. Where do you come off talking to me like that?"

Her wide eyes darted to Captain Garner's closed door.

He glanced at the same door, snorted a laugh, and eased back into the chair. "Had a little chat about me?" he said, poking a thumb toward the captain's office.

Head tilted back, she folded her arms.

"So," he said, "this macho crap, that's to show me you're tough? That you got my back if I need you?"

"Captain said you think I might be a little soft," she said, chin still raised. "I'm not. I'm a good detective, whether you think so or not."

Smiling, he shook his head. "See, that's just stupid.

Nobody's a good detective in three months." He plucked the yellow note off his computer and twiddled it between two fingers. "Here's the scoop on this one, Ram-bo-lina. We got ourselves a nothing hit-and-run." His nose wrinkled. "A Volvo, for crissake. When we find it, the driver's probably gonna be a middle-aged woman who had too much to drink."

"Witnesses say they heard male voices. Sounded like kids."

"Don't fall in love with eyewitness stories. You know that. Or should. But let's say that turns out to be right. It's gonna be a panicky kid, driving mommy's car. We don't need tough. We need smart and hard-working. Good detectives find leads, run them down, and make arrests. That's what we're gonna do, and you're gonna do your part the way I tell you."

She flinched when he rose and reached for the jacket hanging on the back of her chair.

"Oh yeah. Born to be bad." He chuckled and left her sitting at the desk.

Chapter 13

Frank didn't want to leave the hospital, but he'd finished his coffee, the girls were done being cheerful for Torrie, and Angie's fidgeting was only making everyone more nervous. He leaned over the side rail of Torrie's bed. "Gotta go, honey. Love ya." His lips brushed her forehead. Near tears, he stood and sawed a finger under his nose. "Beth, Monica," he said, "time to go."

Looking puzzled, Angie edged into the doorway. "Go where?"

"Daddy," Monica said, "we promised the nurse we'd go back to our room first. She was all blah blah blah about we have to leave in wheelchairs. So stupid to make me sit on a sore butt."

"Okay," he said, "we'll meet you in your room. C'mon, Angie. Almost ten. Gotta clean up before we open."

She widened her eyes. "You can't work today."

"*We're* working today," he said, circling his finger at all of them.

"Not me," she said, folding her arms.

He pulled her out of the doorway by her elbow. "Girls, say goodbye to Torrie, then take off."

"I'm not leaving my baby, Frank."

He held a shushing finger to his lips and pointed to the bed.

The two girls approached Torrie. "Bye, big sister," Monica said, swirling a finger on Torrie's forearm, the only exposed skin without a tube or monitor wire. "See you tonight." Beth kissed her fingertips and touched them to Torrie's cheek, but didn't say anything. Eyes glistening, both girls hurried from the room.

"Frank, what kind of mother would leave?"

"She doesn't even know you're here," he whispered. "We have a business and customers that count on us, too, and we're gonna need the money." His arms stretched out to her. "C'mon."

Angie slapped at his hands. "She may wake up."

"You heard the doctor, Babe. They zonked her." He snapped Angie into a hug.

"She has to see me when she wakes up," Angie said, twisting in his hold.

"It won't be today. You know that." He hugged tighter against her squirming. "Babe, stop." He pulled even tighter. "Please...Please."

She hung loosely in his arms, face against his chest. "Frank, don't ask me. She could wake up. They don't know."

If things were normal today, he'd be free to tend the fields, then swing by the stand for some late-day grunt work, but it looked like that wasn't in the cards. He'd have to run the register, boss their daughters, handle deliveries, and man the phone. Just as well. She'd be pretty useless in this condition anyway, and the corn could survive a little while without him. He kissed her salt-and-pepper hair. "Okay," he said, leaning his face away. "But how about we do this? I bring you home. You take a shower, get something to eat, maybe take a little nap. Later, I'll have Pop bring you back. Whadaya say?"

She left her cheek against him and shook her head. "I'm not leaving my baby."

"Angie, even the best mother in the world—which I'm sure is you—gets hungry, and sleepy, and smelly after too long." He felt the bounce of her small laugh. "Go home for a little while. Give the nurses a break."

"I'll do it tonight after you finish work." She squeezed hard then relaxed her arms. "I gotta say goodbye to the girls."

Angie blew a kiss and waved to them as the elevator doors closed. When they opened again in the lobby, he waited for the volunteers to guide the wheelchairs past him. As his little group approached Patient Information, he noticed a woman behind the counter fanning a hand in their direction, but her gaze pointed somewhere else. He searched to where she was looking. A pretty blonde in a dark pants suit nodded at the woman's signal and scrambled from a chair in the waiting area. She trotted toward them. "Mr. Califano?"

Probably a lawyer or a reporter, and he wanted no part of either. He kept walking.

"Lindsay Marx-Warner," she said, swapping a microphone to her left hand and sticking out the right. "Channel 9, News at 6:00. Do you have a few seconds?"

The volunteers slowed and checked over their shoulders.

"Keep going," he said to them as he brushed past the reporter and ignored her extended hand.

"Mr. Califano," she said, skipping sideways next to him, "is there something you'd like to say to the coward who hurt your family?"

"Burn in hell," he said without turning his face or making eye contact.

"Very understandable. Hold that thought until we get outside. Hospital rules." She beckoned to someone in the waiting area. Lugging a shoulder-mount camera, a sleepy-looking young man joined their march to the exit.

"Folks, this is my cameraman, Randy."

Gazing forward, Randy flipped his free hand.

"Awesome!" Monica said, eyes sparkling. "Are we gonna be on TV?" Beth covered her face.

"Six tonight, young lady." The woman's sunny smile for Monica clicked off. "Mr. Califano," she said, eyes narrowed, "how is Torrie this morning?"

This woman saying "Torrie," like she was a relative or a family friend, got him mad. "Well as can be expected."

"You must all be devastated," the reporter said. "I understand you're a farmer. Do you carry medical insurance?"

His "yes" seemed to disappoint her.

"Will it cover everything?"

"We don't know what 'everything' is yet."

"Good enough," she said. "Randy, get us coming out, and I want a shot before the girls are out of the wheelchairs." Under the covered entrance, the reporter positioned herself in front of the Overlook Hospital lettering. She smoothed her hair, tugged down the front of her suit jacket, and patted the neckline of her blouse. Her face rolled through some goofy-looking exercises. "Everything okay?" she said to Randy after scrubbing a finger across her front teeth.

The cameraman, his eye to the viewfinder, popped

a thumb up and flipped on the camera light.

"Mr. Califano?" she said, crooking a finger. "Over here, next to me."

He couldn't see how any good could come from talking to her but took his spot anyway.

"Us, too?" Monica said.

Randy shook his head to the reporter. "Not if you want close-ups."

"We'll get you two later, if there's time. Action," she said, poking a finger at Randy. "I'm standing in front of Overlook Hospital with Frank Califano, whose three teenage daughters were mowed down by a hit-and-run driver last night, not thirty feet from the safety of their own home. Daughters Beth and Monica…" Randy panned the camera toward where she'd tilted her head. "…have been discharged this morning, but sixteen-year-old Torrie remains upstairs, in a coma."

The camera returned to the reporter. She pushed a foam-topped microphone at Frank's mouth.

"Mr. Califano, is there any way to describe your feelings right now?"

That stupid question. He should have known it was coming. They did it to everyone. *How do you think I feel, you idiot?* is what he wanted to say, but he didn't. Worse, he got emotional, mumbling and sniffling through his answer, words he couldn't remember as soon as she pulled the microphone away. They had no right. Soon as Randy flicked off the camera's light, Frank itched to yank it off his shoulder and smash it on the concrete. Lindsay Marx-Warner would be next. He'd spin her by the shoulders and kick her so hard in the butt her feet would leave the ground.

"Aw, we're not in?" Monica said to the TV crew as

they were leaving.

"Not today," the reporter said. "We'll use you if there's a follow-up."

Frank plodded back to where Beth and Monica waited with the volunteers.

"What did you say, Daddy?" Monica said. "We couldn't hear."

"C'mon." He rolled his hand as he walked. "We're going."

"Mr. Califano," Beth's elderly volunteer called to him, "the girls have to be picked up here. It's the rules."

As he headed alone to Visitor Parking, the new reality for his family got clearer. Lindsay Marx-Warner was only the first intruder. People in the headlines draw flies. Nobody was going to allow them to be afraid, or sad, or angry in private. Opening the stand this morning, which felt like a welcome slice of normal a few minutes ago, was now something he dreaded. A day full of questions. Well-meaning friends, regular customers, even strangers who'd seen or heard the news, all of them would crowd into their faces, try to become part of what happened, or at the very least, make them explain their goddamn feelings.

Removing the wrapper from their lives scared him. One of the few things he remembered from high school biology was that anything put under a microscope, even if it started out alive, ended up dead. That wasn't happening. Not to his family. It was time to close ranks, count only on each other. They didn't need anyone yesterday. Weren't going to need anyone tomorrow. For the first time since his girls got hit, he smiled.

Chapter 14

Diane slogged up the four front steps and stopped on their home's broad landing. Behind her, slow-moving tires crackled on pavers in the circular driveway. Thumb on the latch, she waved until her sister, Roberta, returned the wave, pressed heavier on the gas, and drove off. The prospect of going inside sapped her. Any talk about today's news, both hers and Wyatt's, would only make it more real. Everyone would have to talk about everything. She wanted to call Roberta, ask her to come back and help her escape, as if that would make her healthy and Wyatt innocent.

Jordan didn't come to her when she opened the door. Hands in his pockets, he stood at the kitchen end of the hallway. "Where should we do this? Office?" His voice sounded restrained, like he didn't want Wyatt or Kevin to know she was home, but his litigator's baritone always filled everything.

Nodding, she pressed the door shut and headed into the great room.

He caught up and cupped a hand on her shoulder. "Where's your car?" he said, looking confused after a quick glance out a front window.

"At Roberta's." The day's awful developments didn't stop her from locking eyes with him at the mention of her younger sister's name. She did it every time, her way of letting him know she knew.

"Roberta's? Why?"

She pushed her palm at him and walked into the office. After tossing her handbag onto the cherry desk, she crossed in front of the fireplace, sat on the edge of the sofa's middle cushion, and dropped her face into her hands. Weight on the next cushion tipped her in his direction.

"Sorry about the phone," he said, trailing his fingers on her spine.

That touch both repelled and amused. It had often been a prelude to sex, created a sensation that brought an involuntary arch of her back, pressed her body into him, and somehow knocked their clothes off. She elbowed his stroking arm away and rested her clasped hands on her knees. "Before we start on Wyatt, I have some news. You like it straight, so here it is. I have cancer." She glanced at his stunned expression. "Breast cancer. How about that? None in my family, but all traditions start with a first time."

"Jesus." He grabbed her forearm and squeezed. "Are they sure? Biopsy and everything?"

"That's where I was today. They'll never tell you something like that on the phone. I guessed it was bad when they said I should have someone along." She fell back against the cushion and shut her eyes. "This is turning into quite a day." Casual bravado might keep him away, and she'd already invested a good bit of the morning in sobbing and terror. Roberta had lifted her spirits a bit, but Wyatt knocked her back into the abyss.

"You had Roberta take you? Why didn't you say something to me?"

"I didn't want to make a big thing out of it. If the biopsy was negative, the storm would have come and gone while you slept." Eyes still closed, she smiled. "With no irritating dramatics." Her cushion wobbled when he stood. Footsteps tapped on the hardwood and hushed on the carpet.

"So what did they tell you? What are they going to do?"

"Scans, then surgery. Scans on Monday, surgery Tuesday, tentatively. Then they'll do some other tests and see if it's spread." She hoped that going through the clinical process would dull the shock. Instead, it made her more aware that horrors awaited, and her children would witness them, possibly see her die.

"Surgery's next Tuesday? Five days?"

She nodded, still distracted by her sons' looming ordeal.

"Why tentatively? All the pre-op?"

"That'll only take a day."

"I don't get it then."

"Jordan, if you throw Wyatt under the bus—"

"*Jesus*," he said, knees dipping, "Wyatt."

"If you call the police, or make him do it, I'm canceling everything, and we're not even telling him. I'm not making him go through both things at the same time."

"That's ridiculous." He let out a deep breath. "You need to be all over this. Right now."

Hugging her middle, she rose from the couch and strolled past him to her "thinking" window, a double-hung that overlooked the rear of the property and the ravine. Years earlier, her road to redemption had begun at this window. It was here she'd first come to understand her life's undoing, her unpardonable participation in a modern madness: men didn't have babies, so women shouldn't be required to have them either. Strokes of pens had allowed half of humanity to deny their biology, to murder for convenience without consequence or remorse. Being weak at the time, she'd permitted a rising party star, her own useful idiot, to bully her into submission. Clearheaded now, she feared time might be running out to protect her surviving innocents. "I want to show you something," she said, surprised at her willingness to invite him into a special privacy.

His hands rested on her shoulders. Foggy snatches of their happy, striving times whispered at her, permitting a wistfulness for used-to-be's and might-have-been's. Tears nearly remembered their way out, but truth spared her the humiliation. Those gentle hands were just more of his manipulations, the tactic of a sociopath. She'd spat that very word in his face on the day he suggested she abort Kevin.

"This is my favorite spot in the house," she said, wriggling her shoulders until he removed his hands. "I stand here during the day sometimes. The changing light, it's like the ocean, or the tides. See that line of sunshine? The way it hits the lawn?"

"What about it?"

She painted a finger at the view. "All that energy. But it dies on its way into the ravine. The colors and shapes lose their vibrancy. And then it's gone. But more always comes. It's like eternity, or infinity. The birth and death of the same thing at the same time. Some days I stand here for an hour or more." She tapped fingertips to her temples. "I think better here. Important things become simpler."

"Does that mean you're ready to fight this thing?"

"Right now, my concern is Kevin."

"Did they give you valium or something?"

"Jordan, you're fifty-eight, and I'm sick. Who's going to be here for Kevin if we're gone?"

He edged around to her side. "If you do what you're supposed to, there's a good chance that won't be important for a long, long time."

"The answer to my question is Wyatt. I've known since Kevin was born. No matter what happens to us—and it will—Wyatt has to be there." The fact Jordan even needed this explanation reconfirmed his detachment from the truly important. "He has to." Fear and fury shook her voice.

"Ssh," he said, wrapping her in a slow, rocking hug.

Gagging back "Don't touch me!" she stiffened in the arms that once assured her she was cherished and safe, a haven she was near desperate for at the moment. Horrified, she found her cheek on his chest, hands on his broad back. She sniffled and leaned back. "Now, tell me you're not calling anyone."

His shoulders sagged. "You know I can't do that."

"You can!" She shoved out of the embrace. "Just like I waited out the biopsy, we're going to see what happens to the Califano girl. If she makes a full recovery, case closed."

"Not that it will matter, but if she doesn't?"

"Then someone will still have to convince me that a wonderful person like Wyatt needs rehabilitation." Her face rose to within inches of his. "That putting him in a cage, to be sodomized by psychopaths, restores harmony to the universe." His head shook the whole time she'd been speaking. That infuriating, superior dismissiveness.

"This is my profession," he said. "I know how it's going to play out, and even if the police drop the ball, too many people know. Over time, Tanner or Billy will blab to the wrong person." He poked a finger at her. "Even Roberta could slip. Talking about it in front of her was a mistake."

"Good God. You think my sister's going to tell someone?"

"Secrets are uncomfortable. And there's no point in speculating. The evidence is going to mount very quickly. The police have gotten quite good at solving hit-and-run cases. It wouldn't surprise me if they identify the make of the car by the end of today."

His ease with such facts concerned her. "How?"

"Traces of paint on the girls' clothes or skid marks on the street. Once they identify the car, they'll run it through Motor Vehicles. By lunchtime tomorrow, they'll have a list of every blue Volvo registered in New Jersey. They'll start with addresses close to the accident scene, then spiral outward from there. Sometime Saturday there's going to be a knock on our door, and they're going to ask to see the car. If they see it, they'll know it's the one. If we say no, they'll *really* know it's the one. They'll be back in an hour with a warrant, see the dents, and impound it. When the lab finds fibers from the girls' clothing in the dents, Wyatt's going to be arrested. And I can tell you from experience, it's a tactical mistake to wait for the arrest."

"You sound like you're enjoying this." She glanced to him and back out the window. "Maybe everything's falling into place for you."

"What the hell does that mean?"

She smiled and lowered her hips onto the deep sill, propping her arms on the edge. "You've always been lucky. This could be how you get away. Wife gets sick and dies. But then there are those pesky children. What to do? What to do?" she said, tapping a finger to her chin. "Oh, I know, put one in prison and institutionalize the other. Not much of a stretch for a man who's already killed—"

"Shut up!" He spun away from her, his hands balling in and out of fists. "You only blame me to absolve yourself."

"As if I had a choice."

"Stop it!" he said, spinning to face her. "We have more than enough going on right now. And what are you talking about? Me, wanting to be free. I don't want anything like that. I love this family."

She stood and smiled. "You love us. How nice." The backs of her fingers pushed against his arm as she made for the desk. "Jordan, I may be dying," she said without turning. "Perhaps it's time to set things right, risk the consequences, the unpleasantness." Dragging her purse off the desk, she stepped toward the door but paused. "I have a suggestion for Wyatt's situation. You seem to know exactly how the police will catch him. Why don't you use that information to confound them? You're the smartest man I've ever known, and it sounds to me like we have at least twenty-four hours." Had it dawned on her sooner, appealing to his vanity might have saved a lot of time.

"I see. So, you want me arrested, too. Are you familiar with the term 'accessory after the fact'?"

"Darling, if your great friend, Bill Clinton, can get away with perjury to avoid a little embarrassment, I'm sure you can be excused for a bit of accessorizing under the circumstances." She resumed walking, knowing he'd follow. "Are they in Wyatt's room or Kevin's?"

"Wyatt's." Long strides brought him in front of her. "Shouldn't I come with you?"

"Don't call anyone, Jordan," she said, trying her best to remove any hint of demand. "Please."

Brow furrowed, he shook his head slowly. "Diane, how can you ask that?"

"To save my children? How can I not?" She inched closer and locked eyes with his. "Please, help me. This time, *help* me."

His gaze drifted around the room, dropped to the floor, and rose to her face.

She sensed penetration into his long-buried decency. Ghosts and shadows swarmed in her head, but without screaming this time.

He walked into her spread arms.

Chapter 15

Wyatt stood at the window of Kevin's room, elbows propped on top of the lower sash, hands cupped over his ears. His fingertips combed soft, slow strokes through his hair. Unseeing eyes pointed toward the darkness of the ravine.

"Fire truck," Kevin called from the desk.

"Nice," he said without interrupting his trance.

"Look," was accompanied by the crinkle of flapping craft paper.

"In a minute, Kev." A tug on his belt startled him.

"Dad's mad at you." Head tipped away, Kevin's gaze drilled into him. "Why?"

Wyatt roughed his brother's crewcut. "Let's see that truck." Arm on Kevin's shoulder, he guided him back to the desk. Each time he glanced down, Kevin's face pointed forward, but the eyes were pulled into the corners, checking him. "So," he said after helping Kevin onto the chair, "did you do ladders and everything? Show me."

"Smoke." Kevin's finger swirled on a brown squiggle. "From the house." He grabbed the crayon, bit his tongue, and slashed on more strokes. His eyes peeked out of the corners again. "Dad yelled at Tanner. Why?"

Dropping to one knee, Wyatt pulled the drawing closer and squinted at the confusion of colors. "We did something he didn't like. Did you draw hoses? Point to them."

"What did you do?"

"Kevin…" His eyes filled. "We hurt someone, by accident."

"Did you say 'sorry'?"

"We did." He blotted his eyes with his shirt sleeves. "So, what about ladders? Maybe you can still—"

The door handle clicked.

His mother walked in, arms reaching, mouth curled down at the corners. "Wyatt," was all she said. His father drifted into the room behind her.

"Mom, I'm so sorry." More ashamed than he could ever remember, he stooped his face onto her shoulder and locked her in a tight hug.

"Ssh. I know, honey." She patted and rubbed his back, stroked his hair. "I know."

His father joined them, surrounding him and his mother with his arms. That wasn't like him at all.

"He said sorry," Kevin shouted.

Everyone rolled their face toward the desk.

"He said sorry," was a whisper this time. Head shaking, Kevin tipped his face to the floor, his gaze still on the group. "No yelling."

The instant his mother relaxed her hold and headed toward Kevin, his father let go, too. That group hug thing was weird. He couldn't remember the last time he and his father had even shaken hands, and his parents hardly spoke to each other.

"No yelling, sweetie," she said, pressing her cheek to Kevin's. "I promise."

"Boys, your mother has something to tell you."

His father sounded way different. Not angry anymore. More like dazed, or sad maybe. If they'd come to tell him Torrie died, no way he'd be able to handle it.

"C'mere." She lifted under Kevin's arms and helped him off the chair. At the bed, she sat and pounded her open hands on the spread. "Sit with me, both of you." Taking a hand from each of them, she clasped them in hers and rested the tangle on her knees. "Boys, I'm sick."

"Throwing up?" Kevin crinkled his nose. "I don't like that."

"No, a different kind of sick. It's something called breast cancer." Her gaze darted to Wyatt.

"Oh, no," he said, covering his mouth. His beautiful mother. He peeked at her chest. Something was eating her, trying to take her when he needed her most.

Lips pressed tight, she nodded at him and lowered her face closer to Kevin. "Mommy needs to go to the hospital, honey, and then I have to do some more things after that." Her gaze found Wyatt again. "Things I have to be strong for."

Wyatt's chin dropped onto his chest. He wasn't just a coward. He was a terrible son.

"This isn't the time to collapse, Wyatt. This is when we fight the hardest. All of us." She shook the knot of fingers until he looked at her. "Your dad will explain."

He glanced at his father's blank face, then back to her. She didn't look sick at all. Maybe it wasn't so bad. "What did they say about, y'know, getting well?"

"Positive," she said. "Very optimistic. But it's

going to be long and difficult. And I'm going to need all of you to help me." She stood and kissed the top of his head. "Your father and I talked about the other thing, so you two discuss that while I get Kevin his lunch. "Hungry, sweetie?" she said, smiling at Kevin.

Every inch of his brother's face got happy. "Grill cheese," he shouted and rushed toward the back staircase.

"Listen to your dad," she said. "If anyone can make this turn out right, he can."

"Mom," boomed up the stairwell from the kitchen.

On the way out of the room, she reached a hand toward his dad's face. He flinched like she was going to smack him. She paused, ran a light touch over his cheek. "Thank you," she whispered. The door closed behind her.

He and his father shared the silence. Gazes found the door, the floor, each other. He'd never seen his dad so spaced before.

"She really gonna be okay, Dad?"

He shrugged and shook his head. "I only found out five minutes ago. Her doctors will have more to say after the surgery, but for now, who knows?" His shoulders bounced again.

"Dad, I'm so sor—"

"Stop with the fucking sorries! Do you understand?" He rushed at Wyatt. "Do you?"

"Yes," he said, hands raised in defense. First f-bomb he'd ever heard from either parent. Whatever they were going to talk about had to be real bad.

"Okay then." His father covered his face and blew a loud breath into his hands. "What your mother means." He dropped his arms and blinked at the ceiling.

"What she's talking about, is that we're going to try to make this thing go away."

"What? You're not making me go to the cops?"

"Your mother doesn't think she can deal with both things at the same time."

"But she has no choice. Does she?"

His father stared, jaw muscles big as walnuts. Nodding, he paced near the windows. "With any luck, the Califano girl will make a full recovery. If that happens, the investigation will drop off the radar like that," he said, snapping his fingers.

"What if she doesn't?" He'd have to kill himself if that happened.

"It won't change what we have to do now." His father sat on the other side of the bed. "Okay, we have to assume every cop in the county is already looking for your car, so it can't go on the road again." Eyes closed, head shaking slowly, he rubbed his forehead. "So, we have to get rid of it. Right away, before they come here and want to see it."

"Dad, what are you doing?" he said, springing off the bed.

"Sit down!"

His father's furious face told him he could either sit down or get knocked down. He lowered back onto the bed. Being a coward was one thing, but now he was turning his father into a criminal. Maybe his mother, too. He had to go to the police and tell the truth.

"I must be losing my mind," his father said under his breath. "Okay, so the car's gone. We don't know how yet, but the car's gone. That means we have to tell the police it was stolen. Soon as they hear that, they're going to suspect it was the one that hit the girls. They'll find out we bought it for you, so you were most likely driving it before it was stolen. They're going to ask where were you? Who were you with? What were you doing? Who saw you? At what time? How do you know it was that time? Why did it take so long to call it in?" He stood and massaged his temples. "And that's a very good question."

Wyatt could tell his father was speaking to himself, making up and ditching stuff at the same time.

"We have to put a story together, then get Tanner and Billy back here to get it straight. The detectives are going to be relentless with the questions. Tanner will probably hold up, but Billy could be a problem. Can we just cut him out of the evening?"

"Dad, *I'm* the one you should worry about." He didn't recognize this man. "Let's just go to the cops and tell them the truth. What can happen?"

"What can happen?" A laugh puffed out of his father's nose. "They'll crush you. You're a media wet dream. Son of a wealthy judge, joyriding in his new car, indifferent to dangerous driving conditions, snorting cocaine—"

"Dad, I swear."

"Shut up. Snorting cocaine with other privileged sons, running down the children of simple farmers, tenders of the hallowed family ground, one they're struggling to keep away from greedy, earth-raping developers, yada yada."

"I've never been in trouble before. What about all the good things?"

"Good things?" His father snorted another laugh. "Wyatt, the law wasn't my business. It was understanding how the game is played. It's big guy versus little guy. Always. And no one champions big guys. Ever. Not even when they're right. Create a victim, then get out of the way of flying cash."

He'd never heard his father talk about the family wealth before. Sounded like he saw it as a scam, like he was a con man.

"Ironically, now I'm the big guy. The whole family is. Raw meat for hysterical media. There'll be one drumbeat. Wyatt Carpenter, silver-spoon, overindulged, probably a drug user. Left three girls to die in the street. You'll be portrayed as depraved."

"You know why I left."

"I have to tell you, Wyatt, if this was my case, and I learned you fled to keep a friend from being arrested on a misdemeanor drug offense, I'd probably ask the jury to crucify you. And if things go badly for that girl, you could be looking at five years, maybe a lot more." His father's face turned stony, as if it was the first time he realized how serious this was. He shuffled to the window, laid his forearms on the sash, and stared into the ravine.

The quiet while his father concentrated gave Wyatt a chance to picture himself as a prisoner...*five years, maybe a lot more...* His college and grad school years. Years of constant danger. He hadn't been in a fight since second grade. Defending himself would be next to impossible. They'd do things. Make him do things. Stuff he'd never be able to clean away or forget. His mouth dried. They were right. No jail.

"Wyatt."

His father's voice startled him.

"I'm going to drop your mother at her car, then take mine to the dealership. Call Tanner and Billy. Tell them to put on some work clothes and be here in two hours."

Sounded like the plan had come together. He hoped his father was as smart as everyone said.

Chapter 16

The young man behind the Mercedes service counter wrinkled his brow when Jordan slipped through the door. "Judge Carpenter, hi," he said, checking a lighted appointment board on the back wall. "Are we supposed to be doing something for you today?"

"No," he said, squinting at the name stenciled on the clerk's shirt pocket, "Darren. A little body work, unfortunately."

"Aw, not that beautiful McLaren," Darren said, his face crumpling.

"I'm afraid so." Nodding, he bobbed his thumb toward the parking lot.

Darren strode around the counter and toward the door. "How bad?"

"You tell me," he said, trailing at the clerk's shoulder.

"Does she even have five thousand miles on her yet?"

"Twenty-nine hundred."

Darren's head snapped back, knees buckled. "Judge, you're killing me." He pushed the door open and let Jordan pass. "So, what happened?"

"Somebody hit the rear end yesterday. It's just over here."

Squatting behind the car, Darren trailed his fingertips over the damage as if it would hurt the car to press any harder. "What a shame. I love this car." He stood and patted the crunched trunk. "Let's go back inside and start the paperwork. Your insurance or the other guy?"

"No insurance. It was a hit-and-run, and I carry a very high deductible."

"Man, this just keeps getting worse." Darren leaned his face close to the crushed metal. "Interesting." He took a quarter from his pocket and squatted in front of the damage. "You said this happened yesterday?"

"Had to."

Using the coin, Darren scratched at the paint in the dents. Small flecks dropped into his cupped hand. He wet a fingertip and dabbed it into his palm. "See that?" he said, holding the finger in front of Jordan's face. "There's blue in with your silver. The car that hit her was blue."

Jordan swallowed, shook his head, and shrugged.

"About three hours ago we got a fax from the Readington Police." He laughed. "Can you believe they're still using faxes? Anyway, we're supposed to be on the lookout for a late model, metallic blue Volvo. That's the car that hit those girls last night. Hear about that?"

His speculations to Diane turned out to be correct. The police had already identified the make and color of the car. He nodded. "Just awful."

"Oh yeah. Absolutely. And now *you're* in here, hit-and-run by a blue car." Eyes wide, he slapped his forehead. "How nuts would it be if you got hit by that same Volvo? Bizarro, huh?"

"Why would they contact Mercedes if it was a Volvo?"

"We have all the equipment. No reason we couldn't do body work on a Volvo. I don't think we ever have, mind you, but I guess the cops try to cover all bases." Darren tilted his head toward the office. "Let's get the estimate started and set you up with a loaner." He laughed and shook his head. "Wouldn't that be something if it was the same guy?"

Jordan held up one hand. The other dug a phone out of his pants pocket. He checked the face. "Darren, I have to take this. See you inside. Judge Carpenter speaking," he said to the non-existent caller.

Darren nodded, pointed to himself, and then to the waiting room. "When you're done," he whispered before trotting toward the door.

Jordan waved and nodded. Panic pressed at him. He wasn't even ready for Darren's questions much less a detective's. Under the heat and glare of the high sun, he meandered in the parking lot, phone to his ear. Now and then he'd smile, shake his head, or scratch at the blacktop with the tip of a shoe. All the while, he manufactured more details, sorted through what he and the boys needed to know. No more surprises or gaps.

Back inside, a set of keys and a clipboard sat on the counter.

"Judge," Darren said, patting the counter, "great idea. I'm gonna have the cops look at your car, take some paint."

"You're not doing that."

"Don't worry about it. They're in. They're out."

"I said—" He cleared his throat. "Darren, even if it was the same car, it's not relevant. Thanks anyway." He picked up the keys. "Is this my loaner?"

"Judge, most people don't know that the insurance

is on the car, not the driver. When they catch this guy, his coverage will have to pay for your damages." He tapped both thumbs on his chest and smiled. "Who looks out for you better than us, huh?"

Jordan leaned across the counter. "I don't care," he said in a hushed voice, "and if I don't care, neither should you. Don't involve me. Do you understand?"

"Sure. Absolutely." A puzzled expression stayed on Darren's face as he slid the clipboard forward and handed Jordan a pen. "Initial inside the circles, sign where I've marked the X, and you're good to go. The loaner's a 300 series, I'm afraid, but you won't have it long."

A deep breath helped steady his writing hand.

"Where were you when she got hit?"

He hoped a slump of his shoulders conveyed the message. "Darren," he said, just in case the point had been missed, "I appreciate what you're trying to do, but let it go."

"It's just, y'know, if you were at a mall or something, they have surveillance cameras. You could—"

This time he stood to his full height and spread his arms wide.

"I know," Darren said, pushing his palms out, "let it go. Sorry. I just hate to think someone's going to get away with this."

****

Driving home, Jordan pulled the loaner into a supermarket parking lot and stopped in front of a liquor store. He pinched the flesh between his eyes. This thing had to stop. His mind didn't work the right way. He had criminal insights, but not instincts. A wily detective lurked out there, someone who'd herd him into a corner, make a fool of him, and unfrock each detail of the deception until he surrendered the truth out of pure exhaustion. He'd done the same to witnesses many times. The prospect of such a public humiliation was paralyzing.

A tap on the driver's window caused him to flinch. "Jordan?"

He lowered the window. "Hi, Tracie," he said to a fellow Baltusrol member and one of his former evenings. Chardonnay and Chinese food at her sculpting studio, followed by some naked time on her sofa bed. She giggled during sex, and it always made him uneasy as to why.

Red plastic caps on three oversized bottles poked out of the bag she hugged to her middle. "What are you doing in this car?" she said. "Where's that hot McLaren?"

"Having a little work done. You look great. How've you been?"

"Just peachy. Oh," she said, nose wrinkled, "I'm so sorry to hear about Diane, but she'll beat it. She's a fighter. Anyone who's ever been across the net from her knows that."

"Thanks. Did she call you?"

"We, uh, don't really talk much anymore," she said with a wink and smile. "Blair phoned me just before I left the house." She hiked the bag and backed away. "Gotta go before I drop these. If there's anything I can do, I know you won't be shy. See you soon, I hope."

Diane picked up on the second ring. "It's me," he said. "I just ran into Tracie outside Bi-Low Liquors."

"Shocking."

"She said Blair told her about your cancer. Did you call her from your car?"

"My, that *was* fast."

"This isn't like you. What's going on?"

"Just creating my support network. The more positive energy I'm around, the better, so they tell me. We're even going to let the police know, if they show up. A dash of sympathy might keep them at bay a bit longer, might buy you more time to save our sons. Are you still not telling me how you're doing this?"

"You can't get caught lying about what you don't know." He shifted in the seat and switched phone hands. "Diane, I had a rough time at the dealership. Even the kid behind the counter was tripping me up. It's not too late. In fact, in a crazy way, your cancer could help Wyatt if he turned himself—"

"No!"

"He's going to get caught."

"You promised!"

He pictured her, lips pulled tight across the teeth, throttling the phone in her fist.

"And maybe you don't keep all your promises, Jordan, but this one you are. He is *not* going to prison."

"Well, neither am I."

"Then I'll do it. Tell me what you were going to do, and I'll do it."

"You can't ask me to do this. All we've built." He noticed passing shoppers were slowing and staring into the car. "All we've built," he said, lowering his voice, "I'm supposed to throw it away? When he's guilty?"

"Built what?" she said. "God almighty, Jordan. A family. That's all we've built. That's all I care about."

She had some pair of gonads. Freezes him out for

eleven years, but now, because she wanted something, they were a family again. "He's going to get caught. That's all I meant. Trying to stop it is a fool's game."

"I've been thinking," she said, her tone almost breezy. "What if we tell the police I was driving?"

"You?" A laugh popped out. "So it's your cocaine in the car?"

"That's why I didn't stop. Makes sense."

"Where'd you get it?"

Silence.

"So you came home from *The Arc* dinner, jumped into Wyatt's car, and snorted coke. Why weren't you in your own car?"

"You took my keys."

"Why? You had nothing to drink at the dinner."

"I got drunk after we got home."

"I see. You got home, and within twenty minutes, you got drunk, took drugs, and hit those girls."

Silence.

"And where were you going?"

"Nowhere. Driving. We had a fight."

"What about?"

"Let's see. How about you and Amanda smiling when she stroked a finger between her breasts during your speech?"

She missed nothing. On the day of the banquet, Amanda told him if he caught her doing that, it meant she was thinking about them making love, reminding him of her perfume and how much she enjoyed him nuzzling there. "Don't start," he said. "Not now."

"Jordan, get home. You're either taking care of this like you said, or you're coaching me." The phone went dead.

Chapter 17

Jordan pulled the loaner into his driveway. As he'd instructed Wyatt on the phone, one honk got the garage door to rise.

Tanner and Billy, hands stuffed in their pockets, drifted into the early afternoon sunshine. Wyatt followed, wearing a backpack and holding a forest green blanket. None of the boys made eye contact with him as the car approached and entered the garage. He killed the engine.

Diane, in gray gardening clothes, marched from the basement. "You're not keeping me out of this," she said, brushing past him as he opened the car door.

"Get back inside."

She grabbed a pair of leather gloves and a broad-brimmed hat from shelving next to the garage's side door.

"Diane!"

Without turning or slowing, she strode to where the boys waited.

"God damn her," he muttered as he stomped out of the garage.

Arms folded, head back, she stood next to Wyatt.

He scanned the faces, stopping at hers. "Let's talk," he said, beckoning with a finger. "In the house."

She wiggled her fingers inside the gloves. "You said work clothes. Let's go."

"Why did you tell her?" he screamed at Wyatt.

Tanner and Billy glanced at each other and dropped their gazes to the ground.

"Leave him alone," she said before Wyatt could answer. "I overheard him on the phone with Tanner."

"Diane, you're not doing this." He made eye contact with each one of them. "I've changed my mind. Go home, boys." His eyes found Wyatt. "I'm sorry, son. There's no way."

"Jordan." Diane darted in front of Billy and Tanner, blocking their departure. "Yes, we are, and you're wasting time. Now, start giving assignments."

"This is no game." he said, stepping toward her.

Her advance matched his. "Get on with it," she said, her teeth never parting.

He'd seen that look before. Not often, but enough to know there'd be no point in further discussion. "You figure it out." He turned away from her and headed for the house.

"Stay here, boys," she said. "Jordan, wait." She caught up with him inside the garage, hopped in front, and pressed her hands against his chest. "I thought about this a lot after we hung up. It has to be me. I'm the driver."

"We went through this."

"I wasn't drunk. We had a fight, and I took Wyatt's car because it was blocking mine in the garage."

He rolled his eyes. "And the cocaine?"

"It was in my purse. I had the accident because I was trying to, y'know, drive and snort at the same time."

"The cops are too good. They'll break you down."

"Tell me what's in Wyatt's backpack. And why the

blanket?"

"Give it up."

"We're wasting time."

The faster she understood how ludicrous the plan was, the faster her enthusiasm would disappear. "All right. So, we have to ditch the car and then report it stolen. There has to be a plausible reason why it's taken so long to report it. That's why the backpack. I put three empty bottles of *Plumpjack* in there. Screw-caps. If they were going to take wine from us, that's the kind they'd probably take. Reasonable?"

Nose wrinkled, she nodded and rolled her hand.

"Okay. I was going to have Billy plant the bottles at their fishing spot on the Rockaway. The story would be they took the wine from us, parked at the Whittemore Preserve, walked to the fishing spot, and drank the wine. Wyatt decided they got too drunk to drive, so they left the car in the parking lot and walked back here. When they went for it today, it was gone. Wyatt was afraid to tell us, and that's why it took so long."

"Hmm." Diane's eyes narrowed. "That's pretty good."

The surprising compliment energized him. "Billy worried me. I was going to have him so drunk he passed out and had to be dragged back here. That way he wouldn't have to remember any details, couldn't be broken down."

"What about the car?"

"I just told you, stolen."

"No," she said, patting his chest, "I mean really. How do we get rid of it?"

"The only thing I came up with is the ravine.

Anything else meant someone new would have to know. The blanket was to cover the car after we pushed it over the edge."

Her head rocked side to side. "I don't know."

"Exactly. That's why we're not doing it. It can't work. I'm sorry." He stepped around her.

"Do it anyway," she said, hooking his elbow. "How can it hurt?"

"For one thing, it's another crime. Several, in fact."

Sneering, she flapped the back of her hand. "Maybe they won't look, and if they do, that's when we say I did it. The boys helped me. You never knew a thing."

"Diane, forget it."

"No." She pressed her fingers to his lips. "Jordan, we're screwed. I get it. I also know the consequences would be much worse for you. That's why you're the one who's staying out of it. Now, tell me what to do here, then *you* take the bottles to the river." Eyes wide, she leaned closer. "I'm saving my sons. If I have to kill people, I will."

He pulled her hand from his mouth. "Are you threatening *me*?"

"Get going. You can't be here if the police show up while this is going on."

A softening in her expression confused him. First time in years she'd wanted them to be a team, and it could land both of them in prison. As with suspicions about her dangling and denying sex, he wondered if he was responding to another call of the Siren.

Chapter 18

During his short drive to the river, Jordan revisited the instructions he'd left with Diane. Remove the center rail from the fence along the ravine. Back the Volvo up the bridge's incline. Turn it off and leave it in neutral. Release the brake and have Wyatt steer through the window while they all pushed. Build enough speed for it to clear the rim. If the car leaves marks on the edge, spread a dusting of earth over it. She and Billy reattach the slat while Wyatt and Tanner climb down to the car. On the way down, they trim any undergrowth damaged by the car's fall. Cover any exposed metal with the green blanket. Use leaves and the trimmed branches to camouflage the landing area and the blanket. Send Tanner and Billy home with the story they never left the basement after getting there around ten o'clock last night.

He parked in the gravel lot of Whittemore Nature Preserve. Even with the windows closed, thunder from the normally sleepy river filled the car, making him even more anxious. The plan seemed ridiculous now, but back at the house, the operation had begun. His part had to happen.

Backpack dangling from a shoulder, he high-stepped through thick undergrowth. The path he remembered, the one leading to where he'd taken Wyatt fishing for the first time, was now beneath the overfed river. Frequent stumbles on tripwires of tangled brush pitched him onto his hands and knees. Whip marks of plant juice streaked his tan slacks. Welts and slashes reddened his hands and forearms. Blood leaked from multiple tiny punctures, courtesy of briars and twigs.

He recognized the fishing spot, even though most of it was five feet below the churning water. Their first bit of good luck. If the boys had been there last night, no evidence would have survived. With his heels at the water's edge, he removed one of the bottles from the backpack and tomahawked it against a nearby boulder. That's what a drunken kid might do, and he wanted the pattern of scattered glass to pinpoint the direction of the tosses. Same again with the other two. "That's that," he said, although he realized it wasn't. Using the backpack as a cushion, he sat and pinched mini-daggers from his fingers, palms, and ankles. Nothing to do now but dunk his throbbing hands in the cool water and wait for Diane's all-clear call.

Around him, noise, not sounds, filled the woods. A one-time sanctuary had become a crime scene. He'd fouled the spot where an exuberant, gap-toothed Wyatt hooked his first trout. He recalled his son dropping the pole and tugging the line hand-over-hand. "Dad, got one!" he shouted again and again as he squatted and hopped in the shallow water, snatching at the panicky fish. Like it was a video taken today, he pictured Wyatt beaming at the illegal-sized catch wriggling in his clutch.

Those times should have been unending. Perfect. Lives in ascendancy. Giddy, limitless, certain. Their pre-abortion lives. Life before the mating war that produced Kevin. A war he'd lost without knowing it had been declared. The Diane of those days glowed in his mind. Elegant, yet touchable. Confident beauty. Intelligence, grace, and presence. She loved him. He knew it absolutely. She made him feel worthy, spurred him to live above his weaknesses.

Even now, lightness filled his chest as he replayed the seminal hospital visit. One-day-old Kevin locked onto a breast. Diane's serene face tilted up at him. With no hint of emotion in her voice or expression, she delivered her summation. He'd killed one of her babies and campaigned for Kevin's death. Abstinence would foreclose pregnancy, so that would be her future. He could have a divorce, though she believed their sons would develop better in a nuclear family. If they stayed together, she would sleep in the same bed, thereby preventing gossip by the help. She would also participate in their public life without complaint. When he felt the need for women, all she asked was that he be discreet.

A numbing blindside, with no receptivity to counterarguments. For weeks afterward he credited temporary insanity, some post-partum aberration that would pass, but her abstinence and Kevin both arrived at a first anniversary. A bit drunk at Kevin's party, he celebrated by hooking up with Diane's sister, Roberta, a free spirit who'd often found reasons to touch his hand, or brush a strategic body part against him and smile. She became his inaugural "evening." Keep it in the family. *Take that!* sex in his driveway, against the trunk of her car. Both of them facing the house, daring the silhouettes in the windows to catch them.

He pushed to his feet, flexed and twisted aches from his joints. Before heading to wait for the call in his car, he took a last look around. One of the dwindling number of places on the planet where he'd had wholesome experiences was now sullied as well. Regardless of today's baby step toward reconciliation, the possibility existed she'd sent him here just to spoil another memory.

Chapter 19

Detectives Moseley and Dalton left the pro shop of North Branch Country Club in Flemington. A quick interview with the head pro and an inspection of his vehicle cleared him, at least for now. In little over half a day, they'd eliminated five out of a possible seven Volvo S40s or V40s, Pacific Blue Metallic.

"Who's next?" Moseley said as they settled into the car. Sharing close quarters with Connie Dalton was even more difficult than he'd feared. Forty-eight years old and nervous as a high school kid. He should have known. In the five years since he first met her at the double homicide, she was a frequent visitor to his mind. At that crime scene they'd exchanged maybe three sentences, but that was enough. Each time their paths crossed after that, she loitered in his head for days. Killer body. Eerie amber eyes. A smile that suggested intimacy. Bawdy, smoldering laugh. Flashes of humor and intelligence.

In his life, only two other women had affected him like she did, and he married both of them. At least this time he recognized the warning signs. Two ex-wives keeping him broke and depressed was all he was going to risk. Ever. Jerking off to porn might not be the fuzziest love life, but it was better than finding another note on the kitchen table. Better than coming home to a stripped apartment. Better than jittering a cool barrel against his temple, unsure if everything might end through an act of will or an unexpected twitch.

Dalton grabbed a list off the seat and ran her finger down the names. "Who's next, the man asks? I'll tell you who's next. Wyatt Carpenter, four-four-six Still Hollow Road, Tewksbury."

"I know where that is." He started the engine. "It's beautiful up there. When I'm off duty, I ride those hills on my motorcycle."

"No way." She popped forward in the seat. "I ride, too. Suzuki GSX, candy apple red. What about you? Harley? I bet it's a Harley."

"GSX, that's a racing bike." She had to be good to handle a beast like that.

"I'm right, aren't I? A big-ass Harley."

"So what?"

"Classic overcompensation. I realize this is a scary question, but how big is it?"

Dick jokes? His cheeks and neck buzzed. If he even hinted her boobs were big, he'd risk suspension.

She spit out a cackle. "Blushing? I don't believe it."

"Gimme that name again," he said, snapping his fingers. "Was it Carpenter?"

"First name Wyatt." She laughed again. "I had no idea you were so proper, Lenny."

"Hold it." He pointed to himself. "It's Moseley." The finger swung to her. "And you're Dalton. Capeesh?"

She tipped her face away and raised open hands. "Whatever."

"I wonder…" he said after a mile of silence. "Pretty sure there's a Judge Carpenter lives up that way.

Check with HQ. Have them find out if Jordan Carpenter lives at that address."

"Why would we care?"

"Would you question a Federal judge's family the way we just questioned that golf pro?"

"I wouldn't?"

He caught her gaze. "If it is his house, don't talk."

"Y'know, *Moseley*, that kind of crap doesn't really help me very much. If I'm going to learn anything during this toothache, could you at least think out loud a little? Maybe I'll overhear something useful."

"Hey, I didn't ask for this. You did. I don't owe you shit. Now, check out that address like I told you."

After some muttering hesitation, she began Q & A with the dispatcher.

Good. Keep it chilly.

She signed off. "It's him."

"I'm not deaf."

"Moseley, has it occurred to you that your slimy partner went out on disability one day after you put in your papers? You know what I think? I think he figured a bullshit back injury would keep him from having to spend one more minute with you."

He shrugged and hid his surprise that she'd say something like that about anyone's partner. She couldn't know if he'd lash out, or even worse, repeat it and maybe create a dangerous feud. More evidence of her being unfit. And new on the job like she was, he wondered how she even knew about Karcher.

Maybe he just liked taking the other side of anything Dalton said, but he liked Karcher, even though the guy was dirty. Man's man. Easy laugh, direct, savage in tight situations. Karcher's problem was that they left him undercover too long as a young cop. Moseley had seen it happen to others. Bit by bit, they drift across the line, get off on the action, the adrenaline, being accepted and respected by powerful scumbags. Once that happened, access to easy money, and even easier sex with danger groupies, sealed off the exits.

That was long before he and Karcher had become partners, but even after all those years, it wasn't unusual for them to stop for an envelope during their car time. In spite of many tempting offers, he never took a penny. Occasional head from Karcher's hookers in Trenton, but no money. And that wasn't corruption. He saw those as very short, very successful blind dates.

A quick glance at Dalton's hangdog face got him feeling guilty. It wasn't her fault she looked the way she did, or hypnotized him so easily. Forty-six more days. He could stand on one hand for that long if he had to. "Hungry?"

She glanced at the dash clock. "Who eats at 3:30?"

"No meal times when you're single."

"That's not true. I stick to a normal schedule."

He shifted in the seat. "Thought you were married."

"Divorced over two years now." She snorted. "Kept myself in better shape than a stripper for that bastard, and he took off with a fat waitress. Seven years in the toilet."

"Well, I hope she's not working at the Wagon Wheel Diner. It's just up the road, and I'm getting something to eat. Sit in the car and do your nails if you're afraid."

"No, they moved." Her soft words bounced off the

side window. "Delaware. Texas maybe. I forget." Radio squawks were the only sounds during the short ride to the restaurant.

After selecting a booth, he sat and let his gaze follow her to the Ladies. He pictured her on the throne. Water hitting water. A rumble or two of the toilet paper roll. He missed those sounds. In a home, they meant two people were comfortable with each other. Five years since he'd heard them.

"Much better," she said, sliding into the seat across from him. "Guess I could eat a little something. Wanna split a sandwich?"

"No." He lifted the menu in front of his face.

"Is it just me?"

He lowered the menu to nose level. "Is what just you?"

"I'm raw. I admit it. Happy?"

"Those burgers smell good." He craned his neck around the edge of the booth. "I'd order one if anyone would come to the goddamn table."

"Moseley?"

Her voice going softer got him to face her again.

"Look, I know you think I'm being pushy, but I got into this whole cop thing kinda late. Late as a uniform. Late as a detective. I love it. Feels like something I was meant to do, and I want to be great at it. But I'm thirty-eight."

That news made him examine her face. He still would have guessed no more than thirty-one or two. *So the difference isn't fifteen years.*

"I don't have time to let knowledge, y'know, dribble at me. Captain Garner says you're the best. I thought you could help. And maybe it was naive, but I hoped it might even be fun."

He understood this would cross a line, but he just had to. "Doesn't matter what I try to teach you. You're not right for the job. Never will be." Across from him, her face tightened. "You can get killed out there, Dalton, but you're the kind who won't see it coming. That means whoever's with you goes down, too. I'm trying to save that person."

"Is that right?" The blood squeezed from her lips. "Know what? I'm going to be a good detective whether you help me or not." She glanced over both shoulders and leaned closer. "And I'll tell you something else, you fucking jerk, I'm not putting up with forty more days of your crap. You want out? Fine."

"Nice mouth. Is that how you biker chicks talk?" He dug a dollar from his pocket and spun it onto the table. "Lost my appetite. Let's go. We got a Volvo to check out. And it's forty-six days."

Chapter 20

Jordan slowed the loaner Mercedes to a stop at the beginning of his driveway. The grandeur filling his windshield was something he'd seen a thousand times. It had always pleased, reassuring him that his life was important and being well led. Today he stared and sought out details as if appreciating a new painting. Gentle bends in the driveway pulled his attention, first to the stone bridge, then to the house. Surrounded by a ground-fog of shrubs, the mansion posed on a sprawling lawn. Slate roof over stone walls suggested a fortress, but bay windows, delicate ironwork, and double-doored balconies softened the severity. Splashes of red, yellow, and purple spilled from flower boxes under first floor windows. Wings stepped down from both sides, toward woodland that framed the edges. A masterpiece. His masterpiece. Spoiled only by the unseen canker in the ravine.

Ten minutes earlier, Diane's call assured him that dumping the car had gone well, but time on the bench had shown him criminals always believed they'd covered their tracks. Even the truly clever overestimated their cunning, became proud and careless with details. Most importantly, they underestimated the police. He pictured Wyatt's crumpled, cocaine-dusted car at the bottom of the steep drop, an absurd drape of green blanket and chopped plant stalks the only defense against professional investigators. His imagination jumped to handcuffs, orange jumpsuits, and humiliations, both public and private. But it was done. He took his foot off the brake, tapped the horn once, and rolled toward the house.

Diane ducked from under the rising garage door and ambled into the sunshine with Wyatt, Tanner, and Billy following behind. She smiled as he glided past and parked inside.

A smile. For him. He couldn't remember the last time she'd done that, unless preceded by a slicing comment. He killed the engine and peeked into the rearview once more. Her happy face continued in his direction. Though misplaced under the circumstances, her pleasure resurrected a long-ago time when they enjoyed the sight of each other, welcomed the sound of the other's voice and footstep.

"My God," she said as he got closer, "were you attacked by something?"

He'd forgotten the scourging administered by the underbrush. "Never send an old man on a young man's mission." He hurried past her concerned expression, to the fence along the ravine. "Let's have a look." He inspected the parking area one small section at a time, certain they'd overlooked something obvious. Nothing caught his eye. "Good job up here."

Faces of the work party cracked into tiny smiles.

If there indeed was something suspicious on the driveway, and it caused an investigator to check over the edge, the next view was the one that could snap the trap. He stepped over the fence and peered into the ravine. The Volvo rested thirty-five or forty feet down the severe drop. He knew it, but couldn't see it. The path of the plummet, which he feared would resemble a brush-hogged lane, was pristine, and shade from the ancient tulip trees, oaks, and ironwoods that clung to the slope darkened the car's resting place so completely it vanished.

"We covered it with the blanket, like you said." Wyatt's voice was next to him.

"You guys must have gotten it going pretty fast. Never even skinned the slope."

"Near the bottom it kinda did. It landed on the nose and like flipped onto the roof."

He followed Wyatt's pointing finger.

"Right there," his son said. "See where it whacked some bark off that tree? It knocked out a pretty good chunk of ground next to that, too, but we covered it with leaves and stuff."

Once Wyatt pinpointed the spot, his initial relief faded. In the murk, an inexplicable hump bulged from the ground, tented in four corners.

"Why the face?" Diane said near his other shoulder. "I think everything went very well."

"Judge, please." Billy sounded near tears. "Can we go now?"

"He's right, Jordan. Are we done here?"

Maybe there's still time to get those wheels off.

"Honey." She shook his shoulder. "I asked if it's okay to take the boys home."

"I guess." His gaze had returned to the botch in the ravine when it registered. *Honey?*

"Wyatt," Diane said, "stay here and keep an eye on Kevin. He should still be in the kitchen. You two, in the car. We'll rehearse on the way."

"Diane, wait. Let's think a minute." He wandered

toward her, one hand massaging his taut, painful neck. "So, they get drunk, walk back here, and spend the night. Next morning they have some breakfast and then what? What's Wyatt's plan to get his car back without getting caught?"

Tanner raised his hand. "Judge C, if it was me, I'd wait for you to leave and then tell Mrs. C we needed a ride to Whittemore. I'd just, y'know, confess to the drinking and say we left the car so we wouldn't be driving drunk. Sort of a smart thing that a stupid kid would do. Almost makes him look responsible. Parents love that stuff."

"That fits," Jordan said, reminded once again why Tanner's friendship with Wyatt always had a shadow on it.

"But there's something bigger that doesn't fit, Judge C," Tanner said. "Why would we even go to the river? Rain was coming down like a fire hose."

"Yes, why indeed." Pacing, he rubbed his chin. "How about this?" he said directly to Tanner. "You guys went there to get a little buzzed before the party, but Billy drank so fast he got puking drunk. Then the storm caught you by surprise. Wyatt was afraid Billy would barf in his new car, and everyone was already drenched, so you two agreed to walk him back here and get the car the next day." He scanned all the faces. "How about that?"

The three boys glanced at each other and nodded.

"And one more thing," he said. "Wyatt, when you guys got home, you couldn't find your keys. That way, you might have left them in the ignition, making the theft easier. Or, it could mean you lost them at the river. Either way, both are plausible reasons why the car wasn't at the house."

More nodding from everyone.

Diane raised her eyebrows. "Well, now are we done?"

"I suppose," he said. "Boys, you're all going with my wife. You two," he said, his finger rocking between Wyatt and Tanner, "talk about what you did in the basement until you went to sleep. You know, what games you played, who won, things like that."

"And you'll watch Kevin," she said to Jordan. "That works. So, can we go? Are you calm enough yet?"

She was right again. He had to react casually to everything until the police revealed details. Then it would be reasonable to be agitated. He nodded. "Oh, and don't call the police until you get to Whittemore. Cell calls show location. Wait, call me first. I'll say I told you to call 911. If phone records are ever subpoenaed, that would look proper. And turn your phone off now." He pointed to Wyatt. "You, too. And don't turn them on again until you're going to call me. If I've called for some reason, you'll see it when you power up."

"Wyatt," she said, "run upstairs, will you? My purse is on a chair in the kitchen. Tanner, Billy, wait for me in the Rover. Billy, you're in the front." She waited until the three boys disappeared into the garage. "Impressive," she said, facing him. "I'd almost forgotten."

He shrugged and shook his head. "We're going to need a miracle."

She walked a smile close to his face. Her fingers slid along his cheeks, linked together at the back of his neck. "Thank you." She pulled his face close for a kiss.

"Are you crazy?" He grabbed her wrists and pulled them against his chest. "You think it's that easy? Two smiles and a kiss? That squares us?"

"Jordan, I know. But we can't do this now. C'mon," she said, shaking her hands, "let go."

"This is my redemption, isn't it? Forfeit one life for another." He strained not to shout. "That's it, isn't it?"

She stopped avoiding his gaze. "Jordan, I know."

"You know?" Ten-year reservoirs of anger and humiliation overflowed. "What do you know?" His voice and body trembled. He fought the urge to lift her by the throat, march her flailing body to the fence, and see the horror of understanding when he launched her down to the Volvo.

"I have to go," she said, voice calm, her body slack in his grasp. "We'll talk when I get back."

He threw her hands aside. "Talk about what?"

Her damp, cobalt eyes searched his face, like trying to memorize it. "Life?" She scuffed backward a few steps, turned, and hurried to the car. The Range Rover curled from the garage and stopped next to him. "Don't forget Kevin," she said, gazing forward. The driver's window rose as she drove away.

As always now, the said and unsaid had been reversed. He wanted to run after the car, wave his arms until she saw him in the mirror. What he couldn't imagine was what he'd do if she stopped. Leaden steps carried him into the garage. He opened the basement door and leaned a shoulder inside. "Everything okay, Kevin?"

"Apple juice, Dad? Please?"

"In a minute. Still drawing pictures?"

"Big farm."

"Draw me a nice cow. I'll be up in a second." She'd reached out, and he booted it. He slipped his phone from a front pocket and called her cell. Voicemail. "Oh, right," he muttered, remembering he'd told them to turn their phones off. Behind him in the driveway, sounds of an approaching car mixed with the static and garbled voices of a police radio. He spun his back to the noise. Hair on his neck rose. Showtime. He resisted turning until the buzzing in his face ebbed.

A car door opened. Another. "Judge Carpenter?" a man said. Both doors banged shut.

He turned to see a man and a woman standing on the driveway, each with a leather ID holder open for his inspection. "Don't know if you remember me, Judge," the man said. "Detective Len Moseley. I helped on the American Foreign Trading case a few years back."

"Absolutely," he said. "Driver murdered during a hijacking. FBI took the credit, but everyone recognized you solved it. Excellent work. First rate."

"We all get lucky once in a while."

Being in the garage was a mistake. He should have closed the door and forced all arrivals to the front door. When the officers stayed in the sunshine, each one scanning the surroundings, he took a step toward them.

"Man," Moseley said, "this is some place." He wandered toward the fence, turning a 360 along the way. "If you don't mind me asking, how much property you got here?"

"A shade under two hundred acres." A heavyweight like Moseley pulling this assignment troubled him. Their slim prospects for success were now anorexic. "If this is your partner," Jordan said, holding up his scratched and welted arms, "you'll forgive me if I don't shake hands."

"Oh, sorry," Moseley said without looking at her. "Judge Carpenter, Detective Dalton." He pointed at Jordan's wounds as he headed for the garage. "Looks nasty. Piss off some pussy?"

Jordan caught Dalton rolling her eyes. "A burst of madness, I'm afraid. Gardeners should garden. Judges should…" He smiled and tapped a finger on his chin. "I'm not sure what judges are good for. So, something new come up on that old chestnut?"

"Actually, Judge," Moseley said, "we're here about a hit-and-run in Readington last night. Hear about that?"

"On TV this morning. Dreadful. They said it was the Califano family. My wife and I were wondering if it's the farm stand people. Is it?"

"Judge," Detective Dalton said, stepping forward, "is Wyatt Carpenter your son?"

Moseley narrowed his eyes at her.

"Our older son. Why?"

"Sir, is he home?" She shot a glance at Moseley. "We need to see his Volvo and ask him a few questions."

He sensed tension between the detectives and wondered if somehow it could help sidetrack the investigation. "Strike one, strike two, I'm afraid." Arms spread, he swiveled his face to the two empty garage spaces. "We're standing in his spot. Do you mind telling me what this is all about?"

"Judge," she said, "where was your son last night?"

"Dad!" Kevin squatted on a lower basement step. "Apple juice, please? Thirsty."

"Detectives, would it be all right if we continue this upstairs?" he said, beckoning them to follow him inside. "I'm Mister Mom right now, and after apple juice and popcorn, I'm pretty much out of weapons."

One quick stride positioned Dalton in front of Moseley for the trek into the house. The man's lips thinned and nostrils widened, but he said nothing.

"Go upstairs, Kev." He pushed a button to lower the overhead door. "We're coming." He strolled toward the stairs, exhaling slowly. Each stride away from the ravine produced more relief. *Thank you, Kevin.*

"Sir," Dalton said as they filed through the basement, "I asked where Wyatt was last night."

He stopped the procession, glanced over a shoulder, and affected a concerned expression. "Do you suspect he's involved in the hit-and-run?"

"C'mon, Your Honor." Moseley grinned from behind his partner. "You know this is the part where we ask the questions."

"Of course." He smiled and began the climb to the kitchen.

"Sir," Dalton said, "where was he? Did he go out?"

"For a while with his friends, as far as I know."

"What time was that?" she asked.

He swallowed to clear some cotton from his throat. "I really have no idea. The family got home from an award dinner around eight-thirty, so it was sometime after that."

Kevin looked up from his artwork as the threesome entered the kitchen.

"Detectives," he said on his way to the refrigerator, "this is our son, Kevin. Say hello, Kevin."

"Hello." Kevin held up his drawing. "Big farm."

"My goodness." Dalton bent at the waist, tucked her hands between her knees, and smiled at the swirls of bright colors. "That's beautiful."

Kevin pounded a finger on a squiggle in the center. "Car's in a big hole."

Car. Big hole. His pulse jumped. Kevin understood. Not much, but too much. He must have been watching from the window. "Stop being silly, Kevin. Where's that cow you drew for me? Show her that."

Grinning, his son circled a finger around a red scribble.

Jordan set a half-full glass on the table and edged between Kevin and Detective Dalton. "Okay, here's your juice. Now, do your picture and be quiet. I have to talk to these people." He swapped smiles with Kevin and rubbed his hair. "Okay?"

Juice trickled around the edges of Kevin's mouth when he nodded mid-sip. "Oops," he said, slapping at blots on his shirt.

"It's okay." Jordan was concerned how much Wyatt may have told Kevin. "And you'll be quiet, right?"

"Yeah."

"Judge," Moseley said, "everyone's out looking for blue Volvos, and we don't want to pull your son over if we don't have to. How about you call him? If he's nearby, have him come home. We'll clear his car off our list and get out of your hair."

"I'll try, but it better not work. It's for emergencies only." He dug his phone out and called the stored number. "Ah, as I said." Phone held out to the detectives, they listened to Wyatt's recorded greeting.

Chapter 21

Diane's attention ping-ponged. Road, rearview. Road, Billy. The rearview checks weren't for traffic. They were to watch Tanner coach Wyatt on their phantom activities of the previous evening. Her son was a reluctant pupil. Expressionless. One-word answers to Tanner's stream of specifics.

Each time she glanced to the right, Billy's face pointed at the side window, hands sliding on his thighs to the rhythm of his rocking. Forearm muscles rolled under the skin with each squeeze of his fingers. A child in a man's body. Wyatt, too. Only Tanner seemed grown up. Behind her, his mentoring in deceit was patient and parental. The interplay reinforced what had made her wary of him since the boys were in first grade together. She stopped the Range Rover in front of Billy's house.

Gazing out the window, he stayed in the car, palms continuing to stroke his legs.

"You'll be fine, Billy." She touched his shoulder.

He spun his back to the door. "I didn't *do* anything." Redness ringed his eyes. "Mrs. C, please, I didn't do *anything*."

"You did, Billy," Tanner said. "You didn't go to the cops. Helped us dump the car. You're in. Do your part, dude. Wyatt needs you." He poked his fist over the front seat and held it in front of Billy. "We all agreed."

119

Billy kicked and elbowed the door open and scrambled out. "I didn't do anything," he shouted into the car. He slammed the door and sprinted to his house.

"I'll call him when I get home, Mrs. C. He'll be okay."

She tilted her head and caught Wyatt in the rearview. "Honey, I want to speak to Tanner for a minute. Why don't you get out and stretch a leg cramp or something?"

Appearing dazed, Wyatt left the car.

"Sit up front, Tanner. Easier to talk." She inspected him during the seat exchange and tried to fathom the source of his influence. He wasn't physically imposing. Not tall, like Wyatt or Billy. Not athletic, almost pudgy. Not even good looking. Thick, brown waves, combed straight back. Doughy face, bulbous nose, beginnings of a second chin. But he moved with grace, and without reluctance. His eyes and the set of his mouth said he was unafraid, ahead of you, in on every joke.

"Really, Mrs. C, he'll—"

"Be quiet, Tanner."

Eyes narrowed, he tilted away from her.

"This is your fault. All of it. I know it. You know it."

"Well, I don't think the police would agree with you on that." His brow wrinkled. "Where's this going?"

"If hiding the car goes badly, I want you to tell the police you were driving."

His eyes grew large. A smile crept onto his face. "How about...no."

"You can't let him take the blame for you."

"With all due respect, Mrs. Carpenter, you're being delusional. Wyatt was driv—"

Her open hand against his face sounded like the crack of a pistol shot.

Glaring, he rubbed his cheek.

"Parasite," she said, disappointed at the quaver in her voice. "You've always been a bloated tick on this family. Wyatt's generous nature, his popularity. Our wealth and status."

His smile returned. "You can't touch me. Not without hurting him worse."

The fact he was right only made her angrier. "You're so goddamn smart, Tanner, answer this. What's the most dangerous animal on earth?"

"There's no consensus on that."

"Wrong. It's a mother who thinks her young are in danger."

His eyes rolled. "Mrs. C, give it up. He's my Kevlar vest."

"I'd watch my back if I were you, little man."

Smiling, he raised an eyebrow and faced the windshield.

"Now, get in the back seat." She lowered the window. "Feeling better, honey?" she said to Wyatt. "We have to get going."

"What happened?" Wyatt whispered as the boys passed each other outside the car.

"Dude, she just lost it."

Wyatt ducked into the car and shut the door before Tanner got in. "You hit him?"

The rear door closed.

"Mosquito." She twisted her neck to check traffic before pulling out. "Can't have him getting West Nile."

During the short, quiet hop to Tanner's, she wondered if death was lurking, and somehow she realized it. Perhaps her subconscious had begun decoding mayday calls from organs being overwhelmed by the cancer. That could explain why history and consequences had become irrelevant. Participating in the cover-up, offering herself for prison, fleeting urges to kill Tanner. None held any peril because nothing included a sense of future. Even her new feelings for Jordan were a need for a confessional experience. Closure, not some steamy seclusion, a panting reconciliation where she inhaled his Old Spice, tangled bodies with him, and thrilled to his passion for her. Her desire was to forgive and ask forgiveness before that became impossible.

His life, on the other hand, would continue. Someone would take her place, although not from the collection he'd been defiling on his evenings. Highly doubtful there was a worthy jewel in that lengthening necklace, particularly the ones she knew personally. Those women, even her sister Roberta, were of a type. Independent, discreet, unfulfilled, but only in a sordid, kindred way. She'd never detected a glimmer of someone staking a claim. No dead-air phone calls minutes before he arrived home. No notes, lipsticks, or flavored lotions planted in his jacket pockets. He was too clever to risk a woman of ambition. With the possible exception of now.

His current receptacle was so trite the insult had to be intentional. Amanda, a former Miss South Carolina or something, nearing forty and still only a secretary. That tramp couldn't help but be dazzled by his life. The recklessness of it all. He had to know office romances never escape detection. Risking everything for a few moments of grunting domination. The slut could cash him like a Lotto jackpot when the fling burned out. And that vulgar kiss at the banquet, not five feet from her and the children. Lips parted, eyes nearly closed, one moment from ecstasy. He should have recoiled from it, shown every witness that a boundary had been crossed, that he wasn't about to tolerate such a slight to his family.

"Mom, you gonna stop?"

The car skidded to a halt just beyond the driveway of Tanner's house.

"I presume someone will call me?" Tanner said from outside the car.

The rear door banged shut when she sped off without a word. Speaking might have released the tears.

Chapter 22

Moseley chewed his lips during the drive back to the office. *Stupid bitch.* He'd instructed Dalton to keep quiet at the Carpenters. Not only did she talk, but she stepped on his lead in the interview. The right questions, but they were his to ask. If today wasn't going to be their last together, she'd get an earful.

In the passenger seat, Dalton tapped her heel on the floorboard and shifted in the seat every few seconds. She obviously had something on her mind, but he wasn't going to ask.

"What do you figure that place is worth?" she said. "Five million?"

Thought she was pissed. "Might as well be a billion," he said.

"Wasn't that kitchen something? Bigger than my whole apartment. Some sweet life…Oh, and that poor boy. Always makes me sad to see a retarded person. One crack at life, and that's how they go through it. Seemed happy, though."

This is detective talk? He shrugged, kept quiet.

"You must feel good Judge Carpenter remembered you, huh? Seemed real positive, too. Maybe you should ask him for a cushy corporate job when you retire. People like him are always—"

"Dalton, shut up."

"Shut up?"

"I have a crime question for you."

"Shut up? Who the hell—"

"Yeah, shut up. Our Volvo, think it might be the Carpenters'?"

She snorted. "Right."

"Uniform's report says two voices, maybe three. Arguing. Possibly teenagers. I was waiting for you to match it up, you being such a great detective and all."

"Can't be…Can it?" Sounded like she was thinking out loud. "And by the way, kiss my ass."

"Gotta see the car. Then we'll know."

"Uh-uh. *You'll* know." She pumped a finger at him. "We're done, pal. I was serious. Soon as we get back, I'm talking to Captain Garner."

"What if he keeps you on this case and dumps me? Maybe you need to keep that keen mind of yours trained on this one a little longer."

"You're a total asshole."

"Aw, see? Now you hurt my feelings. I thought women were supposed to be sensitive." He checked the long silence to his right.

She'd angled her face from him, hand covering her mouth.

No. Don't be smiling. He checked the Caller ID on his buzzing cellphone. "What's up, Captain?" Garner contacting him by cell was puzzling.

"Couple things. First, a call just came in about a stolen blue Volvo."

"Let me guess," Moseley said. "Wyatt Carpenter's the owner."

Dalton twisted toward him.

"How'd you know?" the captain said.

"We left their house about ten minutes ago. The car

wasn't there, and neither was the kid. Are you aware he's Judge Jordan Carpenter's son?"

"Great," the captain said after a short silence.

"Is the kid at the station?"

"The mother called it in, from her car."

"So they're coming in now?"

"The kid was in the car with her, but she said she was sick, and they were going home. I told her you'd swing by to take a statement."

"Crap. Almost got through the day. All right. I'll check with you later."

"Lennie, there's, uh, something else," the captain said, his voice lowered. "I was hoping to talk to you when you came off shift, but I can't be here tonight. Hang on."

Moseley heard a door close, footsteps, and the squeak of a desk chair. "Still there?" the captain said.

"Go ahead."

"You know that Internal Affairs has been investigating Karcher."

Moseley switched the phone to his left ear and pressed it tight to his head. He tipped away from Dalton. "How would I know that?"

"This is serious, dammit. He's admitted to shaking down hookers for sex and cash. Says it was both of you."

He hoped his grin camouflaged the shock. "Well, that is something."

"Is Dalton sitting next you?"

"Absolutely."

"You can't say anything about this."

"Won't be an issue, Captain."

"They want to see you tomorrow. Ten in the small

conference room."

"Thanks. So, guess I'll see you then."

"Lenny, I.A. says they have you cold. Tell me that's impossible."

"C'mon, Captain."

"All right. Watch yourself with the judge."

He couldn't believe Karcher rolled on him. It wasn't like they were friends, but he deserved a little loyalty. A lot of money went into that bastard's pocket without him saying anything, or even taking a skim. Blowjobs now and then from the guy's hookers, but that was it. And those were nothing. The girls joked and took care of business. Never any money. If this was about an occasional freebee, he'd deny it. If the girls signed complaints, his word would trump theirs. Unless there was video.

Tires squealed as he ducked into a mini-mall parking lot.

"Hey," Dalton yelled, retrieving her purse from the floor, "how about a little warning?"

"We're going back to the Carpenters."

"So I gathered from the phone call."

"Is that a problem for you? Got a hair appointment or something?" Tires screeched again as he swung onto the main road. *Women. Time bombs.*

"What's wrong with you?" she said. "Want me to drive?"

"Save your questions for Wyatt Carpenter." He could tell she was leaning forward, watching him, but he refused to make eye contact.

"Moseley, I wasn't listening, but I heard something about Karch—"

"Stay outta this!"

When he glanced over, she'd tilted away and was glaring at him. "You need help, pal. Professional help." She batted her back into the seat and faced forward. "Goddamn psycho," she said under her breath.

Her slow burn gave him a chance to settle his mind. While he'd enjoy pumping a .44 through Karcher's head, not much chance that was going to happen. But he was sure as hell going to talk to him, find out what he said and why. "Dalton," he said, trying to appear and sound sorry, "I was way off base just now."

"No, really?"

"Look, this could end up being your case, so when we get there, you handle the interviews."

"Yeah?" A little smile pulled at a corner of her mouth. "Serious?"

"Absolutely. I think you'll do a good job." He'd use the time to slip away and call Karcher.

Chapter 23

Jordan waited at the kitchen table with Kevin. On the opposite wall, an episode of *SpongeBob SquarePants* played on the flat panel TV. Over Kevin's giggling, he caught the hum of a garage door rising. At least Diane and Wyatt had gotten home before the detectives showed up. "Kevin, will you be okay here for a minute? I have to talk to Mom in the office. Wyatt, too."

Face forward, Kevin pulled his eyes into the corners. "Mad at Mom?"

"I'm not mad at anyone, except myself."

Kevin turned to him, full face, head shaking. "No yelling?"

"Just talking. Promise." He smiled and rubbed Kevin's back until his son smiled back.

Diane preceded Wyatt into the kitchen. She paused at Kevin's chair. "Oh, *SpongeBob*, your favorite." After a peck on the boy's head, her gaze found Jordan. "Did I tell you the police are coming here?" she said, discomfort tightening her face.

"Any minute, I assume." Jordan's attention bounced between her and Wyatt, who was shuffling to the windows overlooking the ravine. Plodding at the same lethargic pace, Diane headed for the center island. She set her purse on the counter, leaned over the double sink, and massaged her forehead. "God," she whispered, "does cancer cause migraines?"

Seemed impossible, but every time he focused on Wyatt's situation, Jordan forgot Diane's cancer. He jumped from the table and hurried to the island.

"Leave me," she said, a stiff arm pointed his way. Her face relaxed. "I'm sorry." She squeezed his fingers and let go. Head back, she stroked her forehead again. "So, is there anything we should be doing?"

"Yes, but let's go in the office."

Her knees dipped. "Why?"

"You'd be surprised what he understands," he said, dropping his voice and bobbing his chin toward Kevin. "And when they show up, keep him in his room."

"Honey," she said to Kevin, "stay here until I come back. Okay?"

"Yeah," he said, not looking away from the TV.

They filed down the hallway to the foyer. In the great room, Palladian windows looked out to the front of the house and the driveway. Passing the first window, Wyatt glanced out and ran to the glass. "Oh, no. They're here." He tottered away from the window, eyes shut tight. "I can't do this."

"Yes, you *can* do this," Jordan said, trying to sound unconcerned. He sidled to the window in time to see Detective Moseley's car crest the stone bridge in the driveway. When it hugged the bend leading to the circle by the front door, instead of to the garages, he blew out a long exhale.

"Stop it, Wyatt," Diane said. "You know what to say. It's very simple." She scattered magazines on the coffee table and sofa. "That's better. Casual. Jordan, you'll get the door. I'll make some coffee." She headed toward the kitchen.

"Dad, please," Wyatt said, a quiver in his voice, "I can't do this."

She spun toward their son. "Goddamn you!" Face contorted, Diane charged, fists shaking. "Do you want to go to prison? Grow up!"

Jordan jumped between her and Wyatt, palms raised. "You're not helping." He slid side to side, blocking her continued rush. "Forget the coffee. Take Kevin to his room. He shouldn't be hearing this anyway. I'll stay with Wyatt."

Peeking around Jordan's shoulder, she poked a finger at Wyatt. "Be strong. For me as well as yourself. Do you understand?"

Wyatt had either ignored her or only nodded.

"Answer me!" Wavy, blue veins plumped in her neck. Tendons stretched like tent ropes. A burst of fury that recalled the moment he suggested Kevin be aborted.

"I understand," Wyatt screamed.

"Ah, crap," Jordan said under his breath.

Kevin stood in the foyer, head down, watery eyes watching, lips pressed tight.

"It's okay, Kev," he said. "Mom had to explain something to Wyatt. Now she needs you to go upstairs. G'won. She'll be right there." He turned a reluctant Diane by the shoulders. "Go, and if they ask to talk to you, leave him up there."

"Wyatt, be strong," she cried, teeth bared, fists pressed together. "This will be over soon." She followed Kevin up the front stairs.

Jordan faced Wyatt and rested a hand on his shoulder. "Okay. Real quick. First, you don't have to rush your answers. Take time to think. It's perfectly

131

normal. Second, it's okay to say you don't remember. Nobody can be expected to recall every detail of what they did yesterday, especially if they'd been drinking. Last, and most important, only answer what they ask. Don't volunteer *anything.*"

Wyatt nodded. Breaths heaved through his open mouth.

Car doors closed in front of the house.

"I'll stay with you during the questioning," he said, easing toward the door. "That'll make them cautious about what they can ask."

The doorbell chimed. Hand on the latch, he popped Wyatt a thumbs-up, and opened the door. "Detectives, please come in. Peculiar turn of events, eh?" He closed the door. "Detectives Moseley and Dalton, this is our son, Wyatt."

Wyatt nodded and shook hands with each.

"Can I get either of you something?" he said, rubbing his hands together, "Coffee, soft drink, fruit juice?"

Detective Moseley fanned an open hand to his partner. "Your case. I'll follow your lead."

"Nothing, thank you," she said, sounding preoccupied. Lips parted, she scanned the appointments in the mansion. "Wow. Like a movie set."

"Thank you," Jordan said, smiling, "unless you mean one of the Frankensteins. This way." He led them down the hall to the kitchen, pleased to know Detective Dalton was heading up the investigation. He had no idea how competent she was, but Moseley was flat-out excellent. At the table, he shut off *SpongeBob* and pulled out a chair for Detective Dalton. "Please."

"Judge," she said, sitting and opening her notepad

to a fresh page, "are you staying for this?"

"Any reason I shouldn't?"

Across the table, Wyatt and Detective Moseley took seats next to each other.

"As his attorney?" she said.

"Are you saying he needs one?"

"Do you want an attorney present during this interview?"

Impossible, but she sounded like they were about to make an arrest. "Detective, my son's a victim. He doesn't need an attorney."

The two investigators exchanged glances.

Wide-eyed, Jordan shifted in his seat. "You're joking. Wyatt's a suspect?"

"There's certainly a possibility it was his car," Dalton said. "At the very least, he's a person of interest."

As he'd done to many a witness in his past life, he leaned his bulk forward, intruding into her space until she retreated. "Is he a suspect? Yes or no." He stared until she blinked.

Her gaze darted to Moseley.

"Judge," Moseley said, "pretty sure the car's going to tell us that, once we find it. So, Dalton, let me see if I understand this right. Are you saying their choice is to let Wyatt make a voluntary statement here, or we question him at the station, in the presence of an attorney?"

Jordan felt like a first-year law student for not anticipating the drill.

"Yes," she said, "exactly."

He caught Wyatt flipping his attention from speaker to speaker like a cornered animal. There was no way he could carry this off yet. "Well," he said, "as long as there's any chance my son could be a suspect, I think we'll have to take the attorney route. I'm sure you understand."

"Your call, sir," Dalton said, closing her notepad.

"Wait," Moseley said. "We're already here. Let's at least do the stolen car report."

Slow, heavy footsteps descended the back staircase. Diane looked half a sniffle away from a meltdown. "Hello," she said softly, gaze wandering.

"Diane," Jordan said, pushing to his feet and gesturing to the officers, "this is Detective Dalton, and this is Detective Moseley."

"Thank you for coming," she said, her voice feeble. At the center island, she paused and braced stiff arms on the countertop.

"Diane?" He took a step toward her.

"I'm fine," she said, fluttering the backs of her fingers at him. "Just a little shell-shocked." She inched toward the table. "May I join you?"

Moseley scraped his chair back from the table. "Take my seat, Mrs. Carpenter." He fished a phone from his pants pocket. "I have to make a call, anyway."

"Now?" Dalton said.

Moseley shuffled backward down the hallway toward the front door. "I won't knock when I come back in, if that's okay."

"Of course." Jordan studied Detective Dalton's face. After Moseley left, her gaze lingered on the hallway while her fingers readied the pad and pen for note taking. She obviously wanted him there. Confidence? Insubordination? Affection? The reason wasn't important. Any might present an advantage.

"All right," Dalton said, turning her attention to Wyatt, "where did you last see the car?"

"Detective, wait," Jordan said. "Is this going to require Wyatt's signature?"

"Yes, sir."

"Then I'm going to have to stop you. It's all part of the same thing, really." He stood and sidestepped toward the fridge. "Here's what I propose. We'll meet you at the station tomorrow at 2:00, with our attorney. Orange juice, anyone? I'm having some."

The detective shook her head. "No thanks for the juice offer, and 2:00 should be all right, but I'll confirm."

"Honey?" he said to Diane. "Some OJ?"

Diane, who'd been holding or stroking the back of Wyatt's hand, paused before shaking her head.

He recognized what she was up to. She'd even removed her makeup. The ghoulish appearance was effective because Dalton's glances often found Diane's face since she'd joined them.

"Ma'am, are you all right?"

Eyes half closed, Diane nodded.

"Mrs. Carpenter, is there something you want to tell me?"

"Sorry?" Diane wrinkled her brow.

"Is there something you want to tell me?"

Jordan rubbed away a smile.

"I'm not following," Diane said.

Dalton slowly scanned the kitchen. "I can't imagine replacing the car could be much of a hardship to your family, but you seem very upset. I just wondered if it was something else."

"Detective," Diane said, leaning forward, "today

I've learned my son's car has been stolen, and that I have breast cancer. How should I be acting, exactly?"

"Oh," Dalton's face pinched. "I'm so sorry."

"Yes, well..." Diane sagged back in her seat.

"May I be excused?" Wyatt said.

"Of course, darling, and check on Kevin for me, would you? I think he's coloring in his room."

"Kevin's very sweet," Dalton said, her gaze following Wyatt as he raced up the stairs two at a time. "He showed me a drawing when we were here earlier."

Tingling rose in Jordan's face. *Car's in a big hole.* "Detective," he said, "how about something other than juice?"

She stowed the notepad in her purse. "No, nothing. I'll just wait outside for my partner."

"Sit in a hot car?" he said. "No, please stay. I'm sure he'll be right in." He poured a glassful of juice, wandered to the windows, and left the women in awkward silence. Outside, tranquil colors and swaying foliage in the ravine eased his tension. Even better, progress of the afternoon sun had created a near blackout at the bottom. Other than night, the Volvo couldn't have been less visible. His calm evaporated when Detective Moseley meandered into view.

Phone to his ear, the detective zigzagged toward the ravine, an ant losing and relocating a pheromone trail. He paused every few steps, index finger jabbing at the mouthpiece. Next to the fence he stopped and rested the tip of his shoe on a slat. Still talking, he stepped over to the ravine side and sat on the rail. Gestures became more frantic. His voice rose, loud enough to be audible through the window glass. He jumped to his feet and stared at the screen of the phone. A few seconds passed before he returned it to his pocket.

Arms immobile at his sides, hands curled into fists, Moseley stomped along the ravine's rim. His head shook slowly, as if disbelieving something. He swung one leg, then the other, to the driveway side of the fence and sat where the rail joined the fence post. Elbow on top of the post, head drooping, his gaze stayed toward the ground. A finger picked at one of the lag bolts they'd removed and replaced. He dropped onto one knee and eyeballed the bolt from different angles. Bending close to the driveway, he swept a hand around the base of the post and examined whatever had collected in his palm.

On his feet again, he strode along the rail to the next bolt, one that hadn't been undone, and repeated the inspection. Back at the first bolt, he continued along the fence in the other direction and inspected the connections at the next two posts. After returning to the original spot, processional strides carried him back and forth between the set of disturbed bolts. Squatting like a baseball catcher, he pivoted his face toward the stone bridge and followed an imaginary path to the fence. Standing again, his gaze traced the path one more time.

Returning to the ravine side of the fence, he roamed the edge, hands cupping his eyes. Every few feet he paused, tested his footing, and peered into the chasm. He held point briefly before standing erect. Fingers rubbing his mouth, he stepped back onto the driveway. His gaze drifted from the parking area, to the garages, then upward, until locking with the eyes at the kitchen window.

"Son of a bitch," Jordan said under his breath. He raised his juice glass to the detective, and followed the man's slow paces back toward the front door. Mouth dry, palms wet, he anticipated Moseley's progress. The latch click made him twitch. His breaths quickened as steps approached the kitchen and stopped.

"Dalton," Moseley said from the hallway, "if you're done here, let's go." Foot strikes headed toward the front door.

No questions? Jordan battled the jitters as Detective Dalton gathered her things and stood.

"Your Honor," she said, "I'll confirm the two o'clock for tomorrow. And Mrs. Carpenter, I hope things work out for you."

Diane dismissed her with a blank-faced nod.

"I'll see you out, Detective," he said.

Diane joined Jordan at the great room window.

In the circular driveway, Dalton climbed into the passenger side and slammed her door. Moseley opened the driver's door, paused to return Jordan's stare, and eased behind the wheel. Face pointed forward, he sat frozen, hands at ten and two.

"Go," Jordan whispered. His nerves refused to stand down. An accusation or probing question when Moseley returned to the house would have almost been a relief. Start the fight. Make the opponent thrust, so he could parry. He'd learned over the years that anticipating an ambush was more debilitating than the attack. Already beginning to flag, he also understood fatigue could lead to carelessness.

Detective Dalton must have said something because Moseley snapped a quick snarl her way before starting the engine.

"Moseley knows," Jordan said without turning away from the window. He followed the car as it curled around the front circle and rushed down the driveway. "I watched him figure it out. Took him about thirty seconds. The bolts. The wrench must have knocked some paint off. Stupid," he screamed into cupped hands.

"If he knows," she said, "why isn't someone arrested?"

"Wyatt," he shouted toward the front stairs, "get down here."

Clunking footsteps descended to the foyer.

"They're gone, Wyatt," he said. "C'mon, speed it up. Everyone in the office. Let's go."

"Jordan, why would they leave if he knows?"

"I have to call Marty Bender," he said, marching toward the office. They needed a great lawyer, and right now.

"Who's Marty Bender?" she said, trailing at his shoulder.

He paused at the office door and hooked a finger at Wyatt. "Goddammit, move. Marty Bender," he said to her, "is the best defense attorney I have ever seen."

"Shouldn't this have been done already?"

He snorted and shook his head. "Must be wonderful to know everything."

"I still think you're overreacting."

Wyatt slipped into the office and leaned his back against a wall near the door.

At his desk, Jordan pulled a plastic box of business cards from a side drawer. "Right now, Moseley is on the phone requesting a search warrant." His fingers tickled through the cards until he found Bender's. Repeating the number under his breath, he punched it into the handset. "If they're not back here within the hour, with a tow truck, I'll be stunned." He held the phone to his ear and cleared his throat at the sound of ringing.

"This is Judge Jordan Carpenter," he said to the receptionist. "Put Marty on. It's very important."

"Mr. Bender's in court, Your Honor."

"Page him."

"Certainly. Where can he reach you?"

Diane's puttering during the call irritated him. She repositioned a box containing his hole-in-one golf ball, lifted the base of the phone to sweep dust from underneath. Everything was unraveling, as he told her it would, yet she seemed oblivious. He gave the receptionist his cell number and hung up.

"When he calls back," she said, "tell him I was driving."

He slumped into the desk chair and shook his head. "No more insane suggestions, thank you. I'll handle this."

"If they really are coming back and find the car," she said, sitting on the edge of the desk, "someone in this family must have been driving. I'm not being insane. We have to tell them something."

"Listen to me." He poked a finger at her and Wyatt. "From now on, we don't tell the police anything unless Marty Bender gives the OK. He'll ask us only what he needs to know. And this is important, he won't ask if anyone's guilty, so don't volunteer it. Do you understand?"

"Dad, how can he help if he doesn't know the truth?" Wyatt's legs jittered.

"He once told me he does his best work when he believes, no matter what, there's a possibility his client is innocent."

"What if the police are back here before he calls?" Diane said. "Shouldn't you at least try someone else?"

Even her good suggestions were annoying. "To do what? Fire them an hour later? He'll call."

"Honey," she said to Wyatt, "would you see if Kevin's all right?"

"I just left him. He's doing one of his drawings."

"Check again, and please close the door."

Wyatt's gaze flipped between the parents. He shook his head and pulled the door shut as he left.

"Jordan," she said, smiling across the desk, "I had some time to think while I was dropping off Billy and Tanner. With all we have going on right now, how about you put Amanda into temporary mothballs?"

"Oh, no!" He jumped to his feet, arms crisscrossing. "No, no, no, no. We're not doing this now." She'd waived the right to this conversation years ago.

"Well, at least that confirmed my suspicion."

"Shut up." Acting as if she was the clever lawyer. He wanted to bash her smug face.

"Oh, I'm sorry. I'm violating the treaty."

"Stop. Now."

Her smile faded. "Jordan, of all the mistakes we might be making right now, she's the stupidest."

"Are you deaf? We're not doing this."

"Aw, embarrassed?" Her smile returned.

"I'm warning you." He stabbed a finger, kept his arm extended. If she got close enough, he wasn't sure he could stop himself.

"Actually, Jordan dear, I'm warning you. No Amanda."

"She has nothing to do with this."

Diane inched closer, legs brushing along the edge of the desk, her fingers crawling across the top. "You know I don't care about the sex. It's her."

"Stop saying it's her."

"Jordan," she said, pushing her palm at him, "you're making an ass of yourself."

Trembling, he resisted rushing at her. "Don't make me." Her triumphant face. He needed to quiet her face, remove the smirk. A fist. Strangling hands. Something.

"I know it's her," she said from even closer.

He understood, at that moment, how a person could be driven to uncontrollable violence. While he was piling sandbags against the flood, she was dynamiting dams. Lights bubbled in his narrowing field of vision. He dropped into the desk chair rather than fall to the floor. Chilly beads grew on his forehead and upper lip. *Heart attack?* Eyes shut, he monitored for constricted breathing or pain. Nothing, at least nothing telltale.

"I know you too well," she said, her breathy, growling voice close to his face. "If you're caught protecting Wyatt, at least that smacks of noble intent. You could stand that."

She doesn't see I'm in trouble?

"But when that trailer trash takes you down, you'll be just one more aging crotch-sniffer, popping Viagra and chasing his hard-on. You couldn't bear that. And this time it'll be too late to buy a new image.

She's guessing about the Viagra.

"And file this away, too, Your Honor. If I'm still alive when it happens, I won't be one of those asinine, reflected-glory wives, standing next to her husband at the microphone while he whimpers about his sins. The boys and I will be elsewhere, with our half of whatever she doesn't take."

His lightheadedness passed. No longer in danger of keeling over, he pivoted the chair away from her and stood. "Just couldn't leave it alone, could you?" He wiped his forehead and blew out a deep breath. "You drive me away, then pull this crap." Head shaking, he stepped toward the door.

"Dammit, you're not listening." Dashing around him, she positioned herself between him and the exit. "I'm not asking you to forego your evenings. Just not Amanda. For God's sake, she's your employee. She can ruin your career. Why can't you..." Her eyes widened. Fingertips covered her lips. "Oh, my God. You're in love with her?"

"Absurd, and stop saying it's her."

Eyes closed, she let her head flop backward and bonk against the mahogany door. "Of course. What else could explain the colossal idiocy?"

"This conversation is over." He pumped a thumb sideways. "Move."

She pressed her back into the door and spread her arms against the frame. "Tell me you won't see her."

"Do I have to move you?" He edged closer.

"Tell me."

His hand cupped her neck and easily swept her to the side.

"Don't touch me!" Wild swings rained slaps and scratches at his face and shoulder.

He shoved her away and yanked the knob.

Goggle-eyed, Wyatt hopped back from the threshold, sprinted through the great room, and out the front door.

Chapter 24

Workday or weekend, late afternoon traffic into Flemington ran slow. Any other day the stop-and-go would have frustrated Moseley enough for him to hit the horn and flashers, creating gaps in the traffic he could slalom through. Today, that strategy didn't find its way into his crowded mind.

From the moment they'd gotten into the car at the Carpenters, Dalton peppered him with noise. Now and again, a word registered—"bully" "cancer" "mansion"—but none captured his front brain. "Asshole" was the last to get through before she folded her arms and stared through the side window.

He welcomed the chance to concentrate. His conversation with Karcher in Judge Carpenter's driveway had confirmed the worst. They did have video of him with at least three of the hookers. How they got it, he had no idea, but Karcher confirmed he was cooperating to bring him down. That dirtbag accused him of being a rat, said Internal Affairs knew things only he could have given them. A classic *Fuck me? Fuck you!* "Lucky you're still alive," was the last thing Karcher said before hanging up on him. Then in the middle of all that, he'd stumbled onto the Volvo. At least he was pretty sure he had. Probably his last discovery as a detective.

Detective. For the first time since putting in his

papers, he realized it was over. Regardless of what happened tomorrow, that conversation with Karcher was the moment his career ended. He was a civilian, driving a detective's car. Next time he entered the precinct, his home for fourteen years, it would be as an accused. The life he loved and hated was over. The few specks of time when he believed his existence mattered were finished. To his surprise, other than imperiling his pension money, going out under a cloud didn't much concern him. Of all the people in the department, only two good opinions meant anything: Captain Garner and Dalton. The captain would listen and believe him. There was nothing his boss could do to help, but he would stand by him. Dalton, if he'd guessed her feelings right, would be different. Her disappointment would be like a child for a fallen parent, disillusioned more than outraged.

He refocused on his immediate problem, the hookers pressing a case against him. It made no sense, especially since he knew they worked for Karcher. They would never sign complaints unless he told them to. And both men had to be in the videos. Since Internal Affairs must have his old partner on other issues, shaking down hookers would only make it worse. This had the stink of a deal. I.A. must be keeping Karcher out of that charge. Editing the videos would be easy enough, then they could turn his own nothing infraction into a corruption case. It might be a nice feather for someone if they could chop a pension six weeks before someone was going to start collecting. "Snakes," he said, whacking a backhanded fist into the door.

"What?" Dalton said, gawking.

"Nothing."

"Hey." She pointed forward.

A tug on the steering wheel jostled the car away from the center line. "Go back to your shopping list," he said.

"Just watch the damn road."

Her delayed chuckle annoyed him. "Something funny?" He glanced over to see her pinching away a smile.

"I really was doing my shopping list."

Not that it would ever happen, but he wondered what they would be like as a couple. She was tough enough to kick him out of his black moods, and maybe he wouldn't even have so many with her around. They could be sarcastic with each other, ride together, and screw until their brains rolled out their ears. "Dalton, tomorrow, you may hear something." An explanation would be pointless. Her respect, if that's what she felt for him, wouldn't survive the news. Suspension was going to mash him and Karcher into a two-headed scumbag.

"Tomorrow I may hear what?"

"I'm off this case."

"You son of a bitch." She twisted toward him. "You called Captain Garner from the Carpenters. What did you say about me?"

"Jesus Christ." They couldn't be a couple. "I just know, all right?"

"Bullshit." She pounded her back into the cushion. "So, I guess this means you're not going to be there for the two o'clock with their lawyer."

"Two?"

"That was the first thing I told you when we got in the car. It's tomorrow, at the station."

"I'm out. Come ten o'clock tomorrow morning, you're on your own."

"But you…What's happening at ten?"

"Just be ready to solo."

From the passenger's seat, rustling mixed with noisy exhales. "Well, what if I ask Garner to leave you on? You know, through the interview."

"You'll be fine." He doubted that was true.

"Oh, no question," she said, pushing herself taller in the seat. "You saw him try his big man, intimidation crap on me." She snorted. "I can handle him. But, y'know, we were trained to do this in teams. Who's going to be with me? Garner?"

He shrugged.

"You think the whole Carpenter family will try to sit in?"

"No idea." He regretted breaking the silence.

"Hope not. Wife got kinda lippy with me. I know she has cancer and all, but—"

"Cancer?" *Lenny, shut up!*

"Breast cancer. I told you that half an hour ago. Christ," she said, facing the side window, "it's like being married again."

At the station he parked under the shade of a sprawling maple and left the engine running. Last chance. He understood he should tell her the Volvo might be at the bottom of the ravine, but that would have been a detective-to-detective thing. That wasn't him anymore. Let someone who's still on the payroll solve crimes. "Your interview," he said without looking at her, "your report."

"You're not going in?"

He shook his head, stared forward.

"Sure you don't want to tell me what's going on?" she said.

"Beat it."

Dalton snatched her purse off the seat and shouldered the door open. "Thanks for nothing, jackass."

The door slammed so hard his ears popped. He dropped the car into reverse but left his foot on the brake. His insides hollowed even more as he watched her hurry across the parking lot. A graceful hop onto the sidewalk, up the front steps on her toes, then gone. Foot off the brake, he headed home. The evening would include too many beers and at least a few minutes of videos on the computer. After that, he could sleep, and when he awoke in the morning, maybe he wouldn't be hearing that sketchy whisper anymore, the one suggesting another reason he withheld the info about the Volvo.

Chapter 25

Wyatt wished he'd rammed a fist into his father's face, not run away. His mother was back at the house, helpless, and here he was, two miles away, stumbling along Rockaway Road, nose running, tears still blurring his vision.

The sound of an overtaking vehicle rumbled between the walls of the narrow valley. He darted into thick woods on the river side of the street and peered from the underbrush. A landscaper's rusty pickup glided past. At first, he was relieved it wasn't his mother, or father, or the police, but then he checked where he was and what he was, a pair of eyes in the brush, senses on high alert. This would be his future. A mouse, existing in dark places. A victim's life. A coward's life.

Two days. That's all it had taken. His perfect life— past, present, and future—down the toilet. Everything was bad, but some stuff was worse than others. The accident and taking off afterward was horrible, but things could end up sort of okay if Torrie got better. A no harm/no foul kind of thing. His family could never be fixed.

No way he was going back home. Liars and strangers. Both of them wearing masks, probably for his whole life. What he'd heard through the office door was between extraterrestrials, not people he worshipped. His father would never cheat, but if he did, his mother would walk out. She wouldn't vet his partners.

Eavesdropping on their fight explained a lot. All those dinners without his father. The evenings his mother spent reading in her bedroom after singing Kevin to sleep. He assumed his father was busy doing what powerful men did, but some of those times he must have been screwing other women. The idea of parents, most of all his, having sex was sick enough. Now he had to drive away the image of his father and Amanda doing it. She was epic, and he could see himself with her, but not The Almighty Judge. And then there was Torrie. His car put her in the hospital, but no one seemed to care. Neither parent even asked the cops how she was doing. He didn't either, but The Judge had told him to keep his mouth shut, so that was what he'd done. Always the good son.

"Baloney," he said, hand in his pocket for his phone. That made him laugh. A felon, alone in the woods, and he said "baloney." His parents wouldn't tolerate swearing. They said it was ignorant and immature. An occasional "damn" from them, and his father's f-bomb this morning, but that was about it. Two people, both willing to cover up a crime, one who cheats and one who approves of it, would ground him for a weekend if they caught him saying "fuck."

He clicked his phone on. Too many texts to go through right then, so he checked for missed calls. Four: his father, his mother, Tanner, and one more from his mother. No way he was listening to the parents, and he was sort of headed toward Tanner's anyway, so he returned that one.

His friend picked up so fast he must have had the

phone in his hand. "Dude, talk to me. I'm dying here."

"Nothing to tell yet." He heard a door click shut.

"No cops?" Tanner said in a whisper.

"They came, but The Judge wouldn't let them question me without a lawyer."

"And they left? Just like that?"

"We have to go to the station tomorrow at two."

"Do they know Billy and I were with you?"

"I just told you, The Judge shut it down. Nothing until tomorrow."

"Y'know, with everyone afraid about Billy, there's still time to keep us out of it."

He knew Tanner didn't give a crap about Billy. "I don't know. The Judge may have already said something about you guys."

"But if he didn't?"

"Tanner, why would I go to Whittemore by myself, leave the car, and walk home in the rain?" Anticipating the logic of the questions gave him some confidence. Maybe he could get through a police interrogation. "We're sticking with Plan A."

"I guess…Must be brutal there. Are they crushing your onions non-stop?"

"Worse."

"Worse how? Dude, what happened?"

He couldn't tell anyone about his parents. Ever. "Nothing. Look, I gotta give Billy the update. Call you later."

Seated on the ground, with his back pressed against a giant tulip tree, he pushed the phone's *Contacts* button and selected *Billy.* Instead of calling his friend, he scrolled to *Home,* pressed *Send* and closed his eyes.

"Son," his father said, "where are you?"

"Put Mom on."

"Wyatt, I'm sorry."

"Put Mom on."

"You can't overhear part of a conver—"

"Hey! I'm not talking to you. Put Mom on."

"I'll come get you. Where are you?"

"Tell her to call me from her cell." He hung up.

A few seconds passed before his phone buzzed. Caller ID showed it was his mother. "Mom," was all he could get out before he started bawling again.

"Honey, come home."

Questions and accusations muddled together, preventing him from forming a thought he could put into words. The sobs he hadn't seen coming added to the shame. His first serious encounter with life's ugly surprises had him wailing like a newborn. Head hanging between his knees, a string of drool stretched toward the crushed leaves of the forest floor.

"I won't ask you to understand," she said, "and I'm not going to explain. These are private matters between your father and me."

"Bullshit!" He swiped the back of his hand across his mouth and eyes.

"Wyatt, don't judge what you don't know." Her tone was gentle, patient.

"Fucking liars!"

"Don't speak to me like that." Again, she sounded calm. "You shouldn't have been listening. And what you heard doesn't concern you."

He clamped a hand over his eyes. "Holy God. You make me sick. Both of you."

"Honey, please."

"It's all fake. You're both fake. How many times

152

has he said, 'Be proud of what you do, not what you are?' You think he's proud?"

"This is between your father and me. I'm not discussing it with you."

"How proud are you, Mom?"

"Wyatt, your dad and I are devoted to this family." Her words got sniffly. "We love—"

He killed the call, shut his eyes, and tipped back against the tree trunk. His ears filled with bird songs, skitterings in the brush, and thunder from the normally trickling Rockaway. Combined with the smell of damp earth, those sounds would have excited him three days ago. Now they were relics from when he carried a fishing rod and regarded females as absurd. Eyes open, he returned to the road.

Kevin popped into his thoughts as he slogged home. His brother was coloring, or watching TV, or eating something. Whatever he was doing, he was happy. Each time one of the despicable parents passed by, he'd have a smile for them, maybe rush for a quick hug. The parent would return the affection, send him back to his enjoyment, and he'd be even happier. Not that long ago, his own life was something like that.

Soaked with sweat after the long climb up Stillhollow Road, Wyatt rested in his driveway. In no hurry for what waited inside the house, he rested his hips against the capstones of the bridge, imagining how things would go depending on who he encountered first. He blanked on what to do to his mother, but his father was in for a surprise. Shaky but ready, he continued to the house and eased the front door open. His mother stood in the foyer. "Where's Dad?" he said, pushing the door closed.

Small steps brought her near to him. "He's out."

"Amanda? Or did you find him someone better?" A slap lashed across his face.

"Who do you think you are?"

First smack of his life, at least from her. He stared, hands at his sides.

Another slap. Teeth showing, she raised her hand again.

"No!" Kevin shouted from the landing overlooking the foyer. He squatted at the railing, hands hooked over the top, his face pressed between two spindles.

She winced and spun toward Kevin. "I'm sorry, honey. Sorry. All done. Y'okay?"

Kevin screamed like he'd been scalded. He dashed into his room and slammed the door.

"Damn you," she said, backing toward the staircase. "Your father is out because he's looking for you." Midway up the steps, she slowed to a stop. "Life isn't..." One hand grasped the banister, the other gripped her forehead. "All couples have secrets. Grow up." Fingers still massaging her temple, she finished the climb at half speed. "It's me, honey," she said, poking her face into Kevin's room. "I'm sorry." The door closed.

Soothing sounds drifted down into the foyer until Kevin's crying stopped. She must have made him lie down because soft singing followed. He imagined his brother dropping into a peaceful sleep. For Kevin, "Grow up" would never be a taunt. "I'm sorry" would heal every hurt.

The hum of a rising garage door announced his father's return. Mouth dry, hands flexing, he jogged into the kitchen. As feet climbed the basement steps,

Wyatt bounced on the balls of his feet by the door. First punch had to be a good one. One crisp shot. Backward tumble down the stairs. He'd scramble down, straddle the body, and spit on him.

"Ah, Wyatt," The Judge said, pushing the door open, "you're—"

Hate overwhelmed specks of confused affection. He snapped a fist at his father's face. The punch flew over The Judge's shoulder and hooked his neck, pinning them chest-to-chest.

His father bulled him into the kitchen, spun him to the floor on his stomach, and fell on top. "What the hell?" he said, grabbing Wyatt's wrists.

He thrashed, flailed, and kicked, but no escape. His teeth couldn't reach the hands pinning his wrists, but a head butt found The Judge's mouth.

"Son of a *bitch*!"

A beefy forearm squashed his face against the floor. He felt and heard a snap at the bridge of his nose. Blinding pain. Blood smell and flavor. The force relaxed, and he lifted his head. Drips from his nose joined red smears on the stone floor. He stopped struggling. "Get off me." Exhaustion. Elation.

"Have you lost your mind?" The Judge gasped the words more than spoke them.

"I hope you die."

"Jordan!" His mother's strained whisper approached from the foyer.

"Okay," his father said, heaving breaths, "I'm going to let go. Don't make me hurt you again." His hold loosened even more. "I'm serious. Nothing stupid. Understand?"

"I heard you from Kevin's room," she said.

155

"Omigod, honey, your face."

"Apparently," his father said, "he's still angry." Rising to his knees, he kept both hands braced on Wyatt's back. "Are you OK now? Can we talk?"

"So you can lie?" Wyatt crawled from under The Judge and pushed to his feet.

His mother stood next to him. She lifted his chin and squinted at the damage. "May be broken. Let's get some ice on it." Her furious glare fixed on his father. "And how do we explain this to the police?"

"May not matter." Hands propped on one knee, The Judge labored to stand. "*Jesus.*" He tapped fingers to his puffy lips and inspected the tips. "Looks like we have at least until tomorrow."

Ice cubes tumbled into the dishtowel she held under a dispenser in the refrigerator door. "How do you know that? Wyatt, go sit at the table." She folded the towel into a compress and headed for his chair. "You said they'd be back with a search warrant."

Wyatt tingled at the reminder he could be arrested any minute, and getting his ass kicked by an out-of-shape senior citizen drove home the dangers he'd face as a prisoner. *Get off me* wouldn't be the end in jail. That's when the real evil would start. Memories he'd never be able to live with afterward.

"I spoke to Marty Bender from the car," his father said. "Far as he can tell, none of the judges who might be issuing warrants are doing one for us."

"How would he know that?" She held the wrapped ice above Wyatt's face. "Tip your head back."

"He has his moles, I guess. I'm fine, by the way."

She rested the icepack on the bridge of Wyatt's nose. "Hold that there. I'll get something to clean your face." The paper towel roller rumbled. "Big man," she muttered over the sound of running water, "beating up a child."

"I didn't beat him up."

"Of course. He punched himself."

"You have no idea what happened."

"I'm not blind. You're disgusting."

"Shut up, Diane, unless you want to be next."

The water shut off.

"What's stopping you?" she said.

Wyatt lifted a corner of the towel and caught her swaggering toward his father.

"Goddamn coward," she said. "Beat children. Kill children."

"Shut up." His father shot him a glance.

"Why not a woman with cancer?" Face tipped up, her nose pushed at his. "Go ahead. You're a real lady killer."

His father snatched her hair, twisted her head to the side, and raised a cocked fist.

"Dad!" He jumped to his feet, gripping the ice bag like a blackjack.

Rage melted from The Judge's face. Looking dazed, he let go of her hair and dropped his punching hand.

"Get out," she screamed, rubbing her neck. "All you do is hurt people."

His father trudged to the basement door. One foot down the steps, he paused. "Someone call me if the police come." The door closed with almost no sound. Feet bumped down the treads.

Wyatt listened to the click of the door to the garage and the whirr of the overhead door rising. *Mom, go after him.*

A car started. Engine whine grew fainter. Overhead door hummed. Gone.

He flopped against the back of the chair and set the towel on his nose again, spreading it across his eyes. After hearing a short burst of running water, a warm cloth dabbed at his face. "Hold still," she said, like cleaning a toddler after a meal.

She never asked who started it. Just blamed his father. Again, he'd let someone take his fall. He slapped her hand away and sprang to his feet. "No wonder he hates you." The ice pack exploded against the refrigerator. He dashed up the back staircase to his room and locked the door.

Lying on the bed, he stared at the ceiling. Everything bad was his fault. The accident. The cheating argument he overheard. They wouldn't have had it without the hit-and-run. Now they may be splitting up because he forced their secret into the open. They were right. He didn't understand what happened between them, and he didn't want to. All he wanted was to be happy like two days ago, or like Kevin. No torment would last longer than a hug, a cookie, or a lullaby. But he was afraid his troubles, the ones he knew and the ones to come, would haunt him, every day until he was dead.

Chapter 26

When Frank opened the stand earlier that morning, only half a day had passed since the accident, so he understood Monica's skinned hands would make her almost useless. Still, she'd insisted on being there. He couldn't tell if it was a display of family support, or she didn't want to be left with her grandfather, like she was a baby. Either way, it had been a blessing because while he and Beth busted their tails, Monica handled any customer wanting to talk about the accident.

Never afraid of attention, she puttered near the stand's wide entrance. That way, every customer had to see her. Many knew her, but bandaged hands and a swollen chin were enough to get conversation going with friends and strangers alike. It didn't take long for her to settle into a routine for each retelling. Hand and hip moves were added or tossed based on crowd reaction, and every group smiled at least once during her story. He hoped it wasn't about peeing in the shower, but he wasn't going to change anything. By the time people got to the register, about all he had to say was "Thanks," or "I'll be sure to tell her."

He said goodbye to the last customer at the six o'clock close. After that, he and Beth piled crates of produce, flowers, and potted plants onto handmade dollies. They shuttled them between the sales tables and the cold storage room in the back until all the perishables were safe for the night. By the time they'd hosed the concrete floor, bagged and tossed the trash, and rolled down the metal gates, it was almost seven. In normal times, with so much daylight left, he'd often take care of something in the fields. Tonight, the neck-high corn, deer fencing, and irrigation lines would have to get by without him. Sunrise tomorrow would be soon enough.

"Well, we made it," he said on their stroll to the truck, a daughter on each side, close enough to gather them into a group hug. "Girls, you did great today."

Beth hooked an arm around his waist and tipped her head onto him.

"Even your mother would have said so."

"The heck she would," Monica said as she and Beth left him and circled the rear of the pickup.

He fished a phone out of his pocket, loaded the number for Torrie's hospital room, and opened the driver's door. "Well, we're gonna see. I'm calling her right now." He threw a bag with the day's receipts onto the floor of the passenger side. "Monica, you're in the middle."

"No way." Monica stood outside the open passenger door, wrists on her hips. "She had the window coming here."

"Don't be stupid," Frank said. "You can't even open the door. That means Beth has to do the night deposit." He pushed the *Send* button on his phone and got settled inside the truck. "Get in, for Pete's sake."

"Then we switch at the bank," Monica said, still outside the pickup.

He wondered how someone with a woman's body could still act like a preschooler. "Get in and shut—"

"Hi, honey," Angie sounded like he woke her. "Where are you?"

"Just leaving the stand. How's she doing? Any change?"

"Nothing."

He'd been checking almost every hour, so that answer was no surprise. "Well, she's not worse. That's good."

"I guess...Oh, Frank, you should've seen all the kids that were here today. Cards and flowers all over the place. Little stuffed animals. She has so many nice friends."

"Boys?"

"Here we go."

"Make sure she's covered up good. Those hospital gowns. You know what I'm saying."

"How about a nice burka?"

"Angie, don't gimme that. You make sure."

"So, how was business today?"

"Good. Steady. Maybe even a little heavy because people heard about the accident. Everybody asking about Torrie, wishing her the best. It was good to be busy." *Extra pair of hands would've been nice.* "Babe, the girls were great today. Killed themselves."

"You got Monica to stay off the phone for five minutes?"

"I heard that," Monica whispered. She stuck out her tongue at the phone and covered up after Frank slapped her forehead.

"Well, nobody can outwork Beth," he said, reaching over to shake her knee, "but both of them were terrific. So, Angie, how about when we get there, you and—"

161

"Pop," Angie shouted. "Leave that."

"When'd he get there?" Frank was in no mood to referee a spat between Angie and his father.

"He's playing with the monitors."

"Put him on."

"Pop," Angie's voice sounded far away, "Frank wants to talk to you."

"Frankie," his father said, "you know I'm great with machines. I was just looking. Nothing was gonna happen. C'mon."

"What did I say, Pop? Didn't I ask you not to go unless I was there?"

"Sitting home, Frankie. Nobody telling me nothing. I got scared. My first grandchild. She could die."

"Pop!" Angie hollered.

"And what am I gonna get?" his father said. "A phone call the next day?"

"Gimme that phone," he heard her shout.

"Here's Angie," his father said, the sounds of a scuffle in the background.

"Frank," she sounded winded, "you know I love your father, but sometimes…We're supposed to be positive, right? What if Torrie heard that? How can he be so, so *capo tosta*?"

"Is he still there?"

"No."

"Don't call my father stupid, Angie. He's upset, like all of us. Cut him some slack."

"So, I just let him kill her?"

"You know what I mean. Respect. Always. The girls see you doing that and that's how they'll treat you and me some day. You want that?"

Her "all right" sounded like a child being forced to

apologize. "When are you getting here?"

"A few minutes. And like I was starting to say, how about we get a bite, kiss Torrie goodnight, then get you home."

"We can eat, but I'm staying here."

He faced away from the girls and counted to five. "Angie, you need a hot shower, some good food, and a bed."

"The nurse is getting a cot for me. There's a shower in the room, and I have the cafeteria. I just need some clothes. I'll be fine."

"Babe," he said, knuckles on the steering wheel turning white. "They're keeping her in a coma. There's nothing you can do but make yourself crazy. You gotta take a break."

"My baby's gonna see me when she wakes up, and that's that. Love ya. Drive safe." She hung up.

He tossed the phone onto the dash. Angie had to snap out of it. They all needed her. Watching Torrie sleep was a stupid waste of time. Pretty nervy, her saying his father was *capo tosta*.

Monica rubbed his shoulder. "You okay?"

"Worried about your mother." It was that and all the other things. Torrie hadn't been out of his mind for very long during the day. He was afraid, but he knew she was going to get well. The hit-and-run car took its best shot, but she was still here. That kid was tough as a cheap steak. After Torrie, the business bothered him most. Farming was like breathing. They could only stop a short time before things went south fast, and that meant all the jobs. The whole family did something important. The fields were his. Angie ran the stand. Torrie ran her sisters. With those last two gone, things either weren't going to get done, or would be done half-assed.

He understood, too, that Mother Nature could care less what happened in his life. She didn't pick winners and losers. Corn was no different than thistles, and whatever grew, she didn't decide who ate it. The strongest got it, always. Right now that was him, but bugs never surrendered. Weeds and vines always crept back. Fences needed constant repair. Even then, the deer found a way in. That's why he carried his rifle on the tractor.

The rifle. That could have been useful last night. Maybe he could have pumped a shot through the back window of the car as the bastard drove off. He pictured spider-webbed rear glass, red splatter on the windshield, car in a ditch, constant blare of the horn. Revenge, even if imaginary, settled him. He patted Monica's knee. "Know what I feel like? Ice cream. After the bank, how about we stop at the Polar Cub?"

"Daddy, *awesome*." Monica danced in the seat. "You go, boy."

"What about Torrie?" Beth said, leaning forward of her little sister's rolling shoulders and pumping hands. "And Mom?"

"We'll still see Torrie. And Mom?" he said, rocking his head. "This is a treat for people who worked today."

"I don't want any." Beth turned her face to the side window.

"Ooh, I do," Monica said. "A nasty, gooey sundae."

"Are you stupid?" Beth said, her voice raised. "He said it's for people who worked."

"I worked, you skid mark. Daddy, tell her to shut up."

"Both of you pipe down." For Beth to say anything aggressive, she had to be very upset. "We'll get it on the way home."

Monica threw a shoulder into her sister. "Nice work, skank-a-potamus. Probably be closed."

The truck cruised a short distance down Route 22 in silence. At a red light, he sneaked a peek at each daughter.

Arms folded, Monica chewed her lips.

Beth's head drooped, her shiny eyes fixed on the glove box. A trail glistened down her cheek.

"Beth, what's wrong, honey?" he said.

She shrugged. Blinking sent a new drop to her jaw.

He loved all his children, but Beth needed a little more than the others. She had an extra tenderness for sad things, and now that she was a young woman, a bunch of different hurts waited for her. She seemed to know, clung to the family maybe a bit too much. Sort of like hiding, and that scared him. She could miss her life. As they wheeled into Overlook's parking lot, he found it strange to be more worried about Beth's heart than Torrie's brain.

Chapter 27

She pried Jordan's wine glass from his fingers and set it next to hers on the nightstand. Both hands grabbed the back of his head and pulled their faces together. Plump, sticky lips found his mouth. Even that light pressure stung the gashes made by Wyatt's head butt. He pulled her head to the side. Kisses crawled along his neck while hips bumped him to the edge of the bed. "Lie down." She backed to the door and closed it.

Darkness became so complete he could only trace where she'd gone by sounds of fumbling at the dresser. A wooden match rasped and sizzled. Bright white paled into a tiny flicker that tinted the room a cozy copper. Flame dipped into a candle jar. A second speck of light grew inside the milky glass. The match floated to another jar, then another. Cinnamon and citrus descended around the bed. She circled the room, stopping every few steps to light more. Window sill, armoire, small picture shelf. Each time fire crept to her long nails, she blew out the match, smiled at him, and removed a piece of clothing, careful to smooth and fold it before setting it on the chair at her vanity.

Reclining on a jumble of pillows at the headboard, he drank in the lighting, the aromas, and the delightful tease. Last candle lit, she stood before him in the hypnotic dimness, wearing only the diamond pendant he'd given her for Christmas. A work of art.

Unselfconscious and proud. The din of his life quieted. Affirmation was being offered, and he would accept. Pleasure given and taken. Life in the moment. No limits, demands, or regrets.

"Remember me?" she said, standing at the edge of the bed, fingers laced on top of her head, one knee bent into the other.

"Amanda, you're magnificent." His face warmed, like being caught in a lie. Magnificent had been his special word for Diane, a gift he presented at moments like this. In all his years of evenings, no one else had earned magnificent. The possibility he was transferring nuggets of devotion panicked him. Unlike sex, magnificent hit him as true betrayal.

"Y'know, Jordan, every thirty-seven-year-old woman should have at least one of you." Nose crinkled, she turned sideways and pressed fingers into an almost non-existent tummy. "Not too fluffy?"

Guilt evaporated. "God, no. You're…" He cleared his throat. "You're perfect."

"I always want to look my best for you."

He slid to the middle of the bed and patted the covers.

Eyes glittering, teeth pressed into her lower lip, she crawled toward him. Busy hands swiped pillows onto the floor and ripped back the covers. "Jordan, honey," she said, pulling a comforter to her hip, "you're a bit overdressed if you're thinking of joining me in here."

He scrambled off the bed. Fingers bumbled with buttons, a buckle, and a zipper. Each piece was folded and stacked on the floor next to the nightstand.

"Honey, I don't think you even took off your shoes last time. Why you being so fussy?"

Smiling, he sat on the edge of the bed, peeled off his boxers, and kicked them onto the clothes pile. "Not quite as good as your show," he said as he ducked under the covers.

"Of all the things you do well, sugar," she said, her cheek nuzzling his chest, "being naked ain't one of them."

He rolled on top of her. Laughing was replaced by brushing lips and the rustle of legs against sheets.

"Get comfy," she whispered, pushing his back onto the pillow. "Got a little work to do."

"At this hour? You must have some mean boss."

"The devil himself." She kissed his eyes, nose, and mouth. "Honey, if you knew half the things that man makes me do, you'd blush, I promise you." Her lips teased a trail down his chest until she was a bump under the covers, tending to the one thing that signaled his decline. She peeked from under the comforter and pulled it around her face like a nun's wimple. "How long ago did you take it?"

"Right after you opened the second bottle of wine. Ten minutes?"

"Let's give it a little more time." She wriggled to the headboard, fell back against a large pillow, and tightened a sheet over her breasts. "The girls get a little floppy when my arms are down," she said, laughing.

So comfortable with herself. Life with her would be breezy and high-spirited. Maybe even—God forbid—fun.

"Here," she said, grabbing his wine off the night stand. "No, wait." She set it down and picked up hers. "Save it for after. You're not supposed to drink, if I remember the ads right."

"And I can't be driving half-tanked."

"Oh." She frowned into her glass.

"What?" He tilted away and studied her sullen face.

"It's just, well, the way you sounded on the phone, I thought tonight you'd stay."

He had no idea where she got that notion. After his solo dinner at the bar at Baltusrol Country Club, he'd called her. His mind raced through their brief conversation. *Missed her. Family's going to hell. Only peace in his life was time with her.* No mention of staying over. "I'm sorry if—"

"Don't." Hand raised, she turned away. "I understand." When she faced him again, a smile gleamed on her beauty-queen face. "So, let's talk. What should we talk about?" Careful not to spill the wine, she inched closer and angled her shoulders toward him. "Let's talk about you for a change." The backs of her fingers played across his face and hair. "I want to know everything."

"Are we going someplace bad here?"

"Let's see. I know you ran Wheaton, Weiss & Carpenter, so tell me what happened before that. Y'know, when you were a little lawyer in short pants."

"God, you can't mean childhood."

She smiled into the glass and ran a fingertip around the rim. "We'll save that for a Sunday morning someday. But no," her glittery green eyes snared him, "I mean tell me how you started. How you got so successful, so young."

"Amanda..." He glanced away. "There aren't going to be any Sunday mornings. You're an oasis in my life, but I'm not leaving Diane. You know that."

"Oh, honey, did I scare you? Didn't mean to." She slipped a hand under the covers and rubbed his thigh. "I'm okay with things the way they are right now." She walked her fingers between his legs and squeezed. "Why, Jordan Carpenter, am I feeling a medical miracle?"

He snatched her wrist and threw back the covers. "I'm gonna go."

"No." One hand stayed pressed against his shoulder as she stretched toward the nightstand and set her wine glass down. She held up a small clock showing 9:51. "Still early. We can just talk if that's what you want."

He checked the time and let go of her arm.

"You're here now." She pushed harder against his shoulder. "C'mon, lie back. Be with me. You got nowhere to go."

Knowing she was right cranked up the noise in his head. The mansion he'd slaved and schemed for, the grandest testament to his extreme success, was now enemy headquarters. He eased back onto the pillow and closed his eyes.

She draped both arms around his neck and rolled her forehead against his temple. "You need to relax, honey." Soft kisses found his cheek and neck. "How about it? Want me to relax you?"

Both understood what she meant. After discovering he and Diane had spent four nights in the Lincoln Bedroom, she joked that, like Clinton, all powerful men needed an intern for "relaxation." The following day she'd relaxed him for the first time in a wing chair in chambers.

His mouth dried. Her breathy offer raised more

than the hairs on his arms.

Amanda's fingers crawled along the comforter and found their way underneath.

He flinched and snatched her French twist.

"My gracious, Jordan, you can't go out into polite society with this." Smiling, lips parted, she straddled him. "We better hide it."

Whether exhaustion, or wine, or a combination, their coupling roared to an end without any sense of time, but it must have been short.

She rolled off and laid her face on his chest. "Does this play have a second act?" she said, bumping her hips into his thigh.

Still breathing hard, he rubbed his eyes. "What time is it?"

"Aw, you're no fun." She pitched onto her side and peeked at the clock. "Barely 10:00. We still have plenty of time." She returned to the snuggling. "Oh my lord," she said, rolling her hips, "you *sure* there's no encore?"

"If it was twenty years ago, maybe. You better turn that thing off." He shook his hugging arm and rose onto an elbow. "And we don't have plenty of time. I have to go."

"No." She dove across him, flattening him onto the bed.

He realized instantly how stupid that was. And go where?

"Y'know, Jordan Carpenter," she said, nails digging into his wrists, "a more fragile woman might be insulted right now."

"Sorry," he said, shaking his hands until she let go. He pulled her head to his neck and kissed her hair. "So, what was it you wanted to know about my short pants days?"

Her arms hooked his neck, legs locked around a knee. "I told you, everything."

"Good God, 'everything' in thirty minutes."

She squirmed against him and hugged tighter. "Forty-five."

"Thirty. So, let's see." There would be no mention of his scholarships to Phillips Exeter, Duke, or Michigan Law School. He was grateful for all of them, but each smacked of charity, a pat on the head from his betters. "My first job was at Dewey, Ballantine in New—"

"Why do you stay with her?"

He had no answer she would accept. "Dewey, Ballantine, in New York. That only lasted four months because—"

"Tell me why."

"Ssh. I'm telling you the story you asked for. So, after work one day, I went for drinks with a few of the other rookie lawyers. Martinis, which I'd never had before. For some reason, I returned to the office. To this day I have no idea why. Anyway, I was so loaded I threw up in the lobby."

"Very classy."

"The senior partner had just got off the elevator, and he fired me. Right there in the lobby. That's how I ended up with those bottom feeders, Wheaton & Weiss."

"I don't like that story."

"Thought you wanted to know what makes me tick?"

She hiked herself onto his chest, her face only inches above his. "Sugar, what I want to know is why you stay with her."

"Amanda, I've already—"

She clapped a hand over his mouth. "Tell me why," she said, lips curled away from her teeth.

His vision flashed white. He banged her hand off his gashed mouth. "We're not doing this."

"Don't you think I'm entitled?"

"I'm not leaving her." He shoved her off his chest. "You've known from the beginning. Doesn't matter why."

She sat up, slammed her back into a pillow, and grabbed her wine glass. "I know why," she said, staring forward. "I'm trash. The cliché who crawls under the boss's desk."

"Don't invite sympathy. It doesn't work with me."

"No. I think that's it." Her flicking fingernail dinged the stem of the glass. "She's classy, and I'm your dirty girl."

"Soap opera crap."

"Then you tell me what we're doing?"

"The fun of magic is not knowing how it's done. Leave it be."

"Jordan, your pecker's not even dry, and you want to leave. If she's not gonna take care of you, find yourself a nice little whore. Rent a whole string of 'em. You can afford it." She stabbed a finger at him. "But you better quit thinking you can get an urge, jump on me, and then tip your hat at the door."

"Stop changing the rules."

"Rules? Honey, you're gonna have to deal with what you started. You tried to make me fall for you. I watched you do it. *Knew* you were doing it. Well, it worked. You're all I think about."

Head shaking, he left the bed and stood beside it.

Both her feet thrashed at the comforter until she couldn't reach it any more. "I won't let you do this!"

"Amanda, for crissake."

"Do you even love me a little?"

He re-heard Diane's accusation from earlier in the day. *"My God, you're in love with her?"* Avoiding Amanda's gaze, he stayed quiet.

"Jordan, get out." When he didn't leave, she screamed it.

"Yes!"

"Yes what?" Her leg froze mid-kick. "Yes, you love me? Or yes, you'll go?"

Years of setting word traps, and he'd just fallen into one. "I always hate to go."

The two of them stared. Appearing calmer, she walked on her knees to his side of the bed. "Then don't," she whispered. "Honey, it's just that simple."

"Wrong." Rubbing and squeezing his neck, he paced beside her. "Amanda, no one's going to see me fail. At anything. That includes my home life. I'm not having people speculate about me, revile me, and pity Diane. Understand?"

"Y'know," she said through a small laugh, "the world might not be quite as fascinated with you as you think."

If Diane had said that, he'd be seething, laboring for a counter-barb, but Amanda's zingers included a wink, disarmed rather than assaulted. "There's another reason." Diane's treatment and recovery, or whatever was going to happen, could take a very long time. The last thing he needed was Amanda as a circling vulture, but he'd stupidly opened another wrong door. "I did something terrible, a long time ago, and I need her to forgive me. That can't happen if I leave." Mistakes were piling up. "Forget it."

"What was it?" She sat on her heels and wrapped herself in the comforter. "What happened?"

To buy time while his brain clunked in low gear, he grabbed his shorts from the stack and pulled them on.

"Jordan, tell me." Anger had left her face, replaced by a hint of curious child.

Socks were next. He sat on the bed. "An abortion," he said, crossing a leg and slipping a sock on. "She claims I made her have an abortion." Amanda was the first person he'd ever told. An initial surge of regret vanished. At last, someone would understand he was the victim.

She crept closer. "That's it?"

"Diane was forty. I was forty-six. We were too old for a baby."

Still wrapped in the comforter, she settled beside him. Her face craned in front of his. "Jordan, look at me. That's why you're killing yourself? Honey, I've had three. I admit they're sad. But not the end of the world."

"I believe she'd give you an argument on that." He crossed the other leg and tugged the second sock on. "But there's more." New energy stirred him, like the rush he got from a summation before a slam-dunk jury. "She told me she had her tubes tied when they did the procedure. Four months later, she was pregnant again. We had one hell of a fight about her lying to me, but I didn't even hint at another termination." He stood and stepped into his pants. "And then the amniocentesis showed the baby had Down syndrome."

"Kevin?"

He nodded. "Fool that I am, I said she should end the pregnancy." His arm punched into a shirtsleeve. "She went berserk. First time I really understood how upset she was by the abortion." He buttoned the shirt. "Diane's not a particularly religious person, but she said the Down baby was punishment for killing the other one. We weren't willing to care for a life we created, so God sent us one requiring twice the commitment, and we were going to accept it."

"But that's just crazy."

"Maybe. I don't know."

The comforter fell away when she stood and locked her fingers behind his neck. "Honey, think about this a little. She said no the second time. She could have said no the first. You didn't make her do anything. Don't let her do this to you."

He pulled her hands apart, backed out of the embrace, and slipped into a shoe. "You may be right, but I remember keeping after her about it. Maybe it is my fault." He stomped into the other shoe and checked his fly.

"Your wife plays you," she said, lips pulled into a flat smile. "A strong man shouldn't allow it." She hung her hands on his shoulders. "I'm sorry for being so needy tonight. I won't do that anymore. I want you in my life, so for now, I don't mind seeing you at work every day, and here when you can." She kissed him softly and pushed him toward the door. "Go on. Go back to her trap. I'll be here, for as long as I can take it." Wearing the comforter like a toga, she walked him out.

Their faces lingered in the crack at her front door.

He pecked her on the lips. "See you tomorrow."

"Jordan." She snatched his wrist. "Tell me you love me, but don't shout it this time."

He let a long breath escape through his nose. "Actually, what I said was, 'I always hate to go.' "

"Say it anyway. I'll know."

"Don't do this. I thought—"

"I'm sorry." She rushed out the door and lashed an arm around his neck. "Honey, I'm sorry. Wine makes me so stupid sometimes."

"Amanda," he said, checking his watch behind her back, "what I told you about the abortion, nobody knows that."

"Well, I'm glad you confided. It's important." She kissed the air and backed into the house. "G'night," she said, wiggling her fingers as she closed the door.

Halfway down the walk he peeked over his shoulder and waved back to the silhouette in the window. Even before he'd dug out his car keys, his sense of release had reconstituted as regret.

Chapter 28

The only advantage to a night apart from Angie—their first in nineteen years—was that she couldn't bitch if he had a cigar. With the girls in bed, Frank sat on the porch, chair tipped back onto two legs. He rested his head against the white clapboard and drew on the stogie. Being alone should have helped. Time to think, let off steam, and get organized, at least the farm part.

Instead, the family's troubles took turns poking pitchforks, never letting him focus on any one problem long enough that it got settled. Someone should have been with him, reassuring him that things would be OK, suggesting what they had to do to protect their life. That someone was Angie, but she'd decided sleeping at the hospital, with a daughter who'd been drugged into a coma, was more important than him or her other children. The thought crossed his mind for the first time, if Angie died first, this was how he'd feel for the rest of his life: abandoned, angry, and lost.

He leaned forward, banging the chair legs down hard. Light popped on in an upstairs bedroom, glowed through the window, and brightened the porch. He smiled and waited.

"Daddy?" Beth whispered after opening the front door a crack.

"Sorry, honey. Did I wake you?"

"I was up." She eased the door closed, tightened

the sash of her knee-length robe, and sat across from him on the porch rail. "Mom would kill you," she said, poking her chin at the cigar. Her smile meant the sin would stay a secret.

"Well, she's not here." He blew smoke from the side of his mouth and fanned at it. "How you doing, honey? With everything, it's kinda like you're getting, y'know, the short end." His shy, sad Beth. In the crazy imaginings of a parent, she was the one he most often saw as tragic. An accident, a disease, a kidnapping. If premonitions were real, it would have been her in the coma, not Torrie.

"I'm okay." She shrugged, her glassy gaze pointing at the weather-beaten porch floor.

It was like she'd read his mind, like she knew the short end was her fate, doomed to watch from the shadows. This terrific young woman, his favorite if he was ever forced to admit he had such a thing. Life had to find her somehow, include her, show her a way to blossom. With Torrie in danger of never knowing another day, imagining Beth's gray future piled on one too many hurts. He covered his eyes but couldn't stop the tears.

"Daddy?" Beth hopped off the railing and fell to her knees beside his chair, one hand on his back and the other on his arm. "What is it?"

Still hunched, he forced a laugh and patted her hand. "Some big baby, huh?"

"Is it something about Torrie?"

He shook his head.

"Just sad?"

Nodding, he broke down again.

She swirled her hand on his back. "Daddy, don't."

Her voice trembled.

Can't do this to her. He sat up and checked the tip of the cigar. It was out. The back of his hand swiped at each eye. "Wow. Didn't see that coming. I feel like a dope."

"You're kidding, right?" she said, blotting her eyes with the sleeve of her robe.

"Whadaya mean?"

"You cry all the time."

"Get outta here."

"Daddy, you cried when Monica graduated from middle school, when you saw Torrie in her prom dress." She rose to one knee. "At PopPop's seventieth birthday. Every prayer before Thanksgiving dinner."

"Well, only the important stuff."

"Really? You were so bad watching *ET* we had to shut it off."

"Yeah," he said, smiling, "I do remember that." He pulled her close and kissed her hair. "Ah, Beth. Thanks, honey. I love you." Soon as their watery eyes met, tears trickled again.

"See?" she said, pointing. Her arms snapped around his shoulders as far as her hands could reach. "I love you, too," came out in squeaks.

He pecked a kiss on her cheek. "Go to bed, honey."

"Not tired."

"Another tough day tomorrow." He grabbed her elbows and hefted. "G'won."

"You're not coming?" she said, one foot inside the house.

"Gonna finish this," he said, grinning and holding up the cigar. "While the cat's away."

Chapter 29

Moseley's off-duty time had a pattern. Go through the mail. Throw it out. A few beers while he watched whatever was on ESPN. Soup if he was up for cooking, sandwich if he wasn't. When he got sleepy or bored, a little time in front of the computer. Check his emails, mostly spam. A game or two of Solitaire. Last, a few minutes of porn to release the pressure before he hit the rack.

This night was different. A glance at the oven clock of his rented one-bedroom showed 11:15. Cellphone in one hand, a sweating can of Busch in the other, he sat at the folding table in his kitchen. Eight crushed empties ringed the far side of the table, a flimsy barricade against his troubles. The crazy day kept buzzing in his head. That scumbag, Karcher, cutting the legs off his future. Stumbling onto the hit-and-run Volvo. Toying with the idea of blackmail. Connie Dalton storming off, probably for the last time. She was good riddance, but something kept jumping her back to the front of the line.

After the fifth beer, he'd loaded her number from *Contacts*. The quicker he forgot about her the better, but she was starry-eyed clean, and he needed someone honest to hear his side before Internal Affairs screwed him over. If she agreed he hadn't done anything too wrong, he'd know that he still had some honor left, that he could never be someone who'd invite a judge for a drink, just so he could sneak his thumb onto the scales of justice. While he'd waited for courage, more beers had joined their brothers, and the call remained unsent.

"Probably too late," he muttered. Standing with some difficulty, he shuffled into the living area and paced. He had only a plaid recliner and a TV in the room, so each bump into the chair surprised and annoyed him. "You drunk?" he said after the third collision. He sat on the threadbare arm and slid down onto the cushion. "Yeah, you're drunk. And you're not calling anyone. Loser." Like a free throw, he arched the phone toward the TV. "Moseley shoots." His cellphone bounced off the screen. "He scores," was followed by a breathy impersonation of crowd noise. One long pull finished the beer. "Bullshit," he said, slinging the crushed can toward the kitchen. "Moseley never scores."

He kicked and rocked out of the recliner. On his knees at the TV, he ran fingers over the screen. No chips or scratches, as far as he could tell. He spotted his phone near the baseboard, crawled over, and scooped it up. "Just make the damn call." Sitting on the floor, his back against the wall, he held the ringing phone to his ear.

"Hello?" Dalton sounded dazed.

"It's Moseley."

"What? What time…Moseley?"

"Dalton, am I a good cop?"

"What's wrong with you? It's nearly midnight."

He detected muffled talking. "Not alone, huh?"

"What do you want?"

"Tomorrow, you'll hear stuff. Was I a good cop?"

"Doing a little drunk dialing are we?"

"Why can't women answer simple questions? Was I a good cop?"

"Goodbye."

"Please!" The desperation in his voice embarrassed him. "Just answer that one question." He heard rustling, pictured her sitting up in bed.

"Why does it matter what I think? This is too weird. I hope you're not in a car."

He rubbed a hand over his eyes. "Okay, let's try this. If you heard that a detective, a guy with five commendations…" His splayed fingers waved in front of the mouthpiece. "Five, Dalton. If that guy took a freebie from a hooker. All right, a few freebies. Would you think he was dirty?"

"Omigod. You were shaking down hookers?"

"I said freebies. No money, no threats. Like a date, sorta."

"How can you be that stupid?"

"Stupid." He cocked his fist at the phone. "Stupid how? Stupid to get a free hummer? Stupid to ask if it's corruption? What?"

"You don't see it was wrong?"

"So," he covered his eyes, "you're saying I'm dirty."

"Moseley, you didn't answer me. Are you in your car?"

"Home."

"Good. Go to bed."

"Dalton, wait. What if the hookers say there was force and, y'know, money?"

"Why would they say that if it wasn't true?"

"I. A.'s taking Karcher down. He thinks I rolled on

him. I'm guessing he made the girls sign complaints."

"How could he *make* them?"

"They're his."

"His? What does that—You're *shitting* me."

"Runs about half a dozen out of Trenton. Pretty sure."

"And you just let him do that? What's wrong with you?" She snorted. "And you say *I'm* not right for the job? You got some pair—"

"Hey, Dalton, suck it."

"You wake me up, you piece—"

He killed the call. Dull throbbing above his eyes told him to either keep drinking or crunch a few aspirin and hide in bed. His spinning head voted against more beer. He walked his hands up the wall until he was standing. "Gotta eat something." Back in the kitchen he snatched a bag of white bread off the counter. Holding the plastic sack in the crook of his arm, he wandered back into the living room. Five framed commendations hung at eye level on a white wall. He swayed in front of each one. Using his teeth, he ripped a strip off the bread slice. Slow chewing pulled the doughy ribbon into his mouth while he read and struggled to remember.

Chapter 30

Jordan drove only far enough to get out of Amanda's sight. He pulled to the curb but left the car running. Exhausted and unsure where to go, he resisted the lure of a nap. Last thing he needed was a police flashlight in his face, followed by questions he hadn't the energy to role-play. He opened the glove box for his phone. Two missed calls and four texts from Wyatt in the last hour, three asking him to *call home*, the last read, *moms bad. call.*

"Do I really want to do this?" he whispered, tapping the phone on his thigh. Before today, the end of an evening meant little when he got home. No questions. No explanations. If Diane was awake when he got in, they might even exchange a few words about the needs of the household. Now he had a morally outraged prosecutor to contend with. He typed *bad how* and hit Send. His phone rang immediately.

"Dad," Wyatt said, sounding winded, "you have to come. Something's wrong with Mom."

"Be specific."

"She's falling down."

"Drunk?" He pulled out onto the deserted, tree-lined street.

"No way. We were talking in the kitchen. She was leaning against the island, and just collapsed. I helped her up. She said she was okay, but then she stumbled around and went down again."

He pushed harder on the gas. "And now?" Modest houses flew past at increasing speed.

"I carried her to the couch in the great room. She's sleeping now but was mumbling and moaning for a long time. I didn't know what to do."

"Does she need an ambulance?" Stop signs received his attention, but no brakes.

"That's what I said, but she said no. Just wanted to lie down."

"I'll be there in a few minutes. Call me if—"

"Wait, I hear her."

He accelerated up the entrance ramp to Rte. 78.

"Hang on, Dad. I'm walking to the great room...It's Dad...She wants to talk to you."

"Jordan." Her voice was stuffy, drowsy.

He overtook a speed-limit car like it was parked. "Do you need a hospital?"

"My head."

"Who's your doctor? Where is he?" *Why don't I know that?*

"Madeline Chin, in Summit."

"Where is she affiliated? What hospital?"

The phone clattered on something hard. He heard sounds of retching.

"Oh, God," Wyatt said in the background.

He was still at least fifteen minutes away. "Wyatt," he screamed until his son picked up the phone, "ask her what hospital for Dr. Chin."

"Dad, she's bad."

"Ask her!"

Alternating mumbles and howls poured out of his phone. She had to be in agony to disintegrate like that in front of Wyatt.

"She said Overlook."

"Okay. Call 911. Use the house phone. That locks in the address. Tell them you need an ambulance to go to Overlook Hospital. Not Hunterdon. Overlook."

"Got it."

"Then call Dr. Madeline Chin in Summit. You'll get her service. Tell them it's an emergency, and your mother's being admitted. Repeat that to me."

"Madeline Chin. Admitted to Overlook. Emergency. I'll do it right now." He hung up.

Jordan eased to a safer speed. At the relative calm of seventy-five, a mob of emotions caught up. Anger muscled to the front. At Diane for waiting too long. At her doctor for not finding the cancer earlier. He'd sued many a physician for this exact mistake. Breast cancer, to brain cancer, to funeral.

A peek at the speedometer showed eighty-five. He backed down again. The ambulance was coming. He and Wyatt had done what they could for now. He also realized not everything happening was bad. Wyatt had reached out. And Diane wanted to speak to him. In spite of everything, they were all still connected. Except he had to get out of another woman's bed to answer the siren. The headline *Judge Screws Staffer While Wife Dies* flashed in his head.

No, not die. Her symptoms were ominous, but she could get well, and while she recovered, he'd be attentive and supportive. She'd forgive him. He'd forgive her. They'd have the do-over he often imagined. No more evenings. Amanda would move on to someone else, survive only as a wonderful memory.

Oncoming flashers forced him to the shoulder of

Bissell Road. An ambulance blew by, swung toward Rte. 78, and disappeared. She must be inside, the passion of his happiest years. He dialed the house and pulled back onto the road.

"Dad," Wyatt said, "they took her."

"I saw the ambulance on Bissell. And you told them Overlook?"

"They didn't like it. Said it would cost extra."

"They saw our house and said that? Idiots. And Dr. Chin?"

"I got the service. Dad, the driver said to tell you to go to Admissions at the hospital. I didn't know any of the insurance stuff, and Mom was pretty out of it."

"Okay. I'm close to the house. If you want to come to the hospital with me, call Aunt Roberta to stay with Kevin."

"I should probably stay with him. He's a mess. When he saw them taking Mom, he lost it, tried to pull her off the gurney. You know how strong he is. I had to wrestle him so they could leave."

"Amazing what he understands sometimes. Okay, forget Aunt Roberta. Will you be okay if I go right to the hospital?"

"Dad, she was bad. Every time she barfed, she'd curl up, hold her head, and scream. Something's really hurting her."

He could tell Wyatt was crying. "You know," he said, "I'm going to call your aunt."

"Don't. I can do this."

"All right. I'll call as soon as I know something."

"Don't go yet. Kevin wants to talk."

"Mom's sick," Kevin said, his voice still filled with crying.

"I know, Kev."

"She's in a truck."

"They took her to a hospital, where people can help her. But she may have to stay there for a while."

"Sleep there?"

"I think so."

"Me, too?"

"No, just Mom."

"Will you sing to me?

****

Admissions seemed to require more paperwork than when he and Diane had bought their house. He ran a lawyer's eye over each form, completing or signing until the Authorization for Surgery. "No," he said, sliding it back to the silver-haired woman sitting across from him in the cubicle.

Her gaze flicked away from the computer monitor. "Mr. Carpenter, it's required." She pushed it back.

He glanced at the name plate in the brass holder. "Ms. Jensen, it's Judge Carpenter, and I don't sign blank checks."

"Excuse me?"

"No one's cutting my wife until I know why."

"Judge," she said, pointing to the screen, "the ambulance attendant radioed that they were bringing in a possible stroke. I'm sure your wife's in Radiology right now. If they see something, they may have to act immediately."

"Does it also say she has breast cancer?"

The woman scanned the information. "I don't see that." She shrugged. "And I don't see how it's relevant."

"Does it say if Dr. Madeline Chin has been in

contact with the hospital yet?"

"Um…No."

"Well, I'm here, and I don't plan on going anywhere." He leaned back in the chair. "Once they know something, they can discuss it with me and with Dr. Chin, if she ever shows up."

The woman rested her clasped hands on the counter. "Have you brought the proper medical proxies?"

"They're at home."

"Okay, then you probably know what will happen. If they find something serious, and you refuse surgery, this will go to Legal. While you're tracking down the proxies, another judge will decide in favor of the hospital. During all this, your wife could die. Judge, we're here to help people. Please, let us do that."

Health care had been a target-rich environment when he was in private practice, and imperfect outcomes rang the register. Being on the desperate side of the decision was an eye opener. He grabbed the Authorization, scribbled a signature, and pushed it to her. "Under a lot of stress."

"Completely understandable. Okay," she said, tapping the papers into a neat rectangle, "we're done here, and I'm sure you want to get upstairs." She handed him a laminated pass on a clip. "You'll need this. Mrs. Carpenter is in the Neuroscience Unit, third floor. I don't see that she has a room number yet, so check with someone at the nurses' station when you get off the elevator." Her nose wrinkled. "I hope everything's okay."

Following the signs for Neuroscience, Jordan entered a broad corridor off the main lobby, passing underneath silver block letters that spelled out Overlook Hospital. A snippet of TV news popped into his mind. *"...sixteen-year-old Torrie, fighting for her life in Overlook Hospital..."* One of the shadows on their future was in the building.

Thoughts cascaded while he paced in front of the elevator doors. Wyatt couldn't learn about the girl being there. He might try to see her. No telling what he'd say. And they needed to postpone the police questioning. Except the cops might not allow that. Had to call Marty Bender. He'd make them. Until when? Still had to happen. Why hadn't someone shown up with a search warrant? Maybe he was wrong about Moseley knowing.

The elevator door opened. Inside the cavernous car, he pressed "3." Faint hospital smells grew stronger and more repellant as he rose. Diane became his focus again. One thing at a time. The other harms tracking them were awful, but temporary.

On "3" the elevator doors opened near the nurses' station. A doughy, forty-ish woman, chin resting on her fist, sat behind the counter. Her gaze found him, and she smiled. "Yes sir, what can I do for you?"

"I'm Judge Jordan Carpenter. My wife, Diane, was brought in by ambulance a short while ago. Can you tell me anything?"

"Let's see." She swirled the mouse, clicked it a few times, and hit some keys. "Here she is. I'm guessing they're done with the pictures by now. My suggestion is go to the waiting room. That's usually where the doctors meet with the families." She flapped a hand toward a set of double swinging doors. "Through those. It'll be on your left. You can't miss it."

He took a step and stopped. "Would my wife's oncologist be included with what's going on in there?"

"Would that be Dr. Chin?"

"How did you know?"

"I just saw her. She's never here at this hour. Got yourself a good one there, Judge," she said with a nod. "The best."

He almost laughed. Every doctor was "the best." Someone had to finish at the bottom of every medical school class, but once accepted inside the health realm, they were all "the best." Standard hospital-speak, but since someone actually had to be "the best," perhaps Dr. Chin was. "On the left?" he said, leaning toward the doors.

"Correct, and I'll let them know you're here. Shouldn't be too long."

Sitting in the waiting room was a mistake. His body buzzed and throbbed. Worst day of his fifty-eight years. Crashing the McLaren, Wyatt's confession, Diane's cancer announcement, Detective Moseley finding the Volvo, the fight with Diane, brawling with Wyatt, too many drinks, sex and turmoil with Amanda, telling her too much. And now this. He was defeated. Sleep and some "poor me" time was what he needed, but this night wasn't over yet. Through the half-glass wall, he noticed a young Asian woman approach the nearly empty room.

She leaned her head through the doorway. "Mr. Carpenter?"

He rose to his feet in stages and stood in front of his seat. "Judge Carpenter." Pretentious, he knew, but if he called her Ms. Chin, she'd sure as hell correct him.

"Sorry." She stayed in the hall. "Judge, may I

speak to you out here, please?"

Like a man dragging a boulder, he trudged to the door she held for him.

Her open hand extended toward him as he neared. "I'm your wife's oncologist. Please call me Madeline."

He winced at witnessing his pomposity deflated. This woman had toiled for years to earn her title and chucked it at the first opportunity. He'd bought his, yet clung to it like bread in a famine. "Jordan," he said, clasping her hand. "How is she?"

"I wish I had better news, Jordan. More tests will have to be run, but the MRI is showing a sizable brain tumor."

"Metastatic?"

She studied his face. "I would say yes. Two unrelated carcinomas would be quite unusual."

"When can I see her?"

The doctor wrinkled her nose. "Could be hours. Depends on how long it takes to finish the tests I've ordered."

"Our boys are home. Should I bring them?"

"No. Go to them," she said, patting his arm. "Try to rest. Tomorrow morning she'll be in a room. Sedated, I'm afraid, but at least you'll be able to spend some time with her. I should have seen all the results by 10:00, and I can go over everything with you before surgery."

"And you're sure she'll need it?"

"If we don't reduce the size of the tumor, she'll be in enormous pain." Dr. Chin fished out her cellphone. "What's the best number to reach you?"

They exchanged contact info, and he watched until she disappeared around a corner.

Diane was going to die. He knew it. Not the "someday" kind of knowing, but the ticking clock kind. The regrets, and panic, and anger kind. Their do-over had been foreclosed. They might get around to forgiveness, but even that would be on the back burner. For the children's sake, faked optimism would dominate until the very end. The only upside was an opportunity to begin the healing between him and Wyatt. Treat him as an adult. Feed him knowledge of what was coming, and when that time arrived, include him in post-Diane plans, especially concerning Kevin. As he dialed the house, a rush of enthusiasm for reconciliation with Wyatt struck him as ghoulish.

"How is she?" Wyatt sounded weary.

"It's very serious, I'm afraid." Good a time as any to start including him. "The cancer may have spread to her brain."

Silence.

"Is Kevin in bed?"

"Dad, is she gonna die?"

Wyatt would never have said that if Kevin was there. "We'll all know more in the morning. Son, make sure your brother's okay, then go to bed."

"Are you, y'know, coming here?"

The question caused him to flinch. "I should be there in a half hour. Check on Kevin, then go to bed. And Wyatt, you were great tonight. Thank you."

"Dad, I'm sorry."

"We all are. Get some sleep, son."

"Holy Christ," he whispered after hanging up. Wyatt actually thought he might abandon the family tonight. His son must have believed what he'd overheard Diane say, her foolish accusation about

Amanda being the woman in his life now. No teenage boy could grasp what Amanda was. A primal attraction. A release. Relaxed companionship at times. Some level of friendship perhaps. But not love.

Amanda was one too many balls in the air. He'd been honest with her from the beginning. Their fling had a time fuse, and he set the detonator for nine o'clock the following morning.

Chapter 31

Sunshine through the bedroom window warmed Frank's face, an odd sensation since he was usually up before that could happen. Eyes closed against the glow, he patted and clawed his fingers toward Angie, but her side of the bed was cool. "Oh, right." He kicked out of the covers, strode to the dresser for his cellphone, and stood at the toilet while he waited for someone to pick up in Torrie's hospital room.

"Hi, Frank," Angie said. "I was just gonna call."

"You're coming home."

"Good morning to you, too."

"Sorry. Good morning." He smacked a kiss into the mouthpiece. "Now, you're coming home. I'll be there in half an hour."

"Frank, listen. The—"

"You listen. You're opening the stand this morning, and I'm on the tractor. That's it. Be ready when I get there." He hung up.

Twice while he dressed, his phone rang until voicemail picked up. The house phone rang. Beth picked up and had a short, mumbled conversation. "Daddy?" she said, knocking on his door.

"Can't talk now, honey. Tell your mother I'll be there in a few minutes."

"She hung up, but she told me to tell you the doctor may bring Torrie out of it today. She's doing way better. Isn't that awesome?"

****

Hospital staff and visitors filled the third floor corridor of Overlook. All of them weaved to avoid collisions with gray-skinned patients pushing IV poles. He slowed outside of Torrie's room, still sheepish about cutting Angie off before she could share her news. He'd called her right back, but couldn't melt the frost. She was facing away when he entered the room. "Hey," got her to turn.

"Hey, yourself." She opened her arms and walked into a short hug.

"So, when's this gonna happen?" he said, heading to the side of Torrie's bed.

"Any minute."

He kissed his daughter's forehead. It still didn't feel real. Her eyes should open. "Mornin', Daddy," she should say through a stretch and yawn.

"Ah, good morning, Mr. and Mrs. Califano," Dr. Michelson said, his cheerful voice filling the room.

In the hallway behind the doctor, Frank noticed a man pause and glance into the room. An important looking guy. Not just tall, but big. Stood straight, lots of salt and pepper hair. The kind of guy everyone knew was there even when he was quiet. Familiar, too. TV, newspapers, something.

A tall teenager following close behind the man grabbed his arm. "Dad, that's—"

"Wyatt, please." The man slipped between the young man and Torrie's doorway. "Don't be rude." A short, thick retarded boy stopped near the man and peeked into the room. "You, too, Kevin." The guy pulled the second boy's arm. "C'mon. We're going to see Mom." He smiled over his shoulder at Frank. "Sorry."

"No problem," he said as the man disappeared.

The retarded boy placed the family for Frank. Customers. Beautiful mother. Tall and graceful. She glided through the aisles like she was on rollers. The few times he'd seen her at the stand, he had to force himself not to stare. It was like being around a movie star, a woman so perfect she made him feel cheated somehow.

"Ready for a little good news?" Dr. Michelson said.

"Babe," Frank said, poking a thumb toward the hall as he joined Angie alongside the bed, "those people that just passed by—"

"Ssh." Brow creased, she pointed at Dr. Michelson.

"Okay," the doctor said, "the cranial pressure is down dramatically, enough that we're removing the shunt. If things continue to improve, tomorrow morning we'll begin bringing her out of the coma. With any luck, by tomorrow night…" He wrinkled his nose. "Well, let's not get ahead of ourselves."

Angie brushed Torrie's cheek. "Hear that, honey?" she said, her voice shaky, "God saved you. I prayed that He wouldn't take you, and He didn't. When this is over, you're coming back to church with your father and me to say thank you."

"Good morning, all." A female nurse blew into the room, along with an orderly pushing a gurney. She clapped her hands. "Okay, everyone out. We have to get this young woman ready."

"Good heavens." Dr. Michelson checked his watch and skated backward toward the hall. "I'll see everyone later."

While the staff prepped Torrie, Frank and Angie waited in the corridor outside her door. Not far up the hall, the teenager who'd gone past with his father and brother wandered out of a patient room, his hands jammed into the pockets of his jeans. He looked their way and ducked back inside.

"See that kid, Angie?" he said. "That's who I was—"

"The Carpenters. I know. Nice people. The girls tell me they're rich as Arabs."

"The wife's a patient here," Frank said. "I heard the father say that to the retarded kid."

"Wow. They were in the store a couple days ago. Whatever it is must've just happened. And it's 'challenged,' Frank. People don't say retarded anymore."

He snorted. "You think the kid cares what it's called? Who decides this crap?"

"Such a sweet boy. She lets him hand me the money and carry the bags to the car. So proud of himself. And polite. Always 'please' and 'thank you'. Both of them smiling all the time, like nothing's wrong. Has to be hard. They must be a wonderful family."

"All that money," Frank said, "and they still had bad luck. Makes you think, huh?"

"Watch your backs," the orderly called from Torrie's room. "Hot stuff, coming through." The young man grinned at them as he guided the gurney past. The nurse walked alongside, steadying the IV bag. Angie caught up and grabbed her daughter's hand. She lifted it to her lips, and rubbed it against her cheek during the trip to the elevator.

"Mrs. Califano," the nurse said when the doors opened, "you're going to have to let go now."

"Mommy'll be right here, honey." Angie kissed her daughter's fingertips. "God bless."

Frank cupped a hand on Angie's shoulder and tugged. "C'mon," he said, nudging her down the hallway, "we gotta go."

She fought to free herself. "Frank, please."

He stopped and cradled her face in his hands, "Don't make me the bad guy, Angie. We're a team. You, me, the girls. I let it go yesterday. That's it."

Eyes closed, she nodded. "I'll get my purse."

On the trudge back to Torrie's room, they paused outside Mrs. Carpenter's door. Inside, the husband stood at the edge of the bed, both hands gripping the rail. Bent onto the covers, the retarded son rested a cheek on his mother's forearm. He hummed softly while he stroked her hand. The older son sat in a corner chair, head down, hands gripping fistfuls of hair. He tipped his face toward the door. A piece of white tape stretched across the bridge of his nose. Pale purples and blues ringed each eye. "Dad?" the kid said without turning his eyes from the hallway.

The father's gaze slid from the unconscious woman, to the son who spoke, and then to Frank.

It could have been because the Carpenters were customers, or maybe it was because both their families were going through misery at the same time, but Frank felt comfortable enough to approach. "You might not recognize us, Mr. Carpenter," he said, staying on his side of the opening, "but I'm Frank Califano and this is my wife, Angie. We own the farm stand on Rt. 523. Your wife and the little guy," he said, pointing to the retarded son, "they come in all the time."

The man nodded and held eye contact.

"They're, uh, kinda favorites of ours."

Another blank-faced nod.

"Yeah, well, I heard you tell the boy she's in here, and, y'know, just wanted to say we hope she gets well soon."

"Thank you," the man said, his soft, deep voice making the scene feel even heavier.

"Okay then." Frank slapped the doorjamb and backed away. "Didn't mean to intrude."

"Frank, Angie, wait." Leaving his wife's bedside, the father's long strides carried him quickly into the corridor. "Please, call me Jordan," he said, shaking hands with each of them. "Your poor daughter, Torrie. We heard about it on the news. Just terrible. How's she doing?"

"Better, thank God," Angie said.

"I'm very pleased to hear that," Jordan said. "Kids. They're all we really have, huh? So," he said, leading them down the hallway, "the TV said it was a hit-and-run. Any progress finding the driver?"

Frank shrugged. "Cops ask. They don't tell."

"That's true if they're any good." Jordan smiled at each of them. "Being a judge, I'm required to know a lot about police procedures." He continued walking them away from his wife's room.

"Well, I know one thing," Angie said. "It was a blue Volvo hit my girls." When Jordan stopped, they all did.

"How do you know that?" Frank said.

"A woman detective came by here this morning. She told me."

Jordan's eyes wandered. "Folks, there's something…" He shook his head. "I better get back," he said, retreating toward his family. "Can't tell you how happy I am to hear your daughter's improving."

"Judge, we're gonna pray for you," Angie called to Jordan as he slipped into his wife's room. "See?" she said to Frank. "You can be rich and still be nice." She winked and poked him with an elbow. "If that Mrs. Carpenter's gonna be here for a while, maybe Torrie and her son could get acquainted a little. Wouldn't that be something?"

This felt good. All of it.

Chapter 32

Back at Diane's bedside, Jordan poured some water. It jiggled in the paper cup as he raised it to his mouth. He'd come close to making the mistake he'd feared Wyatt might. Except maybe he should have told them. They were eventually going to learn the police suspected it was Wyatt's car, so when Mrs. Califano said a blue Volvo hit her girls, there should have been no reason for him to withhold that information. And when they *did* find out he knew, they'd have to become suspicious, too. If they asked him flat out, what would his excuse be?

The arguments he'd been having with himself the past two days were exhausting. Lies don't fix themselves. He imagined them as plates, spinning atop long sticks. Each new one required attention that imperiled the preceding ones, and there would be more before the process played out. Even a brilliant acrobat had a finite number he could manage before catastrophe struck.

His gaze roamed over Diane's lovely, sedated face. Only an oxygen tube in her nose suggested the possibility of the lethal attack underneath. Her last day of regal beauty. Within hours his wife's head would be shaven, swollen, and stapled, a chilled portion of her brain in Pathology. Afterward, he'd have discussions with Dr. Chin about aggressive treatment, or, if his fears were right, palliative care.

Cell phone vibrations were a welcome interruption until he saw *Amanda* on the caller ID. "Stay here," he said to his sons. He hurried into the hallway, away from Torrie Califano's room and Wyatt's ears. "Judge Carpenter," he said, just in case he'd misjudged Wyatt's hearing.

"Good morning, Your Honor."

That sugary Charleston accent bumped aside his descending life, substituted one with healthy doses of Amanda's impish smile and playful irreverence, the scent of her hair and silkiness of her body. A stressless existence if he had the courage to grab it and escape. His fingers tightened on the phone. "Yes, good morning."

"Why did you leave that message on my work number?" she said, sounding as if she'd cupped a hand around the mouthpiece.

He revisited the call he'd made from the car last night. *Amanda, please block out 9:30 to 10:00 tomorrow. We'll meet in my office.* Half an hour seemed like enough time to deliver the handshake and get the crying over with. "Where else would I leave a business message?"

"Anything unusual I should be prepared for? Never took thirty minutes before." A cough interrupted her giggle.

Perfect time to end this. She was getting reckless. "No. Nothing like that." He checked his watch. "I should be there by 9:30."

"I'll be ready. Bye."

He turned to see Wyatt, arms folded, staring at him from the doorway of Diane's room. Each new glimpse these last two days found Wyatt more mature. Broader at the shoulders. A tight, angular face belonging to a man. Thin coat of stubble on a jutting chin. Tape on a broken nose and raccoon rings around his blue eyes advertising a capacity for violence.

"You two at least gonna wait for Mom to die?" Wyatt said as Jordan neared the doorway.

His first instinct was to lash out, but he'd earned the reproach. An ember of respect burned alongside his anger.

"Mom's sick," Kevin shouted at his brother.

"Get inside," Jordan growled at Wyatt, pointing into the room.

Kevin rolled his face on Diane's hand like a nuzzling cat. "Mom's sick."

A quick step put Jordan inches from Wyatt's face. "Jackass," he whispered, "watch what you say. About everything."

"Sorry, Kev," Wyatt said without looking away from Jordan. "You're right. Mom's just sick."

Jordan resumed his bedside post and checked his watch again. 8:38. Earlier, when Dr. Chin told him Diane needed surgery, she said they'd meet in this room at 8:30 to introduce Dr. Kornheiser, the surgeon who'd explain the procedure and answer any questions. Jordan wanted everything done so he could attend to the Amanda thing, at least get that anxiety resolved. Marty Bender had been successful postponing the afternoon interview with the police, so after Amanda, his day was clear. The prospect of some time without a swinging sword overhead—other than Diane—and some sleep was nirvana.

Dr. Chin huffed into the room, followed by a

chubby, kinky-haired young man in scrubs. "Jordan, I'm so sorry we're late. And these must be your sons. Madeline Chin," she said to each boy, along with a handshake and a slight bow. "And," she said, presenting an open hand to her colleague, "this is Dr. Adam Kornheiser. He's going to operate on Diane."

The surgeon could have passed for one of Wyatt's classmates.

"Everyone gives me that look," the surgeon said with a smile. "I'm thirty-four and very experienced."

"He's absolutely the best," Dr. Chin said.

Another one.

"We have the O.R. at 10:15," Dr. Kornheiser said, "so if you want any specifics on what we're going to do, fire away."

Lightheaded, Jordan leaned a stiff arm onto the bed's foot rail. "No," he said. "If you're the best, just do it."

"Okay then," the surgeon said, "let's get the nurses in here for prep."

"Jordan," Dr. Chin said, touching her fingertips to his arm, "are you all right?"

"I'm whipped."

"Go home," she said. "Diane won't be out of surgery for at least seven hours. There's nothing you can do here." She flicked a glance at the boys. "I'll phone if you need to come back."

"Might be better for this guy," he said, bobbing his chin toward Kevin. "Wyatt, are you okay going home for a while?"

Wyatt answered with a slow, staring nod.

"Madeline's right," Dr. Kornheiser said. "Your wife won't be in post-op until 4:00 at the earliest, and that's if everything goes as expected."

Nodding, Jordan shook hands with both doctors.

"Hold a good thought, everyone," Dr. Chin said as she and Dr. Kornheiser hurried from the room.

"C'mon, son." He pried Kevin's hands off Diane's forearm. "We're going home for a while. Blanche will make you a nice lunch. How about a grilled cheese? Would you like that?"

Mouth bent down at the corners, Kevin shook his head. "Mom's sick."

Down on one knee, he laid an arm across Kevin's shoulder. "I know. The doctors have to make her well, but we can't stay for that. We'll come back after lunch." He grimaced as he stood.

"Too old for floor time, Dad?"

"Too old for most things, Kev," he said, his next appointment already weighing heavy.

****

After dropping his sons at home, Jordan pulled into his reserved spot at the Federal Courthouse in Trenton. Having no eagerness for what awaited, he shuffled to the entrance. Scenarios played in his head but without any clarity, not that he was particularly concerned. Severing with prior evenings had never followed the expected give and take, so preparing a script was pointless. Anticipate the fastball, stay loose for the curve.

Amanda wasn't at her desk in the anteroom of his chambers, so he continued into his office.

Hips resting against the front of his desk, she'd hidden her hands behind her back.

He clicked the door shut and stayed there.

"Well hello there, sugar. You didn't say what the

meeting was about." Like firing a rubber band, she launched her thong at him. "Could this be agenda item number one?" she said, smiling and batting her lashes.

He was going to miss her. A lot. "Not happening," he said, stooping to hook the panties with one finger. He shot them back.

"Oh," sounded like a wide awake child who'd been told to go to bed. "Why?" She shimmied into the panties and smoothed her skirt.

Don't drag it out. "Diane was taken to Overlook Hospital by ambulance last night."

Amanda cupped a hand to her mouth. "Omigod. What happened?"

"I have to sit," he said. "Working on no sleep." He flopped into his favorite leather wing chair, the one they used when Amanda "relaxed" him. Eyes closed, he let out a long, slow breath. "She has breast cancer."

"Oh, how awful...but an ambulance for breast cancer?"

"While I was with you last night, she lost motor function. Wyatt called the ambulance. At the hospital, they did a brain scan and found a large tumor." He opened his eyes to find Amanda pacing near his desk, one hand holding an elbow, the other rubbing her chin.

"She gonna be all right?" she said, her gaze cast downward.

"I don't know. But I'm sure you see why this thing has to end now. She's going to need all of me, for however long it takes."

Amanda snapped her face toward him. "End what?"

"You know."

"You can't mean that," she said, head shaking.

208

"Not now."

"I'm sorry."

"But that's crazy." She ran to him, dropped to her knees in front of the chair, and grabbed his hand. "Honey, nothing has to change."

"Amanda, it's one thing to step out on a wife who's frigid. It's quite another to do it when she's dying."

Her eyes widened. "She's dying?"

Think! "Well, desperately ill."

"Sugar, you're tired. Said so yourself. Just breathe. Let things happen the way they're gonna happen. I'm okay to wait. I said so last night."

"It could be a very long time."

She rubbed his thighs and offered a weak smile. "Honey, I'm telling you, it's okay."

"I won't ask for that, and you shouldn't offer. Your life—"

"Jordan." She poked a finger at herself. "That's right. *My* life. I know what's best for me, and I know the cost. Don't you go making decisions for me."

He leaned back. "You always knew what this was. I never lied to you."

Eyes moist, she squeezed his hand with both of hers. "Let's don't do this now. Not when your mind's so full."

"Amanda, I'm sorry."

"Jordan, I know you love me." She pulled his hand to her lips.

He let his fingers stay against the soft kissing. "I'm sorry."

Glistening emerald eyes stared through him. Her hands pulled free. "He's sorry," she whispered. Using the armrests, she pushed to her feet and smoothed her hair. "Y'know, Jordan," she said, gazing on the belt she was adjusting, "you're on your way to being one lonely old man, and not all that far off, either. When you get there?" She peeked at him. "Remember, it didn't have to be that way."

"You'll find someone. You're a magnificent woman."

"And you had to do this *here*, you bastard?" Her shaky finger pointed toward her desk.

"Maybe a few days off would help." He realized this was a turn he should never have taken. "I really am sorry, Amanda."

"Or maybe going to HR would help."

He pitched forward in the chair. "I never lied to you."

"Oh, don't worry your little self, Jordan. I don't need HR fighting my fights." She stood in front of him, gazing to the floor. "There is one more thing, Your *Honor*." She raised her chin. "I'm not quitting, and you're not firing me." Nostrils pulsing, her dewy eyes met his. "We clear on that?"

He nodded but had to fight the urge to rush to her, admit his mistake. They'd disappear together. Morning coffee on terraces overlooking rugged coastlines, lunch in chalets beside snowcapped mountains, evenings sipping wine in candlelit restaurants.

"Okay then." She ran fingers under her lower lashes and checked the tips. "Will there be anything else?"

"No." One tiny word that drained the last of his energy, his hope.

As if someone had called, she faced the door and marched off. It closed with a faint click.

Life receded, leaving him in twilight awareness. He slumped in the chair, let his achy eyes roam the nearby trappings of power and success. Rows of thick volumes in dark wood bookshelves. Cherry wainscoting and elaborate crown molding. Marble mantelpiece. Arched windows bordered with thick, forest green drapes. Air scented with leather from the oversized seating scattered everywhere.

The empty chairs recalled his solo dinner at Baltusrol after the dust-up with Wyatt. That night, a stream of club members offered nods or brief greetings as they passed his seat, but not one sat to chat or keep him company. Afterward, in the dark of his car, he'd scrolled through the list of contacts in his cell phone. Hundreds, but not a single confidante. Not one who would smack his forehead and warn him about bad decisions. Not one who'd counsel or comfort him after it was already too late. Only Amanda had shown him the power of an understanding ear.

Gears engaged in the mantel clock, starting the progressive gonging for 9:45. Knowing he'd just torched the only place he wanted to be, Jordan nestled his face against the cool leather, closed his eyes, and longed for some sleep to hide in.

Chapter 33

Moseley couldn't decide if was nerves, a hangover, or both, but since earlier that morning, he'd needed to stay close to a bathroom. Now, at 9:50, he had to sprint from the precinct's small conference room for another surprise vomiting. At least the Internal Affairs guys hadn't shown up yet. They would have made something out of that, for sure.

On his way back from the Men's room, he detoured past Connie Dalton's desk. If she happened to be there, he'd drop a quick apology on her for last night's stupid phone call. Above a partition wall of her cubicle, he spotted the signature plastic clamp on the back of her head. Thick, sandy hair spiked out of the black claw. "Dalton," he said, loud enough to startle her, "why aren't you on the street?"

She wheeled her chair away from the desk and swiveled to face him. "Ah, my ex-partner."

"So it's official?"

"I said I was gonna talk to Garner. We're done."

"Told you not to bother." He turned to leave.

"That's it?"

Glancing over his shoulder, he waited a few seconds and shrugged, even though he understood what she meant.

"Do you even remember calling me last night?"

"Yeah, that." Nose wrinkled, he scratched an ear.

"Sorry."

"Don't *ever* do that again."

"Dalton, when I say 'sorry,' what would be wrong with you saying 'no problem' and letting it go?" Head shaking, he started back toward the conference room.

"Dammit, Moseley, wait."

He paused and turned his body halfway toward her. "Make it quick."

"I meant don't call when you're drunk." Her gaze darted to the surrounding cubicles, "After I hung up on you, I got to thinking."

I hung up on you.

"Just because we're not partners any more, that shouldn't mean we can't be civil. And I was thinking, y'know, it might be nice if I could call you once in a while, ask your advice on something." Her spooky-pretty amber eyes searched his face. "You'd be okay with that?"

"Sure." He resumed his march to the executioners. "See ya."

"Good luck," she called to his back.

Rounding the last corner, he had a clear view into the conference room. Acid boiled in his gut again. His union rep, that pinky-ring-wearing waste of space, was camped at one end of the table. Two suits from Internal Affairs sat across from each other. Cagey bastards. Now he'd have to sit next to one of them. Game on. Good cop, bad cop, scumbag. But who was who?

****

"Lenny, you stupid asshole," Captain Garner said, sweeping Moseley's gun and shield into the top drawer of his desk, "that could've gone a lot worse for you."

"Is that right? I got no credit cards and maybe a

hundred and fifty bucks, plus whatever's on the floor of my car. You gonna float me for the next forty-five days?"

The captain tipped his chair back. He rolled a pen from finger to finger and eyeballed his newly suspended detective.

"The union rep said I should appeal."

Garner popped forward in his chair and laughed as he slammed the drawer holding the sorry end of Moseley's career. "Are you kidding? You break the law, violate your oath, and still go out on full pension, no drop in pay grade. Appeal what?"

"Broke the law, my ass. They're not hookers if they don't charge."

"You got lucky, and you know it."

Moseley slouched back in the seat, crossed his arms and ankles. "You're just jealous."

The captain snorted. "Of what?"

"Not being on the street anymore. Missing all the booty on duty."

"See," Garner said, jabbing a finger at him, "right there. That's why you're not on my side of the desk. You think you're funny, and you're not. And by the way," he said, finger still poking, "if this Internal Affairs thing didn't happen today, we were going to have us a little chat about you breaking Dalton's balls. I mean butt."

"Not so easy, is it?"

"Shut up."

Moseley laughed. The morning's wrist slap was a huge relief. Maybe that's why his attitude about Dalton was different, almost generous. "I already apologized to Dalton. Checked in with her before the meeting. She's cool."

Captain Garner fell back in his chair again. He squinted and resumed twirling the pen. "Unofficially, is she gonna be all right?"

"Time will tell." Far as he was concerned, she was hopeless.

"Lenny, I said 'unofficially.'"

"Leave me out of it. As of ten minutes ago, I'm permanently unofficial."

"I spoke up for you, Moseley. An opinion. That's all I'm asking."

"Do your own job, Captain. Doesn't matter what I think."

"Gonna be a pain in the ass right to the end, huh? All right." The captain rose to his feet and extended a hand. "You knew your stuff, Lenny. I gotta give you that."

"Been a trip," he said, returning the handshake.

He was getting out just in time. Even the good guys were part snake. Garner pressing him on Dalton. He'd already told him she wasn't right for the job when they first got paired. The "opinion" would have been like ratting. Didn't even feel right having to testify against Karcher. Spattering the scumbag's brains onto a wall would be okay, but not ratting.

The thing to do right now was get home for a little celebrating, or some hair-of-the-dog. The technical distinction wasn't important, and with no obligations anymore, neither was the time of day.

Chapter 34

Frank carried two coffees to a corner table in the hospital cafeteria. He should have bought some dinner, too, but Angie didn't ask, and he wasn't hungry. "Already has two sugars," he said, setting one in front of her.

"Maybe it wasn't the car," Angie said, staring down at the wedding ring she was twisting. "Maybe *they* did it. Y'know, those doctors. Tubes in her brain. Coma drugs. How would we ever know?"

"Don't do this, Angie. Only been four days. Four days is nothing. She could still end up good. Have a little faith." He sipped the coffee. "Strong. You'll like it."

"Aphasia." Her gaze flicked from him to her coffee. "Funny word, huh? Sounds like it should be a good thing. A perfume or something. Aphasia," she said, drawing the sound out. Her spoon dragged around the inside of the cup.

Angie looked older, like she was deflating, life leaking away. Always a little big, which he liked, things were starting to flap onto whatever was below. Her face had blotches and lines he didn't remember. A new droop under the chin. Even her hair. Not that there was more gray in it, just less color, less energy. "Angie, she's gonna be all right. Her head heals. A little therapy. It'll be like nothing happened."

Her lips pressed flat. She pushed the coffee away and rested her elbows on the table. "Who's been reading up on this?" she said, punching the air with her finger, "you, or me?"

"Don't get like that. Doctors say be positive. That's what I'm doing." Being the only cheerleader all the time was starting to wear him down. He expected their daughter, Beth, to be her usual gloomy self, but Angie surprised and disappointed him. One more chore where she'd left him with the heavy lifting.

"Frank, please." She wrinkled her nose. "That's not positive. That's being some," she fluttered a hand in front of her face, "I dunno, some kind of dumbass."

"Attitude's important. Doctor said so."

"You're only gonna make her feel worse if the miracle doesn't happen."

"That's enough," he said, leaning closer, straining not to shout. "Y'know, I almost cracked Monica across the face today. She told one of the customers Torrie could end up a vegetable. That's you talking, and it's gotta stop." His fist banged onto the table, jangling the spoons.

Tears swelled in her eyes. "What if it's true?"

He tapped his ear. "Maybe you read, but I listen. Dr. Michelson said it's too early to tell anything. She's still healing. Let it happen."

"It's like a stroke, Frank. If she doesn't recover in a couple weeks, it may never happen. No talking. No writing. Pointing at things like a one-year-old. There's some great life."

"She's only been awake four days, for God's sake."

"Do you see any improvement? I don't."

His chair scraped back from the table. "I'll be upstairs."

"Frank, I'm sorry."

He dropped a backward wave and headed for the elevators. Pull together. Rally. That's what should be happening. Team Califano. What doesn't kill you makes you stronger. Stuff like that. He'd never say it out loud, but in some half-nutty way, he was glad for this chance to tighten the family. Everyone taking on an extra load with a smile. Someday they'd look back on a shared victory, know they'd been tested and made it because they had each other. Seemed like he was the only one seeing it that way.

He slowed in the corridor as he neared Mrs. Carpenter's room. Now that she'd become conscious after the surgery, she and her husband had gotten in the habit of waving or nodding. And the girls knew their older son, Wyatt, from school. Like the father, the kid was some kind of big shot. Nice, though. Visited Torrie's room a lot to see how she was doing.

Smile at the ready, Frank peeked into Mrs. Carpenter's room. The only person with her was the retarded son, Kevin. Big as he was, the kid was on the bed, his back to the door, feet pointed at her face. After eye contact, she wiggled her fingers at Frank and nodded, but didn't stop stroking the boy's calf or interrupt her soft singing.

Out of sight beyond her door, he rested his back against the wall and pretended to be thinking about something, not eavesdropping on a shaky soprano.

Soft the drowsy hours are creeping,
Hill and dale in slumber sleeping
I my loved ones' watch am keeping,

All through the night.

He slid a few more steps down the hallway, feeling a little creepy about sneaking into their gentle moment. But that's what he wanted for his family. Something terrific coming out of the heartbreak. Strong families do that. When Angie came back up he'd ask her if she'd seen the same thing he just saw. If she did, it would be easier to explain how he wanted her to be about everything. Not so angry and down. Play the hand you got and move forward. Like the Carpenters.

Chapter 35

Wyatt leaned a shoulder into the doorjamb of Torrie's hospital room. "Hi, Mr. and Mrs. Califano. Hey, Torrie."

Lying against the bed's raised back, Torrie's eyes got big. She nodded and pulled the covers closer to her throat. The bandages had been off her head for a couple days, but her face was still a little swollen and bruised on the left side. "No sisters tonight?" he said, sneaking peeks at Torrie. He still had to force himself to believe he'd put her in that bed.

"Dinner with their grandfather," Mrs. Califano said. "They'll be in soon."

"My mom and Kevin are sleeping. Thought I'd see how everyone's doing down here." Two days after they'd dumped the car, the insurance company had approved renting a replacement, but other than picking out his new Volvo, it seemed like he'd been at the hospital without a break since his mother was admitted. Hadn't done much of anything for those five days except tend to Kevin, watch his mother's slow progress, and be totally confused by his father. He couldn't understand how a man could love another woman, but still be so tender to his wife. Putting on a show, maybe, or trying to make up. No way he could know for sure, and since he and his father said almost nothing to each other anymore, not much chance he was going to find out. Probably be a lie, anyway.

"You can come in, Wyatt," Mr. Califano said, rolling an arm. "Hey, I see your shiner's almost gone. Never asked," he said, grinning, "how does the other guy look?"

"Nah. Just a stupid fall. I'm not brave enough for throwing hands." Fighting and prison had become Siamese twins in his mind. With each reminder of a punchout, faces of coal-eyed, tattooed skinheads floated in the black.

Torrie followed with her eyes as he shuffled into the room and stood at the foot of her bed.

"Feeling any better today?" he said.

Her lips twitched and trembled. A kind of squeak puffed through her nose, like something he might hear on his volunteer days at The Arc. She got all red and clapped a hand over her mouth.

"It's okay, baby," Mrs. Califano said, stroking the girl's arm. "Doctor said it'll come. Be patient."

Wyatt wondered if aphasia meant Torrie couldn't think straight, or if she knew what she wanted to say, but couldn't get the muscles to make it happen. It probably was the second thing because she got all shaky and scared looking. Didn't seem she'd made much progress in the few days since they brought her out of the coma. That bothered him because her mother told him if Torrie was going to be like before, they'd know pretty quickly.

"How's your mom today?" Mrs. Califano said, still running her fingers over Torrie's arm and hand. "I went by earlier, but her eyes were closed."

He shrugged. "Radiation seems to be working. I think she slept less today. Had more to say. Stuff like that."

The day had been pretty good, all in all. That morning, his father had helped her from the chair back into bed. He'd kissed her forehead as he was leaving for work, but she pulled him back for another one, this time on the lips. Slow and soft. Pretty embarrassing and confusing. Five days ago, the man was screwing Amanda, and his mom knew it. Now, she was treating him like he was Husband of the Century. Lots of hand holding and finger stroking. Some whispering and smiling. Maybe they took out the pissed off part of her brain.

Torrie opened her mouth. Her jaw rocked. The sound that popped out was like some jungle bird. Eyes full of tears, she whacked a fist on the bed.

"I'm gonna go," he said, afraid he might cry, too. "Feel better, Torrie."

"Maybe tomorrow," Mr. Califano said, raising his chin toward the door. "Thanks for stopping by."

"Such a nice boy," he heard Mrs. Califano say after he was out the door. Worst thing she could have said. Made him feel like he was the same as his father. Both of them acting like they were some kind of shining examples. But of cowards and liars.

When he got back to his mother's room, Kevin was exactly where he'd left him, standing next to the bed, holding his mother's arm.

She was awake, adjusting the multi-colored scarf wrapped over the bandages on her head. "Honey, please take Kevin to the bathroom. I know he has to go, but he won't leave me."

"C'mon, buddy," he said, holding his hand out, "you heard. Let's go. I'll watch Mom until you get back."

Hunched, Kevin pounded around the foot of the bed, pulling at his fly. He darted under Wyatt's arm at the open door to the bathroom. "Hurry," he moaned, and slammed the door.

"I hope you weren't down the hall again," she said, eyes closed, forearm lying across her forehead.

"If I can help, that's what—"

"Well, halle-friggin'-luiah," a woman said from behind him. Amanda braced an arm against the doorjamb. "Forgot what room number they said, but here you are." Her big, green eyes twinkled at him. "Hello, Wyatt. My goodness, some jealous boyfriend give you those?" She smiled. "Growing up handsome as your daddy."

He couldn't look without knowing his father had seen this mega-hottie naked, that he'd done all kinds of stuff with her. "Hi, Aman—Amanda."

Smiling, she gave his chin a playful shake. "Shy, I see. Well, that's where you and your daddy are quite different, I promise you. So, how are you feeling, Mrs. Carpenter?" she said breezing toward the bed.

His mother peeked from under her arm. "Get out of here."

"Well, I like that. Can't a body wish someone a speedy recovery anymore?" Amanda's tight, gray dress showed skin to mid-thigh, clung to the motion of her perfect legs and butt as she made her way around the bed.

"I said get out."

Amanda sat on the window ledge and set her purse on it. "Visiting the sick's a corporal work of mercy, sugar." Arms propped on her knees, she leaned toward his mother. "Don't you want me to have a higher place in heaven?"

"Leave." She sounded more bored than angry.

"Oh, you're being silly. I'm just here to cheer you up."

"You're drunk. I can smell it."

"Oh, I can handle it, honey. That is a *lovely* scarf, by the way. You and I seem to have the same tastes."

"You're disgusting."

"Ouch. Sounds like someone needs a nap, so I'll just spread my sunshine and be off. I got something special to tell you. Ready?"

"Wyatt, get Security."

The Amanda he remembered from before was polite and professional. This slutty, witchy version dazzled him. He inched toward the door.

"Okay, here goes." Amanda teetered even closer to the bed. "Honey, you won. You beat me. He won't even let me suck his dick anymore. There, now don't you feel better?"

His face and neck buzzed. Would there ever be an Amanda in his life? God, his poor mother.

"Dammit, Wyatt," his mother said, still shielding her eyes, "get Security."

The bathroom door opened. Kevin peeked into the room and returned Amanda's smile.

"Hello, Kevin. Remember me? Amanda?"

"Don't you *dare*," his mother said, pointing at their drunk visitor.

"Yeah." Kevin said, grinning. "Dad's work."

"Mom, should I take Kevin with me?"

"For God's sake, just go."

"Oh, you're no fun." Amanda rocked onto her feet

and collected her purse. "Don't bother, Wyatt. I'm leaving." At the foot of the bed she paused, her gaze to the floor. "Diane, I hate losing more than anything, but this was wrong. I'm sorry. Breast cancer must be horrible." After a wobbly step, she stopped again. "Course, odds weren't really in your favor, were they? I've heard that women who've had abortions are more susceptible." Without looking at any of them, she hip-rolled out of the room.

What's she talking about? No way.

"Bastard," his mother whispered, eyes squeezed shut. Her body shook. Tears dribbled toward her ears. Both hands covered her mouth and trapped the sobs.

Movement in the corridor drew Wyatt's eye.

Tanner stood against the far wall of the hallway. Eyes bugged, hands flat on top of his head, his mouth formed the word, "Wow."

Anyone but him. Wyatt pushed a palm toward the doorway as he hurried to the bed. Crying hard the way she was couldn't be good for her head. "Mom," he said, dropping to a knee, hand on her shoulder, "do you want the nurse?"

She kept her eyes closed, hands over her mouth. Her head rolled side to side until another rush of crying hit.

"Kev, come over here." His brother was still near the bathroom door, sniffling, wringing his hands, rocking foot to foot.

"She's okay. Don't cry." His eyes filled, too. "I need you here with her, okay?" He held out a hand. "Don't be afraid. She just needs a hug."

Kevin ran toward the top of the bed, arms out.

"Not her head," he said, blocking the way with an

arm. "When I get up, you stand right here and hug her, uh, elbow. Okay?"

His brother dropped face-first onto the bed and pressed her arm to his cheek.

"That's great," he said, rubbing Kevin's back. "Easy. Just like that. Good man."

"Wyatt," she said, eyes still closed, "I…" She started to cry again, softer this time.

Tanner must have caught an earful. "Mom, take this," he said, handing her a box of tissues after he'd ripped out a couple for himself. "I'm gonna see if the nurses think you need something."

"I'm all right now."

"Just to be safe." He backed toward the hall, one arm pulled behind to wave Tanner away from the opening. Hoping he couldn't be seen, he dabbed the tissues to his eyes, blew his nose, and stuffed the wad in his back pocket. In the corridor, he got close enough so his conversation with Tanner would stay private. "What do you want?"

"Dude," he said, tapping the bridge of his nose, "what's going on with your face?"

The fight with his father seemed like a hundred years ago. "Fell. Why are you here?"

A smile popped onto Tanner's face. "So, that awesome specimen's been hoovering The Judge, huh?" He bounced his eyebrows. "Dude, your old man's a rock star."

"You're a fucking moron."

Eyes wide, Tanner leaned back and grinned. "Wait. *You* said 'fucking'? Have I portaled into a parallel universe?"

"I asked what you're doing here."

"Ah, yes. The accident, of course."

Wyatt checked over both shoulders. "What about it?"

"Being a bit paranoid at the moment, I was afraid my texts and phone conversations might be monitored, so I came in person to tell you I gave my statement to the police this morning. Billy, too, I presume. Has he been ducking you, too?

"Not a word, but I haven't tried to get him, either."

"Mistake, dude. That detective's visit was an unpleasant surprise. What happened to the heads up?"

"You're kidding. My lawyer was supposed to call you guys." He pictured Billy flipping out when he saw the cops at his house.

Head tilted, Tanner squinted. "Why would your lawyer call me?"

"With my mother being so sick, my lawyer got the cops to agree to give me written questions. I finished those with him yesterday morning. That's when they got your names. He said his secretary would call you. Christ, Billy. Maybe they got to him but not you."

"Could be. I mean, nobody's arrested, right?" Tanner backhanded him across the arm. "Hey, I hear Torrie Califano's in here, too."

"Four doors that way," he said, pointing down the hall. "You want to go see her?"

"Why would I do something that stupid?" He tilted closer. "Word is she's headed for the drooling academy."

He jammed a forearm into Tanner's throat, driving his friend's head into the wall and keeping him pinned. "Get outta here." His face zoomed so close Tanner looked cross-eyed.

"Dude," Tanner said, struggling to shove free, "have daddy buy you a fucking sense of humor."

A security guard rushed toward them. "Both of you, out," he said, hoisting each by an elbow.

"Officer, wait." Tanner said as they stumbled alongside the beefy guard. "Totally my fault. Totally. I'll go."

The guard stopped and eyeballed Wyatt. "Your mother's a patient here, isn't she?"

He nodded.

"All right." The guard shoved Tanner toward the elevator. "I see you again and you're arrested for trespassing. Understand? And you," he said to Wyatt, "once more and you're on the street, too." Head shaking, he walked back to his post near the nurse's station.

Tanner paced in front of the glowing arrow at the elevators. "Dude," he yelled to Wyatt when the doors opened. His spread fingers made the "call me" sign before he disappeared.

"NFW, *Dude,*" he muttered. Since the accident, everyone but Kevin was different, and each one left him with the same question: *Who is this person?*

Chapter 36

Coldness woke Moseley. Pain thumped behind his eyes and stabbed his neck, shoulders, and knees. He continued to inventory the damage. Scalded throat. Stink and taste of vomit. He cracked one eye, let it adjust to the stinging light. Inches from his nose he recognized white porcelain flecked with brown and red paste. Continuing to scan, the eye located a recessed soap dish.

He activated parts one at a time, a gasp or groan with each repositioning. After he struggled to a sitting position, brain pain competed with nausea. Slow breathing cranked down the intensity of both, enough for him to climb out of the bathtub, peel off his plastered shirt, and throw it in. The rest of his clothes followed. He ran water to the right temperature, pulled the shower lever, and hauled himself back in. Revitalizing water removed the evidence from him, the tub, and his clothes. He let the soothing go on until the hot water ran out.

Dressed in his underwear, he crept onto the bed. The clock showed 9:15. Staying up would have put him on a normal timetable, but sleep was the only way to ride these things out. He'd just settled on his back and closed his eyes when the phone rang in the kitchen. The machine picked up.

"Moseley, it's Dalton. If you're there, pick up.

229

C'mon. Where else would you be? Quit being a jerk. Pick up. I don't know if you have one of those machines that times-out after some quiet, so I'm just going to keep talking until you pick up. Or maybe I'll sing. That'll teach you. Mose-ley, Mose-ley," her laugh cut in, "give me your answer true. I'm half fired, and it's because of you."

Sick as he felt, he smiled, got out of bed, and slogged to the kitchen.

"C'mon. Moseley. Oh, wait, maybe you're out on a ride."

He lowered onto a folding chair at his card table and grabbed the phone.

"That's what I'd be doing on a beautiful—"

"Dalton," he said, holding the receiver a foot from his face, "use your inside voice. Better yet, whisper."

"You're kidding. Not again."

"Why are you half fired?"

"Moseley, do you want to talk to someone about this? I'm in the program. I can get someone right now."

A drunk. Something in common. "Let's just do straight Q & A, all right? Why are you half-fired?"

"Nooo. That was a joke. Garner loves me."

"Then what do you want?"

"This Califano thing. Wyatt Carpenter's Volvo hasn't shown up, and I'm kinda stuck."

"Can't help you."

"There's some interesting stuff happening. Wanna hear?"

"No."

"Mrs. Carpenter's sick as hell. In the hospital. Their lawyer asked for interrogatories, and the Prosecutor's Office said okay. Must be nice being a judge, huh?"

"Your point?"

"Makes me suspicious that they think the kid needs that kind of shielding, y'know? What do you think?"

"I think you should ask someone who's getting paid to answer that question."

"Yeah, I guess. It's just that Garner's not always easy to talk to. He—"

"Dalton, you really picked a bad day. I'm dying here."

"Sorry. Call you later?"

"No. I'll call you. Cell or precinct?"

"Cell. And, Moseley, I've been there. Talking to someone in the program helps. I'm serious. Hey, I gotta go. Later." She hung up.

He felt a little better when he awoke at eleven. Still in his underwear, he put on a pot of coffee. The brewing smell didn't make him queasy. Good sign. If his hands stopped shaking, maybe he would take the Harley out today. Problem was, until his pension started in forty-five days, he could buy gas or wine, but not both, and the guy at the liquor store let him run an account. To try that with a gas station, first he'd have to learn a foreign language.

"Holy shit." He dropped onto a folding chair. It wasn't forty-five days. It was sixty. The deposit was coming on the fifteenth, not the first. Details had been his career, yet they never meant much in his personal life.

He punched in her cell number but hesitated before he made himself hit *Send*.

"Moseley, how you feeling?"

I'm in her Contacts? "Not great, but better." He

closed his eyes tight. "Dalton, any chance you could…?"

"Little busy here, Moseley. Could I what?"

"Nothing. I'll see ya." He killed the call and powered his phone off. What next? Panhandling at the bus terminal? Soup kitchens? Hanging by his belt in the closet? He powered up the laptop. In the search box he typed *cash for motorcycles in NJ*. While he waited, a devil on his shoulder cupped a hand around his ear. *Chump*, it whispered, *go see the judge.*

Chapter 37

Smile on his face, chin up and shoulders back, Jordan strolled through Overlook Hospital's lobby. At the elevators, he nodded a greeting to each person who made eye contact. Always a few glum faces in this crowd, but he was no longer in that camp. His finger played along the perimeter of a jewelry box. Presenting the diamond earrings tonight would continue their celebration. On each of the three previous evenings, her first fully aware days since the surgery, he'd given her a present. Jewelry had always marked events during their happy times, and he wanted to show how each new day represented something important. Her appreciation seemed genuine. Smiles, hand squeezes, soft kisses. Last night, a whispered, "I've missed you."

The elevator doors opened, and he stepped to the side for those disembarking. It took a second or two before he and Tanner recognized each other.

"Hey, Judge C," Tanner said, half of his mouth pulled into a smile.

He waited for Tanner to exit. "This is a surprise," Jordan said, a firm grip on the young man's elbow. He yanked and herded him away from the elevator traffic.

"Seems to be my evening to be manhandled by Carpenters," Tanner said during the clumsy stepping.

He would have preferred breaking Tanner's jaw, but let go of the elbow. "So, were you visiting Mrs.

Carpenter, or someone else?"

"If you mean Torrie Califano, I have no intention of ever meeting her. No, I came to see Wyatt. Of course, I would have said hello to Mrs. Carpenter, but a woman was already in there." His smile widened. "Wyatt said it was someone who worked under you."

Jordan hoped the shock didn't show on his face. "Did, uh, did he say the name?"

"Amanda, I believe."

"Is she still up there?"

"I'm surprised you didn't see her. She just went down, so to speak. Couldn't have been more than a couple of minutes ahead of me."

Jordan's gaze swept the corridor and lobby. "Wish I'd known she was planning to come. We could've carpooled. Oh well." Before facing Tanner again, he slapped on what he hoped was an expression of indifference. "I'm going up now. Goodnight."

"Judge," Tanner said, "I don't know how you can concentrate with that woman in the same building."

"Amanda?"

"Oh, yes," he said, nodding, eyes wide. "Amanda."

Tanner's snarky tone concerned him, but he laughed and sidestepped toward the elevator. "She might as well be three hundred pounds and bald."

"Right." Tanner pursed his lips, nodded, and ambled toward the lobby.

He suspected Tanner must have overheard something, but it almost didn't matter what. Amanda coming here held no potential for good. When the elevator doors opened on the third floor, he forced himself to leave the car. Near Diane's room, he affected a confident stride and breezed in. A nurse blocked his view of Diane's head. The boys stood at the window side of her bed. Wyatt's arms-folded glare told him all he needed to know. "Evening, family," he said with as much nonchalance as he could muster.

"Dad." Kevin ran to him and bear-hugged his waist.

"What's going on?" He patted and rubbed Kevin's back. "Everything okay?"

"Tracie, I'm fine," Diane said to the nurse. "Wyatt, please take Kevin downstairs for a snack."

"Sure you don't want me to give you something?" the nurse said. "It will help you sleep?"

"Let me speak with my husband first. All of you, go."

"C'mon, buddy," Wyatt said, tugging Kevin's arm. "How about some apple juice?"

"I like apple juice."

Wyatt's angry gaze stayed on Jordan all the way out the door.

"Evening, Judge." Nurse Tracie blocked his path to the bed. "Something's really upset her," she whispered. "Come for me when you're done. She needs to sleep."

After the barest of nods, he let her pass. He leaned over the bed rail for a kiss, but Diane shut her eyes and turned away.

Never ask a question if you don't already know the answer. Amanda could have said anything. He stood in silence and waited.

"Your little friend just left," she said, eyes still closed.

"And that would be?"

"That serpent, Amanda. No. I'm being unfair. You're the serpent."

"Why let her upset you?"

"Shut up," she said, an open hand slapping on the covers. "Just shut up, you goddamned…" She covered her eyes. "You told her. The indelible shame of my life. Pillow talk for two degenerates. And now Wyatt knows."

He wanted to track Amanda down and choke her to death.

Tears squeezed through Diane's eyelids. "I want to die."

"Diane, you—"

Her scream stopped abruptly. Mouth agape, back arched, she panted and rattled the bedrail with a white-knuckled hand.

Nurse Tracie shoved past him. "What happened?" She ripped Diane's hand free of the rail and clutched it in both of hers. "Mrs. Carpenter?"

Another nurse and a security guard hurried into the room.

"Sir," the guard said, "did you do something?"

"We were talking. That's all. Talking."

"Everyone out," Tracie said. She lifted one of Diane's eyelids.

The stocky guard maneuvered in front of him. Arms wide, he leaned into Jordan's chest and plodded toward the corridor. "Sir, you have to leave."

"That's my wife," he said, not resisting the nudges.

"Right now she's a patient, and you have to go. Wait out here if you want, but don't go in there again until they say you can. Understand?"

"Yes," he said, nodding. Banishment was a relief. Her interrupted scream echoed in his ears, unnerved him still, not only because she might be in medical crisis, but because now he had twice the mountain to climb. Child killer, and now Judas.

Amanda's visit astounded him. What could have been gained? Tomorrow, Human Resources would let him know if he could fire her for this. Insulting a non-employee hardly seemed sufficient cause, but it wouldn't cost anything to investigate. But then Amanda would most likely drag in their affair.

After some minutes of pacing and weighing options, he decided the best short-term strategy would be to treat this as a setback, not a final defeat. Unless something harmful happened because of the outburst, Diane would be released in the next few days. In the meantime, he would limit his contact, let her process and digest how things were, and maybe how they could be. With no more bombs anyone could drop, and given a cooling off period, she might stop seeing only the horrors in their history.

The nurses were still attending to Diane when Wyatt and Kevin got off the elevator.

"Can't go in yet," Jordan said to them. He ducked his head into the room. "Is she all right now?"

"Settling down," Tracie said, her voice hushed, "but she's done for the night. Give the sedative another minute or two before saying goodnight."

"Some?" A chewed straw poked through the lid of the cup Kevin offered him. "Apple juice."

"Not right now, but thank you." He smiled and roughed the boy's hair. Kevin, the Switzerland in their family war. No alliances or judgments, no grudges, no schemes, no expectations beyond affection and sustenance. Diane had done a wonderful job nurturing the boy to this plateau. Wyatt had the makings of a first rate man, but Kevin was her masterpiece.

"Something happen?" Wyatt said, watching the nurse soothe his mother.

"Amanda's stupid visit set her off."

"Bull. You did something. She was fine."

"You know," he said, advancing at Wyatt, "I'm getting pretty tired of this." He closed to within inches of Wyatt's face. "I'm going to tell you what I've told her a thousand goddamned times. I've made mistakes, and I'm sorry. I can't do any more than that. You don't like it?" He banged a finger into Wyatt's chest. "Go to hell."

"Dad, no." Kevin's head tipped down, but his eyes stayed on him. "No yelling."

"No anything, Kev. I'll see you both at home." As he headed for the elevator, his thumb brushed the jewelry box in his jacket pocket. He couldn't remember feeling more defeated.

Chapter 38

The house elevator would have allowed Diane to convalesce upstairs, but that's where Jordan spent his nights. Even an adjoining room would have been too toxic, so she insisted he refit a haven for her on the first floor. She chose his office, the room with her "thinking" window, the one overlooking the rear yard and ravine.

Three days earlier, coming home had been a terrible drain. Lunchtime arrival by private ambulance, wheelchair ride to the office. A nurse had settled her into the hospital bed, arranged mobile trays of food, drink, and reading materials on both sides. That was followed by irritating repetitions of instructions to all of them before the nurse left. Three days of fitful or drug-hazy snatches of sleep, exhausting trips to the bathroom, early soup and sandwich dinners with the family. Wyatt on one side of the bed, Kevin on the other, Jordan at her feet.

Yesterday was the breakthrough. Her energy had built enough to enjoy the view through her special window. At last, enough strength to focus and conclude. After having Wyatt help her into the wheelchair and position it at the sill, she'd insisted on privacy.

Without Jordan's negative aura, calmness had settled on her, turned down the drumming in her skull.

She'd surrendered to the scene outside, allowed it to clear passion's static. While light and dark marched in its cycle, and shadows crept to her from the ravine, she'd invited her limited options to compete. Each argued and rebutted until only one remained standing. All she would need was the physical strength.

****

"You awake?" Dressed for the office, Jordan appeared next to her bed holding a glass of orange juice. "I thought you might like this." He leaned toward her.

Gazing forward, she tilted away.

He sighed. "I want to help you get well."

She pulled the light bedcovers to her waist, folded her arms, and closed her eyes.

"Diane, please talk to me."

"Running out of things to tell her in bed?"

"There's no bed anymore. Even she told you that."

"You're both liars."

"Diane, I'm sorry about the other thing. I can't say it any differently than the last hundred times. Please," his voice was closer, "take the juice. It's good for you."

"Not after you touched it."

The glass clunked onto her night stand. "Is this how it's going to go? All the way until you die?"

She couldn't prevent a small laugh. "Do you know something?"

"I meant are you going to do this forever?"

"In that case, yes."

"You're punishing the boys as much as me."

She opened her eyes but didn't look at him. "I will deal with my children as I see fit."

"They're not yours. They're ours, and if you don't

recover, they're mine."

"Don't you mean hers?"

"Diane, I've told you. She's told you. It's over."

Her eyes squeezed shut. "You stupid, *stupid* man. That predator isn't done with you."

"Even if you're right, which you're not, it doesn't matter. I'm done with her."

"Jordan, you're beyond stupid. Why do think she wanted to keep her position?"

"I can't believe you're making me defend her, but she does an outstanding job. And why should she pay for my mistake?"

She screamed into cupped hands.

His hand gripped her shoulder. "Diane?"

"Don't touch me!" She slapped his hand away. Eyes closed, her head eased back onto the pillow. Short breaths helped clear the brilliant flashes of pain. "You're so smart, tell me this. Why do you think she told me about your deviant sex, and the abortion?"

"Deviant?" He laughed. "God almighty. Should be fairly obvious, even to someone with half a brain."

"Oh, aren't you clever. And you're wrong, again. It was to show me she can't be removed, in any way."

"Then she was wrong. In every way."

"Leave me."

"Diane, I never wanted Amanda. Any of the Amandas."

"Get out."

"You did that so I'd be even more evil."

"You are."

"Look, I don't want to hate you back, but it could happen. Your choice. I suggest—"

"Ah, the doorbell. Charlene must be here.

241

Goodbye." The nurse's arrival would have driven him away anyway, particularly when she had to change the dressing on her scalp, but dismissing him felt delightful.

"Juice is on the table," he said, so distant she almost missed it.

A productive exchange. That horrid woman would succeed her, and he'd be clueless. No doubt any more. Wyatt would protect Kevin for a while, but then he'd be absorbed by his own expanding life, a life he deserved. She had no choice.

While Charlene finished up, a knock tapped the office door. "Mom? You decent?"

"Come in, Wyatt." Her bed faced away from the door, but she recognized Kevin's stomps running toward her.

"Morning, Mom," he said, face beaming. His feet stayed in motion, fingers patting and pulling at her hand and the covers. "Better?" His nodding head coached her to the answer.

"You know, I am." She pulled him into a hug. "In fact, today may be the greatest day of my life. How about that?"

"Good," he said, arms squeezing, feet still dancing.

Wyatt leaned over the other side of the bed and kissed her cheek. "Morning."

"Charlene, I don't remember if you've met my sons, Wyatt and Kevin."

The nurse smiled and bounced a finger at each boy. "There's the best medicine of all." She snapped her case shut. "Okay then, everything looks good so far. Let's just keep doing what we're doing. You have help coming at eleven-thirty?"

"Plus these two full-time knights," Diane said.

"We're fine. Wyatt, please show Charlene out."

"I know the way," the nurse said, heading for the door. "Remember, time out of bed is OK, but when you feel tired, don't fight it. Someone will be by this evening around six. You have a great day."

Diane checked the mantel clock. 9:10. "Honey," she said to Wyatt, "I need you to do something for me. There's a GNC in Woodbridge. I want you—"

"You mean Bridgewater."

"I don't like that one. The staff is very rude."

"Won't bother me. It'll save an hour each way."

"It's too small. They won't have what I want, and I know Woodbridge will."

"I'll call Bridgewater. What're you looking for?"

"Goddammit!" Pain blasted inside her skull. Eyes shut, she waited for the throbbing to ebb. When she opened them again, two stunned faces stared at her.

Wyatt's head shook in slow motion. "Mom, I didn't mean anything."

"I'm sorry." She tugged Kevin into a hug and kissed his cheek. "I don't seem to have the energy for patient parenting at the moment."

"Hey, you want Woodbridge?" Wyatt said, hands raised, "then it's Woodbridge. What am I after?"

"There's an herbal remedy I read about in the hospital. I forget the name, but they'll know. It's specific for brain health."

"Sounds like junk, but if that's what you want." He shrugged. "Go now?"

"In a minute. Kevin, please sit on the sofa. I have to talk to Wyatt."

Kevin nodded and ran to his assigned seat.

"Sit here," she said to Wyatt, hopping her hips

243

sideways to make space.

Looking puzzled, he crooked a leg onto the bed and sat facing her.

She took his hands in hers and let her gaze wander his face. "Honey, you're going to be all right."

"What are you talking about?"

"Your life. You're a wonderful person, and no matter what, you'll be all right."

"Thanks. That's it?" He rose part way.

"Annnnd," she said, pressing on his shoulder, "you're going to be a fine man. When I'm gone, you—"

"Mom, don't." He drew away, but left his hands in hers.

"Honey, this is important to me, so listen. You're the best evidence that my life wasn't worthless."

"Please stop." He shook his head. Tears swelled in his eyes.

So caring and generous. She recognized traces of early Jordan and wondered how such strength and promise could have devolved into something so craven. "Remember this. You're not me, and you're definitely not your father. Your destiny isn't controlled by anything we've done, or will do. Do you believe that?"

Nodding sent tears down his face.

"Good. C'mere." She opened her arms and wrapped him in a tight, twisting hug. "I love you so much. Never forget that." His arms tightened around her. "Honey," she said, "I want to hear you say it to me."

"I love you. You're scaring me."

She patted his back. "No. Some people make the mistake of waiting too long to do this, and now we haven't. In fact, let's keep it going. Kevin?" She waved him over. "Come over here. Give Wyatt a hug and tell him how much you love him, and what a terrific brother he's been."

Big smile, Kevin ran to the bed, arms reaching toward her.

"Not me, sweetie. Wyatt. If you love Wyatt, tell him, then give him a nice hug."

"Love you, Wyatt," he said, snapping his arms around his brother's waist.

"I love you, too, buddy."

"Okay, now say goodbye to each other. My brain's not going to get better by itself."

"What?" Wyatt dabbed a t-shirt sleeve to his eyes.

"GNC?"

"Oh, right." He stood and rubbed Kevin's hair. "Wanna come?"

"Yeah."

"No. He's with me."

"Mom!" Kevin banged both feet on the floor.

"I said no."

"Sorry, Kev. The boss says no. All right." Wyatt grabbed the wallet from her purse. "What do you think? Fifty?"

"Should be fine. And, Wyatt?"

"Yes, highness?"

"Say goodbye to your brother."

"This is getting weird." He bowed to his brother. "Kevin, my treasured sibling, goodbye."

"Bye."

She listened for a garage door to open, and then close. "Honey," she said to Kevin, "I have to get dressed now, so do some drawing in the kitchen, and then we'll go for a ride. Okay?"

"Yeah." He dashed from the room.

Dressing sapped her, but she still managed a laugh when selecting panties. "Mother would be so proud," she said as she slipped into the cleanest pair in the drawer. The last bit of clothing was a fresh, multi-colored scarf for her head. Bending toward the bathroom mirror, she tied, tucked, and fluffed the fabric several times before nodding approval. A short rest on the edge of the bed recharged her. She grabbed her purse and shuffled into the kitchen. "All set, honey?"

He peeked up, jumped from his chair, and joined her for the slow march to the elevator.

"First we're going up," she said, guiding him into the cramped car. "Do you feel strong today?"

Snarl on his face, he flexed his biceps and growled.

"Good heavens. I should say so." Her precious boy. If Jordan's backwater tramp got him, there would be none of this. Kevin would be a speed-bump on Amanda's dash for everything money. Jordan would be no impediment. Regular rations of fawning and sex would neutralize him.

She leaned on Kevin's shoulder during the slog to her dressing area off the master bath. "Mommy's going to rest here," she said, flopping onto the chair at her vanity table. "Honey, would you please bring me that yellow bag with the seashells on it."

He lifted the large canvas tote from a hook.

"Thank you." She pulled drawer after drawer from her jewelry case and spilled out necklaces, earrings, bracelets, pins, watches, and rings until everything she owned was in a tangled heap on the vanity's marble countertop.

Kevin shook his head. "Too much, Mom."

"Please hand me the bag, sweetie. Okay, I want you to hold it open. Perfect. Just like that." She hooked an arm around the three-million-dollar mound and dragged everything over the counter's edge. A few items missed the bag, but Kevin chased them down. She replaced the drawers in the jewelry chest and closed it. "Can you lift that, honey?"

"Heavy," he said, hiking the straps and arching backward. "Corn's not so heavy."

Carrying groceries was the pride of his day, the reason they made so many trips to the store. That whore would use a service and leave Kevin to shrivel in a contracting world. Jordan would be oblivious as long as he was serviced as well.

"Okay, sweetie, please bring that and follow me." At her water closet, she opened the door and stepped aside. "Set the bag by the pottie."

"Please?"

He was seven before "please" and "thank you" became part of his understanding, but he never forgot, or let anyone else. She leaned over and kissed his hair. "*Please* set it by the pottie." Standing next to the bowl, her legs weakened. Hands propped on Kevin's shoulders, she lowered to her knees and sat back on her heels. Pain in her head built as her energy flagged.

"Gonna throw up, Mom?" Nose crinkled, he shook his head.

"I'll be all right. Why don't we get started? Hand me something from the bag, please."

He gave her a necklace. "Why?"

"Just a little cleansing, sweetie." She dropped it in the toilet and peeked down at the coiled gold near the outflow. Still plenty of room. "Please keep giving me things until I say stop. Okay?"

Birthdays, anniversaries, Valentine's Days, promotions, partnerships, all clustered in roughly equal portions and flushed. The last piece slid off her finger. She wrapped it in toilet paper and plunked it into the water. Not a single pang. Each drop of the handle restored a little more strength, enough that she could return the empty tote to its hook without holding onto Kevin or the walls. Best she'd felt all day.

"Car ride now?" he said, holding her hand at the elevator door.

"More like a journey, honey." Purse under her arm, she smiled at him.

At the Range Rover, she opened a rear passenger door. "Back here, sweetie."

Kevin clipped his safety belt and grinned at her as she closed his door.

She rounded the car, sat in the driver's seat, and started the engine. Before leaving the front, she removed an envelope from her purse and set it on the dash. "We'll let the air conditioner work for a while," she said. "Keep all that hot air outside."

"You're smart, Mom."

"Well, thank you, angel." She climbed into the back seat next to him and patted her thighs. "We have enough time for a song if you like."

He undid his seatbelt and snuggled his head and shoulder on her lap. "You're a good singer."

"And you were the most wonderful gift of my life."

"Yeah." He nodded.

"You know, I don't remember thanking God. Should we go and do that?"

His nodding hadn't stopped since her last question.

"Yeah."

Chapter 39

Chief Justice Lansky insisted his staff car take Jordan home, along with a police escort. After the briefest of condolences, the driver, Martin, kept his full attention on swerving through lunchtime congestion, leaving Jordan to his grief, and anger, and bewilderment. Each siren burst and horn blast was a banshee scream, a jarring reminder of what was waiting at the house.

The only consolation was that Wyatt didn't find the bodies. Diane at least had the decency to send the boy on a three-hour fool's errand. That set up Blanche to find them because she always entered the house through the garage. But if Diane assumed the bodies would be bagged and gone before Wyatt got home, she must not have realized the garage would be a crime scene. Investigators and the Medical Examiner would take as much time as needed to document all details. Wyatt would come home to a beehive of police activity and yellow tape cordoning off access, and that was exactly what his son described when he called with the news thirty minutes earlier.

He'd only been off the phone with Wyatt a few minutes, but if he was feeling this bad, Wyatt must have been a wreck. He fished out his cell phone.

"Hey, Dad."

"Almost home. How you holding up?"

"Not good," he said, his words stuffy from crying.

"Where are you now?"

"I can see her head against the door."

The police should have been keeping him away.

"They just put Kevin on a gurney. They're pulling a sheet around. No, it's a bag."

The view Wyatt described put him in the turnaround outside the garage doors. "Son, don't watch. If they'll let you in the house, go inside and wait for me."

"She was telling me stuff before I left. I didn't pick it up. Oh God, they just closed Kevin's bag. How could she do that?"

"Stop watching. If you can't get in the house, walk to the bridge and wait there."

"Dad, it was so weird. She made me tell her and Kevin I love them. *Made* me."

He covered the phone. "Martin," he said to the driver, "any way you can find out the officer in charge at my house? The idiots are letting my son watch the body removals."

The driver nodded and got on his radio.

"Wyatt, I'm serious. Go to the bridge."

"Then she made me say goodbye, to both of them. Dad, I didn't see." He broke down.

Diane must have been losing her mind. She might have wanted to do this to him, but never Wyatt. "None of us saw. You did nothing wrong. Now please, walk away. We're about two minutes away."

"A guy's opening Mom's door. Why was she in the back seat?"

Their car swung onto Stillhollow.

"Wyatt, for God's sake."

"Judge," the driver said, gazing into the rearview, "a Detective Dalton is in charge."

"Thank you." What was Dalton thinking?

"He's pushing on Mom's shoulder. Holding her up."

"Son, do what I tell you, please."

"Gurney's coming...Dad, was she dying anyway? Kevin, he never..." Sobbing drowned out the rest of his thought.

Near the driveway, the cruiser and Town Car sped past parked cars, all with hazard flashers pulsing. People stood with arms folded, silent, watching the collection of Rescue Squad trucks, police vehicles, and ambulances parked near the house. The staff car turned into the driveway and sped over the bridge. After parking, the driver hopped out and trotted to an approaching woman in street clothes, Detective Dalton.

Jordan pocketed his phone and jumped from the car.

Wyatt waved but held his position at the yellow tape.

"Judge Carpenter," Detective Dalton said, hand extended, "I am so sorry."

"How could you let my son stand there?" he said over his shoulder, leaving her hand floating. At the tape, as soon as he and Wyatt hugged, his son broke down. "C'mon," he said, pulling Wyatt's arm.

One peek into the garage froze him. Two men wearing surgical masks and rubber gloves pulled Diane from the rear seat. Her parts dangled and swayed during the short trip to the gurney. Like folding laundry, they arranged her on the white canvas, flapped the sides up, and zipped her in. A festive scarf was the last of her to disappear. He understood why Wyatt had to watch. An unspeakable finality. This was true death, not the funeral home fantasy of peaceful sleep. Diane was a bundle, not a person. The woman who'd sparked both warming and destructive passion fires for most of his adult life was now debris needing attention. He applied the same detachment to his son but failed. She'd left, but Kevin had been taken, a victim of deluded sanctimony.

"Judge?" Detective Dalton stood at his elbow. "Sir, I have no authority to keep family away from the site, as long as they stay outside the tape."

"I apologize, Detective. Things are…Thank you for the condolences." He shook her hand. "Where will they be taken?" he said as the ambulances left without sirens or flashing lights.

"Hunterdon General." Her nose wrinkled. "Your Honor, I'm sure you know that circumstances like these require autopsies. I suggest you contact your funeral director and let him coordinate with the Medical Examiner to take possession once they're done. That's going to be the first time you'll be able to be with them. I really am sorry."

"Thank you." His glassy eyes followed one half of his family down the driveway for the last time. Ambulances gone, he noticed satellite dishes on two vans idling along the street. "I better get on that now. Let's go inside, Wyatt."

"Judge, wait." Face pained, Detective Dalton handed him an envelope. "I'll need this back, so if you could, y'know, read it now."

Slipping the thin note from the linen paper envelope, he glanced at the detective, trying to glean from her expression if she'd already read it, perhaps already knew if the contents were sad, or venomous, or conciliatory. He unfolded the single sheet and read it as if he was the foreman of a jury, a jury passing judgment on the accumulated sins of his life. The salutation presaged any leniency he could expect.

Jordan,

Death is nobler than a complicit life or permitting the slow torture of an abandoned innocent.

My beloved Wyatt,

Kevin is saved. God will forgive me, and I ask you to, as well. You were born to do great things. Free yourself and live joyfully.

All my love always,

Mom

Inside the house, Jordan unclipped the phone connection. Using his cell, he contacted the family attorney, Arnold Hoffman, and asked him to deal with Kuhn Funeral Home and serve as media spokesman. With nothing more to do at the moment, he joined Wyatt in the kitchen. Each manned a position at the windows overlooking the turnaround and ravine.

As activity wound down, and the cluster of vehicles melted away, he battled the fury Diane had created with her brief apologia. Debate over. She'd hammered home the point, tapped her notes on the lectern, and left the stage. No generosity, even in death. He wanted to ascribe her sentiments to impairment from the tumor, but the hatred he'd warned her about had gained purchase. Going forward, the trick would be concealing it from Wyatt.

The most bothersome aspect, at least so far, was his feelings for Kevin. Never someone with prospects for a long life, Kevin's taking seemed more a fulfillment than a tragedy. He'd never whisper it to a soul, but his unlucky son lived every day under a shadow of resentment, an ever-present reminder of why he'd lost Diane. If, on his deathbed, he was forced to admit to any heartlessness, it would be his reluctant affection for such a gentle, loving soul.

Wyatt had seen the note, too, and had said nothing since they'd got into the house.

"Want to talk?" he said to his son.

Keeping his gaze to the ravine, Wyatt shook his head.

"Not even about the note?"

Wyatt's head continued its slow side-to-side, a facial expression so blank and constant Jordan wasn't sure the question had registered.

"She obviously loved you a great deal. All the rest, though? The cancer must have been affecting her mind."

"I'm not stupid."

"Wyatt, we're past the time to be mad."

Slow head swivels persisted. "I don't think so."

Out with the old feud, in with the new.

"Dad, how is Kevin 'saved'? Saved from what?"

A bad direction, but at least Wyatt was participating. "Being left with me, I suppose."

Gaze still trained on the ravine, Wyatt nodded. Exhales whooshed through his nose, picked up speed. "Why did she have an abortion?"

This had no chance of going well. "She wouldn't want us discussing that."

Wyatt folded his arms and continued to stare out the window. "Then just tell me what you told Amanda."

Amanda, another spiteful move turned catastrophic. "We're not doing this. Now or ever." He patted Wyatt's shoulder. "I have to call Arnold Hoffman."

"No." Wyatt's chin and lips quivered. "This is your fault. She might not have made it," he said, tears leaking to his jaw, "but Kevin…" He shook his head, kept his gaze out the window.

"Wyatt, I promise you I will never speak ill of your mother, but stop thinking she was perfect. If today has a reason, it's because she couldn't forgive. Me or herself. Be careful not to be like that, too."

"You did all the bad stuff. She must have run out of forgiveness."

"Okay, I admit it. I can't keep apologizing to her anymore, so I'll say it to you. I was wrong, and I'm sorry. Now what do we fight about?"

Wyatt's gaze wandered, breaths quickened. He collapsed, sitting lotus-like, wailing, rocking, hands pulling the back of his head toward the floor.

Down on one knee, Jordan rubbed his son's back, massaged his neck, and stayed quiet. After only a few seconds, pain in his knees and back forced him to reposition every limb. *Too old for floor time, Dad?* Tears blurred his vision. How could she think he wouldn't take care of Kevin?

Chapter 40

Wyatt straightened his tie in front of the restroom mirror at Kuhn's Funeral Home. Final night for the wake, and he wasn't sorry. It seemed the point of wakes was to get the family so busy and tired, they forgot to be sad. If so, it was working. The double funeral tomorrow would almost be a relief. He and his father were supposed to be at the wake from 2:00-4:00 and 7:00-9:00 each day, but his father had so many political and social connections, and he had so many school friends, people couldn't get through the line without sending the thing into overtime, especially the night sessions.

His father did it way better than him. Solid, patient, a warm thanks to everyone, even those he couldn't stand. Probably how he got so good at politics, but it disgusted him to see that phony part. For three days, powerful people and their posses strutted through. The governor, both senators, congressmen, judges out the ass. Both Clintons called and said they hoped to come, but hadn't so far. Maybe for the funeral, they said, if they could clear their schedules. His father acted like he wanted them there, but Wyatt didn't. The media would make it about them, not his mother and brother. He blew out a big breath and left to take his place near the coffins, right in the middle of that waxy stink of funeral flowers.

Jordan adjusted Diane's portrait on the top of her casket. Kuhn couldn't get her wig right, so he decided she and Kevin would have closed coffins. Her picture was recent enough that she almost certainly had cancer, but the image showed nothing but beauty and serenity. Common belief was that suicides produced anger in those left behind, but as he took in details of her face, gratitude overwhelmed all else. She'd been gracious enough to plow the field of his hatred years ago and nurture it without letup. Now, a bumper crop had come in.

He moved on for a final inspection of Kevin's farewell. As with Diane, his son's joyful smile sat in a frame atop the casket. Had the coffin been anywhere else, no one would have known that's what it was. Over George Kuhn's pinched-faced objection, Jordan allowed Wyatt to paper the coffin with dozens of his brother's colorful drawings. Decorating that box was the only time he'd seen Wyatt cry since the first day. With them still not speaking much, it had to have been a valuable release.

Satisfied with the viewing angle of the portraits, he assumed his position for the evening: legs a bit wide, back straight, one hand gripping the other wrist. He examined Wyatt as his son strode up the center aisle. Camel blazer, navy slacks, striped tie he didn't know how to knot. Collar of his blue button-down shirt hanging loose around his neck, the unmade look of a boy reluctant to turn into a man. Too late. Time was already putting on the finishing touches, and recent life had erased most of his innocence. "You've been a rock," he said as Wyatt arrived next to him and mimicked the stance. "I'm proud of you."

"That's so great, Dad," he said, gazing forward, lids at half-mast.

Knocking Wyatt's teeth out would be a front page humiliation, but it's what he itched to do right then. She'd left *both* of them, taken someone from *both* of them, but she'd spit in only one face on the way out. He was the injured party, and Wyatt should have seen that.

Arriving mourners prevented the angry exchange he ached to begin. In the broad entry to the viewing room, he glimpsed Angie and Frank Califano along with one daughter, all looking hesitant to come in. He smiled and beckoned to them.

"Beth," Angie said from a corner of her mouth as they made for the Carpenters, "omigod, is that eye makeup?"

"Mom, please don't embarrass me," she said, dropping behind her father.

Frank coughed to cover his smile. So that was why Beth hit the Ladies when they first got there. If Wyatt took the job he was going to offer, he'd have to keep an eye on those two.

Angie was the first to reach the family. "Judge," she said, both hands closing around his, "I thought all day about what I was going to say, but there's nothing is there? 'Sorry' doesn't really do it. Wonderful woman, your wife. She and Kevin were so special together. We're praying for them."

"I appreciate that a great deal," Jordan said. "Thank you."

She slid to Wyatt. "Mother *and* brother. What could be more sad? Honey, you just have to trust that God has a reason." She pulled his face down for a kiss on the cheek. "My husband has a question for you," she whispered.

Frank guided Beth to the father, touched by her nervous determination to deliver rehearsed sympathies.

"I'm so sorry for your loss," she said before sidestepping to the son.

"Thanks for coming, Beth." Wyatt's hands covered the one she offered. "You got the short straw for the sisters, huh?"

"I wanted to come," she said, looking offended. "I'm heartbroken for you." Her wide eyes shot to Frank and back to Wyatt. She worked her hand free and pointed to the kneeler at his mother's casket. "Gonna, y'know, say a prayer."

Frank's eyes welled. Not real smooth by Beth, but she tried. And it wasn't one of those loud-laughing, hip-throwing, hair-flipping tries. She was attracted by the kid's kindness. Maybe he could relax a little about her future. His heart was so full, "Sorry" was all he could risk saying to Jordan without bawling. He kept pumping the judge's arm until the feeling passed. Arriving in front of Wyatt, he shook hands and pulled his other arm around to the youngster's back for a quick hug and slap. "I'm really sorry, son. Takes time, but you're gonna be all right." His hand stayed on Wyatt's shoulder

"I hope so."

"I'll make this quick," Frank said, checking the long line behind him. "How'd you like to learn farming until you go off to college?"

"Pardon?"

"With Torrie in rehab every day, I could use the help."

"Excuse me one second," the judge said to the

mourner he'd been speaking with. "That's not very practical," he said, leaning toward Frank. "Getting ready for college is going to be pretty much a full-time job."

"I'll do it," Wyatt said.

"Son," his father's gaze scanned the immediate area, "we need to discuss this first."

"Mr. Califano," Wyatt said, "the funeral's tomorrow. I'll start the next day. What time?"

The judge leaned closer. "Frank," he said in a low voice, "don't count on him."

Hands raised, Frank backed toward the kneeler at Diane's coffin.

Jordan's hands jittered from the effort not to attack his son, in word and deed. He needed separation. "I'll be right back," he said to everyone within earshot. Heart thumping, mouth dry, he did his best controlled stroll toward the lobby. From the corner of his eye, he caught shapely hips bumping inside a black skirt. The woman stopped at a distant chair in the viewing room and sat. No need to see the face, but he peeked anyway. *Oh Christ.*

In the lobby, he spotted Tanner near the front door. He stooped to avoid discovery, but his size made that impossible.

Tanner waved and cut off his path to the restroom. "Judge C, I'm so sorry. Wow, are you all right?"

"I'm exhausted. This whole thing may be catching up with me."

"Well, in case I miss you inside, I want to say I'm sorry about Mrs. C and Kevin. She was like a third parent sometimes, until the accident, anyway. She—"

"Tanner," he said, pushing a hand at the young

man, "please take this the right way. My wife didn't like you, and neither do I." He continued to the restroom and banged the swinging door open with both hands.

Wyatt noticed Tanner in the sympathy queue. As the line crept along, Tanner checked over a shoulder or craned his neck around the room. At one point, something he'd seen made him cover a smile and drop his gaze to the floor.

"Dude," Tanner said when his turn came, "I called and texted you likc ten times. You can't answer even once?" They gripped thumbs. He leaned in for a chest tap, but Wyatt held him away. "Sorry about your mom and Kevin," Tanner said, looking puzzled.

"Thanks. I'll call you." He let go of Tanner's hand.

"Had to be that brain tumor. I think she was already losing it the day she slapped me. Remem—"

He snatched the shoulder of Tanner's shirt and yanked him in the direction of the flow. "Thanks for coming."

"I'm done?"

"Totally." He tugged harder.

Tanner slapped his hand away and inched closer. "All you Carpenters, you think you're fucking royalty. But I know better, and you know I know." Tanner's nose dueled with Wyatt's. "Dude, check the corner." He pointed to a beautiful woman in sunglasses and a dark suit. "He brought your new Mommy. Isn't that—"

Wyatt jumped a knee between Tanner's legs. One grunt, one tongue-thrusting cough, and Tanner doubled over, both hands between his thighs. No one acted like they saw him do it. "I think it's a cramp," he said, waving off a man who stooped to help. He slipped an arm under Tanner's shoulder. "C'mon. Let's get you some air."

"Kill you," Tanner repeated between groans and gags as confused faces followed their exit into the lobby.

Mr. Kuhn rushed to them from his permanent greeting station near the main entrance. "Oh my. Is he drunk?"

"He'll be okay. Mr. Kuhn, would you please?" He bobbed his chin at the door.

"If he's going to be sick," the director said in a low voice as they passed, "please use the shrubs."

Out of sight of the entrance, he shoved Tanner, who stumbled and dropped to his hands and knees on the lawn. "You know, Tanner, it was cool hanging around your brain, but I think I always knew you were a shit." He fixed his coat and tie before heading back inside.

Leaving the restroom, Jordan noticed his son re-entering the viewing room. "Wyatt," he said, catching up, "where'd you go?"

Wyatt spun toward him, face taut, fingers rolling in and out of fists. "Did you bring her?" he said, his teeth never parting.

"So, you saw. And no, she just came."

"How could she come?"

"How do I stop her?"

"Then tell her to go."

"She's not doing anything."

"She makes me sick."

"That's not grounds."

"Christ almighty!" Wyatt clapped both hands on top of his head. "I'm not asking you to be a fucking lawyer."

"Keep it down." He scanned the concerned faces turned in their direction.

"I will. Soon as you tell her your wife wouldn't want her here. Soon as you tell her your dead son…" He started to cry. "Your dead son, who worshipped his mother, wouldn't want her here."

"Wyatt," he said, reaching out, but the boy batted his hands away. Eyes from all directions found them.

"Tell her I don't want her here." Wyatt backed away from his father's slow advance. "Tell her my mother did this because of what that bitch said, because of what you told her."

"Son, please." The mobbed building had fallen tomb quiet.

"Tell her you hate her and want her to die, too. She killed your family and you hate her. Tell her. Why are you still here?" he screamed, fists vibrating against his temples. "Tell her!"

No need any longer. Through the opening into the viewing room, he glimpsed a woman in sunglasses and dark suit, tissue to her face, rushing through a side exit.

Chapter 41

While the Director of Human Resources prattled through the phone, Jordan stared out the kitchen window into the cool greens and shadows of the ravine. He dragged knuckles across the stubble on his chin. The receiver against his ear amplified the noise, like tearing Velcro. *Wonder if she can hear that?* Some of the woman's words registered. "…paid bereavement leave" "…seven days, to begin today" "…confirmation by email." They hung up.

He cared nothing about the pay. The only reason he applied for the leave was so his resignation wouldn't follow on the heels of that humiliating wake. When he did resign at the end of the month, wagging tongues around the courthouse might discover other targets. He unclipped the house line and killed his cell.

Sitting at the kitchen table in his underwear and robe, he congratulated himself for remembering to make the call at all. Even before Wyatt's tantrum at the funeral home, stress and lack of sleep had been dulling his mind. Since that tirade, he'd slipped another notch. Every conscious moment had the cloudiness of a standing eight-count. Memories of his wife and son's burial visited him through distorting glare or dream-scene gossamer, out of sequence, short on interaction or participation. The people he recalled seeing at the service or the cemetery maintained an embarrassed and embarrassing distance. Eyes studied him, then Wyatt, then him. Whispers to the next person in the pew or at graveside. Disappointing attendance at the luncheon reception at Baltusrol. Wordless limo rides with his stone-faced son, a willful son who wasn't there when he awoke this morning, and neither was Wyatt's rental car. Presumably, Wyatt was now a trainee farmer. Spite, so it appeared, was not a trait that skipped generations.

He pushed his achy body to a standing position and poured the last of the coffee. Cup in hand, he shuffled toward the foyer, not as a destination but because the hallway offered a path to someplace else. Under the foyer's chandelier, he sipped from the mug and surveyed a few of their accumulated things. Nearest item was a Japanese lacquered commode standing against the wall along the staircase. He wandered to it and stroked the marble top. Each finger left a glistening streak in the dust. Diane's death and Blanche's resignation happened just five days ago, but chaos had already established a beachhead.

Like much of their furnishings, she'd acquired the commode on a trip. Prague, before the children, the Christmas they always spoke about when they still shared themselves. That Christmas Eve, after the best meal of their lives, they'd decided to walk back to the hotel. Two blocks from brandies in the cozy lobby, soaring voices lured them through flurries and frigid temperatures to a nearby cathedral. In the shelter of a side-door, they'd huddled for a private performance, unspoiled by its passage through the centuries-old door. Mystical, joyful sounds. An exulting collaboration. He'd felt the "us" of them in that doorway. Even now he remembered the peace and fulfillment, an almost overwhelming gratitude, but so many years back, the loss of it had long since scabbed over.

"Why did I do that?" He shifted two brass candlesticks to one side of the commode, swept and swirled the sleeve of his robe across the cleared area, then repeated the process for the other side before replacing the candlesticks. "Really is a fine piece," he said, slapping dust from his robe onto the floor.

The doorbell startled him. "Jackals." He tiptoed into the great room and peered around the drapes. It wasn't the press. His sister-in-law's Hummer sat in the front circle. The bell rang again, this time without interruption. Roberta still had her thumb on the button when he ripped the door open. "Enough!"

"I tried to phone," she said, brushing past him.

"Come in, I guess." He stood by the open door, hand still on the knob.

"Jordan," she said, hiking the strap of an oversized purse higher on her shoulder, "this will sound horrible based on timing, but Diane promised me several pieces of her jewelry. I thought it better to come before your women had a chance to pick over everything." Arms folded, she tilted her head back and stared at him.

"Opening with an insult." Nodding, he pursed his lips. "Interesting tactic."

"I know where she kept things. Do I have your permission to go up?"

"You don't have my permission to be in the driveway." He pulled the door wider. "Get lost."

"My sister's keepsakes are *not* decorating your whores, especially that trailer trash, Amanda."

"Roberta, try thinking before you speak, unless having your name on that list is a source of great pride."

"You're a degenerate."

"And how do you know about Amanda?" he said to her crimson face. He pictured this witch listening to Diane offload some hurt and then driving the wedge deeper between them.

She snorted. "I'm blood. I know everything."

"Really? Did Diane know everything?"

"Yes." Defiance remained on her face.

"Bullshit." His bravado was fake. Without a specific accusation, Diane had always made it clear she knew of his brief fling with her sister.

"I couldn't stand the guilt any more. It took a few years, but over coffee, right in there," she said, pointing toward the kitchen, "I told her about the mistake and asked forgiveness."

"You're lying."

"You know what she said? She'd given you permission to screw anyone you wanted, but she was surprised at my lack of taste. My lack of taste, Jordan," she said, laughing. "From then on, you were a shared joke." She leaned toward him and poked a thumb at her chest. "I know more about you than you do."

"Is that so?" He needed to find out if she knew of the abortion. "Do you know why there were lifeless pieces of ass like you? Did she share that with you?"

Her shoulders slumped. Pain dripped from her face. She clasped hands in front of her breasts like a diva. "Oh, poor man. Brutalizes his wife, then wonders where the magic went."

Everyone's crime was forgivable but his, and he was innocent. "I'm not doing this with you." He fanned a hand toward the sunlight. "Out."

"I want to see her will."

He took a long step toward her. "Get out. Now."

"Jordan," she said, giving him a wide berth as she headed for the door, "I know exactly which pieces she promised me. If they're specified for me in her will, and you hang them on some slut, I will sue you."

"Let's do this," he said, walking to the door inches behind her. "Why don't I follow you outside and bend you over a fender for old time's sake?"

"You pig!" she screamed at the slammed door.

Her intrusion did have some value. It reminded him that no one, except a child, is completely dead until the property is divided. Their wills were Arnold Hoffman's bailiwick, but one thing was certain, Diane's personal property was his, unless otherwise specified. That made looking at her will a good idea.

He took a step toward his office but reversed direction and headed for the billiard room. Diane commandeering his office for her recuperation meant his desk had to go elsewhere. The room with the most open space was the billiard room, a spot he might have set foot in five times since they built the house. He entered through a door off the foyer.

Movers had positioned his desk and chair in front of the walk-in fireplace, a recess vast enough to roast an ox. He sat in the soft leather and swiveled to face the cavernous room. During the design phase with the architects, he'd enjoyed planning this space more than any other. It would be the epicenter of fun in their huge lives. Raised oak paneling ringed the walls, unifying the functional areas and warming the entire space. An eight-stool, mirrored bar, with a rear door to the wine room, sat across from the fireplace. Two powder rooms. Regulation-size billiard and pool tables spaced far enough apart so both could be in use at the same time.

But troubles predated any parties, and houses don't tolerate disingenuous merriment. He scanned the room. Not a single ghost spilled a drink on the competition felt. No female shrieked in laughter at an off-color joke. No singing or dancing to the theater-quality sounds. No gatherings of rabid fans in front of the big screen televisions. Not even a political huddle or celebration. He rotated back to the desk and rummaged through the drawers until he found her will.

"Shit," he muttered when he opened to the appropriate page. Of all the pieces she owned, only three had been listed, all for Roberta. The descriptions must have come verbatim from the appraisals, so at least they would be easy to find. Better to give them to her now than endure repeated contact. Papers folded to the schedule page, he headed for Diane's dressing area.

He set the list on the vanity counter and sat in front of the jewelry chest. First drawer slid out too easily. Empty. He closed it. Next drawer. Same. Each subsequent drawer, a quick peek and slam.

Leaning back in the undersized chair, he clicked through possibilities. Blanche? No. Safe deposit box? No, and if he was wrong, the bank had already sealed it. Cops? Too smart to take all of it. Burglars? Maybe. During the wake or funeral? No. He'd set the alarm each time. Or had he? The alarm company might have a record. Panic room?

He jumped from the chair, hurried to the back of her walk-in closet, and yanked open a disguised door. The small room was a fortress if they were invaded. Fireproof to three hours, water, oxygen, telephone, access to surveillance cameras, inside and out. A search of the small space yielded nothing.

He meandered into the master bedroom and sat on the edge of the bed. Another possibility floated in, a sickening one. Murder. Robbers took the jewelry, forced Diane and Kevin into the running car, confirmed they were dead, then left. No. There was the note, and she'd sent Wyatt away so Blanche would find them. No doubt it was suicide, but that didn't explain the jewelry.

Hand squeezing the back of his neck, he rose from the bed and ambled toward the windows overlooking the turnaround and the ravine. Hidden? He rested his elbows on top of the lower sash and massaged his temples. No, not hidden. He might call the police, and they'd search everywhere, including the grounds. They'd find the Volvo and that would hurt Wyatt. Gave everything away? No. Roberta would have already gotten hers. Thrown away? Too stupid. "Oh my God," he whispered. That was it. Spite. Every piece had a sentimental origin. No better way to show contempt.

After a shower and shave, he dressed in denim work shirt and blue jeans. If he was going to sift through trash, may as well do it in the right clothes. He raced down the back stairs to the kitchen and across to the basement door. Hand on the knob, he stopped. The allure of the chase vanished. It was a cursed treasure, and just because she had no generosity, that didn't mean he would retract his. Each piece was a gift. She could do what she liked with them, and apparently had.

One burden had been lifted, the first in quite a while. He was hungry. Not just hungry, but famished. Hunting began at the kitchen's center island, at the ever-present bowl of fresh fruit. Using one finger, he rolled the top pieces of the mound. Soft brown pears had leaked paste onto withering apples. Wrinkled oranges sported patches of green-gray fur. He tossed everything into the trash, and did the same for the contents of the refrigerator, other than cans and bottles.

That minor domestic success was the limit of his abilities and interest. He plugged in the house line, placed calls to three maid services on Yelp, and detached the line as soon as he was done. The first interview would be that afternoon at two. A small step, but a heartening start.

With several hours to kill, he decided to get breakfast at the Oldwick General Store. Afterward, he'd swing by Califano's farm stand to catch Wyatt for a chat, maybe even get him to quit. On the stairs to the basement, he powered up his cell phone and scrolled through the missed calls. "Good God." Five from Amanda, coming in ever-shortening spans. Fat chance he'd return those. Entering the garage, he was about to power off when the phone buzzed in his hand. Caller I.D. showed "restricted." If it was the media, as he suspected, he could always hang up. "Be right with you," he said, his big voice reverberating in the garage. He hit the door lifter button.

"Judge Carpenter?" a man said.

"Hold on." He sat behind the wheel and closed the door. "Who's this?"

"Len Moseley."

"Yes, Detective," he said, eyes shut tight, "what can I do for you?"

"Not detective any more, Judge. I retired."

"Good for you." He started the engine. "Well deserved, I'm sure. So, why the call?"

"First, sir, I'm very sorry about your wife and son.

272

In fact, I was at the funeral home two nights ago, but before I could speak with you, things got, y'know, crazy with you and Wyatt."

"Poor kid. Young people aren't prepared for trauma like that. Then again, who is? But, you said 'first.' There's more?"

"Wyatt's Volvo, Judge. You and I need to talk about that."

His stomach clenched. He swallowed twice to keep his voice from catching. "You found it?"

"Oh, I think you'd know if that happened."

"Wait. You're retired, Detective. Why are we even discussing this?"

"I know you've had a horrible few days, Judge, so I'm not pressing, but you and I have to meet about the car. I'll explain then. Is tonight too early?"

"Can't you just tell me now?" He braced for what was coming.

"No harm, I suppose. Judge, I'm pretty sure the Volvo's in the ravine behind your house."

He covered his eyes. "Absurd."

"Maybe you know, maybe you don't. But I think you do."

"Then why haven't you got a warrant?" He slammed a fist into his leg for asking a question without already knowing the answer.

"I was a good detective, Judge, not a perfect one. That's why I want to see you. You gotta straighten something out, and so do I. What about tonight?"

"Is nine all right?" At least it would be too dark to see the bottom of the ravine.

"See you then."

He wasn't hungry any more.

Chapter 42

Head hanging, knees spread, Wyatt sat on an upright tomato crate behind Califano's farm stand. He always knew the small field of weeds back there wasn't the family's farm, but everything might have felt different if it was. He wasn't learning farm stuff. Just a job in a store. Good smells and friendly people, but sweeping and unloading trucks into the refrigerated storage room wasn't what he'd imagined. He wanted to drive a tractor and throw bales around.

Baking out there in the late morning sun wasn't real smart, but he was too embarrassed to be inside. Around eleven o'clock, when Mrs. Califano had told him and Beth to take their lunch break, he realized lunch had never crossed his mind when he was getting ready that morning. Neither had money. Soon as Beth pulled her brown bag from behind the front counter, he ducked out the back door.

"Ah, here you are," Beth said, peeking around a corner on the driveway side of the building. "Okay to join you?"

He nodded and even managed a little smile for her.

She sat on a nearby box, set a frosted bottle of Peach Snapple on the dusty ground, and slipped a wrapped sandwich from the brown bag. "You finished *already*?"

"Forgot. First day, first job. I was bound to screw

something up."

"Hey, I can't eat all this," she said. "Take half."

"Thanks." He shook his head. "Not really hungry."

"Me either." She rewrapped what looked like ham and cheese on marble rye. Brown mustard, not the yellow stuff he hated.

"C'mon," he said, "don't be that nice. I'll remember tomorrow. Eat your lunch."

"Only if you take half."

"Really, I'm good. Too tired. Too…" He shrugged.

"Sad?" She held out a piece of sandwich.

He bent his head and couldn't keep from crying. The outburst surprised him, too. After last night, he was sure he wouldn't be able to produce another tear for the rest of his life.

"Want me to go?"

Head shaking, he sat taller and dragged a wrist across each eye. "Last night I found something out. People have their own smell. Did you know that?"

"I guess."

"I couldn't sleep, so I got up. Kevin's room is next to mine. I went in and laid on his bed. When I closed my eyes, it was like he was right there. But then I thought pretty soon someone's gonna wash those sheets, and he'll be gone for good."

"Not the memories."

"I took his pillow case. Then I went to my mother's bed and did the same thing. I put them in Ziploc bags, in my closet." He flicked a glance at her. "Totally sick, huh?"

She leaned closer. "Once, I heard about this little boy. Three years old, I think, with a head full of blond curls. Anyway, he went into the hospital to have his tonsils out, and all the nurses went crazy over him. After the operation, something happened and he died, right there in the hospital. In the little bit of time before they could take his body away, the nurses snipped so many pieces of his hair, he had to have a haircut for the funeral. His first big boy haircut, after he already died." Nose wrinkled, she shook her head. "What you did isn't weird at all."

He nodded. "Kevin, he was always coloring, drawing pictures."

"That was so sweet at the funeral, putting them around his casket like that."

"I stuck a drawing in another bag and put it in with his pillow case. That way, I can't get confused someday about which bag is whose." Crying again, he beat a fist on his knee.

"Maybe you should go home. Start fresh tomorrow."

"No," came out louder than he meant. "No," he said, softer this time, his hands pushing toward the ground. "I'm going to do Torrie's work."

Looking puzzled, she tilted away from him.

"Beth, do you guys ever, y'know, talk about the person that hit you?"

Her gaze drifted. "Not really. It happened, and we kinda just keep going." She shrugged. "That's how we are, I guess."

"Do you hate him?"

"Yoo-hoo," Monica sang from inside the cold storage room. "Careful what you're doing. I'm coming out." She opened the door a crack and pushed her smiling face into the gap. "Thought so. Hello, you lucky people. It's me."

He rolled an arm for her to join them. "I was just asking Beth about the accident. Tell me, do you hate the guy that hit you?"

Bending one knee into the other, she slid both hands around the sides of her neck, swept long curls onto the top of her head, and held them there. "Now that I'm gorgeous again, no." Lots of lip action with the "no."

"How about Torrie?" he said. "She got it the worst. Does she hate the guy?"

Monica flapped a hand. "My dad's right. Hating is stupid. You get all psycho and junk, but the person you hate is all la la la." She blinked and wobbled her head. "They like don't even know."

"Hey!" Mrs. Califano called out. The three of them walked to the edge of the building and peeked down the driveway. "What are you doing?" she said, arms wide. "I'm all alone up here. Let's go."

His afternoon went the same as the morning: hosing, sweeping, hauling, and stacking. At a lull around two-thirty, he was sweeping fragments of husk and silk from in front of the corn bins—for about the tenth time—when he spied Beth huddled with her mother near the register. Mrs. Califano sneaked a peek at him. Beth slid a flat of flower seedlings from the counter and left through the wide front entrance.

"Wyatt," Mrs. Califano said, hooking a finger at him. She kept her back to him and fussed with a display of snack-sized baked goods at the checkout counter.

"Yes, ma'am," he said when he got next to her.

"Catch." She underhanded a packet of cookies, a small coffee cake, and a corn muffin. "Eat these. Tell me what you think."

"Mrs. Califano, I just saw Beth—"

"Hey." She held her hand up. "This is a new line, and they're not selling. If they stink, you'll tell me." She pointed to the drinks cooler. "And get a milk or something. That coffee cake looks dry. Go on. Have it in the cold room or out back."

Each Califano kindness made him more ashamed. Tears welled and dropped.

"Aw, honey." Mrs. Califano touched his cheek. "Maybe this was too fast for you. Go home. Be sad for a while if you have to."

"Stop it!"

Her face grew red and tight. "You don't talk to me like that. Not in my place."

"Mrs. Califano, you don't understand," he said, setting the pastries on the counter. "It was me. I hit the girls."

"What?"

He nodded. Confessing felt like he'd taken a breath after being under water too long.

Her expression flashed from confusion, to blank, to shock. "Omigod," she said, eyes searching for her daughters.

"Beth, Monica," he said, catching a glimpse of each one's startled eyes, "I wanted to tell you from the beginning, but...*but my mother wouldn't let me?* I didn't have the guts."

Mrs. Califano looked like she was having trouble focusing. "Then what's all this?" Her head and open arms shook. "Some kind of twisted game?"

"I had to do something to help." Like a wolf pack closing around its victim, Monica and Beth drifted into his peripheral vision.

"How could you leave us?" Monica screamed.

No excuses. It wasn't Tanner who closed the door and stepped on the gas. It was him. "I panicked. That's it."

Tears shined in Beth's eyes. "You hurt us. Torrie…And you just drove away?"

He shook his head and shrugged. "I'm sorry."

Monica stepped in front of her mother and stabbed a finger in his face. "My mom's gonna call the cops."

"I don't care," he said. "I had to tell you."

"Let me, Mom." Monica started for the phone by the register.

Mrs. Califano snatched her daughter's arm. "I'll handle this." Eyes closed, she tapped praying hands to her lips as she paced in front of the checkout. After what seemed like a long time, she cut behind the counter, punched buttons on the cordless phone, and held it to her ear. Her gaze dropped to the floor. "Frank, you have to come…Nobody's hurt, just come…No, now. I know who ran the girls over…Yes…No, when you get here." She hung up.

Hands on her hips, bent at the waist, Monica wrinkled her nose. "You're going to jail, sucker."

Mrs. Califano rushed into her daughter's face. "Listen to me. He and I are going out back for a little talk. When your father gets here, tell him where we are. Don't say one word about this to anyone. Either of you." She glanced at Beth, who nodded. "Monica, you hear me? No calls, no texting, no comments to customers, nothing. Do you understand?"

"Why aren't—"

"Do you understand?" she shouted.

"Jeez, okay," Monica said, hands raised. "Y'know,

he's the criminal, not me."

He passed Beth's sad face as he followed Mrs. Califano out the side door to the driveway. Neither said anything. He could never explain it right, but as disappointed in him as she looked, that's how proud he was. From now on, all the bad would come from outside.

"Know what I'd like to do?" Mrs. Califano said, fist pumping in time to her stomping steps. "I'd like to flatten your head with a shovel."

"Mrs.—"

"Shut your mouth." They stopped at the stacked crates and dumpster behind the building. "Sit down," she said, pointing to his lunchtime tomato box. "Last thing I'm gonna do is talk up to you."

There was nothing she could call him that he hadn't already called himself. Nothing she could threaten he hadn't already imagined. He sat and kept his gaze to the ground so she could blow up without challenge or interruption. She'd earned it.

"Aren't you wondering why I didn't call the cops?"

Her nervous, sneakered feet shuffled back and forth where he was looking. An answer would keep her going, so he nodded.

"I'm a little confused right now. See, my husband is the finest human being on God's green earth, and he's a good judge of people. Always knows who's good and who's a bum. Always. After we got home from the wake the other night, he told me about how proud he was of Beth because it was your kindness that attracted her. Not money, not looks, none of that stuff. Your kindness. He said he saw it in you, too. The way you were with your brother and your mother, and God forgive me, Torrie. I said yeah, I saw it, too, but now I gotta see what he thinks after you tell him."

She widened her pacing area and took frequent peeks down the driveway. "About time. Frank," she hollered, crisscrossing both arms over her head. Mr. Califano must have been coming, because she walked farther from the crate, making room for her husband's turn at the prisoner.

"So, tell me for heaven's sake," Mr. Califano said as he neared the corner of the building. "Why the big—" He halted, looking surprised to see Wyatt. "What's this?"

Mrs. Califano swept an open hand to where he was sitting on the crate.

"What the hell does that mean?" Mr. Califano said, arms spread.

"It was me, sir," Wyatt said, staying seated. "I hit the girls. Couldn't stand it anymore. I had to tell you."

"You?" Mr. Califano squinted at his wife, who nodded. "You?" he said, his gaze wandering but always coming back to him. "And we were worried about *you?*" Looking confused, Mr. Califano dragged fingers across his face and neck. He did it so hard they left white trails in his tan. "My Torrie's talking in two-word sentences, because of you? And you knew all along." Small steps plodded toward him. "I gave you this job. We cared about *you?*"

"I wanted to help," he said, nervous about Mr. Califano stepping closer. The waffle sole of a boot stomped into his chest. Floating. His back flattened a flimsy crate. Wood slivers stabbed through his shirt.

Mrs. Califano jumped in front of her husband, propped stiff arms into his chest.

He spun her to the ground and kept coming.

"Daddy!" Beth raced from the driveway, yanking at her father's belt. "Daddy!" She hopped and skidded behind his advance.

A scary nothing on his face, Mr. Califano hoisted him by the hair. An open hand found the side of his head. Weightless. Dumpster gonged. Shoulder and head scraped along dust. Echoes and flickering light. Tilted images turned from fuzzy to clear. Monica at the corner of the building, crouching, hands to her face, mouth stretched in a scream. Mrs. Califano, arms braced again into her charging husband. Beth, riding her father's back, tugging an arm into his neck. "Daddy, please!"

Mr. Califano stopped and stared straight ahead. His family surrounded him, all of them breathing through open mouths, stroking and whispering like to a spooked animal.

Nothing hurt, at least not a lot. Arms at his side, Wyatt stood tall and waited.

"Go," a panting Mrs. Califano said over her shoulder, her body positioned between him and her husband. Strands of hair fell around her face. Trickles of blood ran from her nose to her lip.

"Aren't you calling—?"

"Go!" she growled, her head bobbing toward the driveway.

In the car, splinters in his back forced him to sit forward as he wheeled onto Rte. 523. Panic and elation chased inside his chest and head. He eased off the gas but still chirped tires at the turn onto Rockaway Road. Slowing the car to a crawl, he fished out his phone and dialed his father. First time he'd wanted to speak to him in a while. Voicemail. "Dad, if the cops show up, it's because I told the Califanos the truth. I figured with Mom gone..." Tears blurred the road. He hung up. No way he was leaving a blubbering message.

Whittemore Nature Preserve's parking lot loomed just ahead on the right. He held it together just long enough to turn in, skid to a stop, and throw the shift lever into *Park*. After this cry was over, he'd talk to his mother, let her know that what he was going to do didn't mean he didn't love her or care what she thought anymore.

Chapter 43

Interviewing a maid service drove home how little Jordan understood about maintaining a household, especially one as large as his. Too disinterested to even consider going through the process again, he signed with the first company and cancelled the next two appointments. What Diane and Blanche used to accomplish every day, without seeming to try, would now require two full-time and one part-time person. The number of occupants had been cut in half, yet somehow the need for labor had doubled. He blamed Detective Moseley's portentous phone call about the Volvo for his unwillingness to conduct stronger negotiations.

Already a bit over-caffeinated, he poured water into the coffee maker for another ten-cup pot. The activity substituted for thinking, and he enjoyed the aroma. Bent at the waist, forearms flat on the counter, he watched French Roast trickle into a carafe.

A knock hit the front door, followed by the bell. He kept his attention on the brown dribble.

The latch jiggled.

"Aggressive son of a bitch," he said.

"Jordan," Amanda called out, "I know you're in there." Hammering and ringing resumed.

Halfway to the door he stopped. "What do you want?" he said, his voice booming inside the foyer.

"I won't take but a minute, promise. Please let me talk to your face."

The anti-Diane. Even with an edge, her sound spun pleasures. Smiles and laughter. Touches and scents. Flickers of long-gone devotion and appreciation. Continuing to the door, he rested his palms and forehead against a raised panel. "Why are you doing this?"

"I never got a chance to tell you how sorry I am about your family."

"And now you have."

"Jordan, please open the door."

"I saw you at the funeral home." He replayed the imprinted motion of her body as she'd made her way to a remote chair at the wake. "What were you thinking?"

"Same reason I'm here. When a person does something hateful, they have to fix it if they can."

"You can't."

"I'm going away from here, Jordan, but I need you to forgive me first."

He covered his eyes. "What do you mean, 'going away from here'?"

"Back to Charleston. I'm already packed."

As a fellow victim, he appreciated that denial of absolution was an awful power. He opened the door.

Both her hands fiddled with the soft leather purse she held at her waist. "I guess we can do this out here if you prefer."

"Oh, sorry." He stepped aside and waved her in. Based on the dark pinstriped suit, she must have spent at least part of the morning at the courthouse. Hair in a French Twist was the only non-work element of her beautiful presentation.

"Mercy," she said, her gaze drinking in everything on her way into the foyer. "I always knew your place would be special, Jordan, but my heavens."

"I just made coffee. Care for some?"

"Thank you. I believe I will. This way?" She pointed down the hallway and strolled in that direction.

No way was he watching from back there. He hurried around her. "I'll get some cups. Have a seat, and I'll bring everything over. How do you take it?"

"Well, this is quite the role reversal. Black's fine." She looped the room on her way to the table, pausing to take in the view to the ravine.

"Impressive, don't you think?"

"Maybe," she said, her voice soft. "When I was a little girl, we had a marsh behind our place. Scared the stink outta me at night, especially if my momma left the window open. Bugs would be chittering, then something would cry out. Or I'd hear some thrashing in the grasses. Sometimes just a splash. Then things would go quiet again until the next poor thing got killed. Anything nasty ever come out of those woods?"

For the first time in years, a woman wasn't filling his kitchen with crackling tension. He wanted to surround her with his arms and assure her he'd never let the monsters get her. After setting two full mugs on the table, he twisted a chair toward her and sat at the head.

"Well, sir, may as well get right to it." She let out a long breath. "Jordan, what I did at the hospital was the cruelest, stupidest thing I've ever done. I meant to hurt you, not her, and certainly not your boys."

"I know."

"Should've quit after you dumped me. I left that place half-crazy after being around you all day. Soon as

I got home, I'd have a glass of wine. Didn't even change my clothes. Then I'd have another. The tipsier I got, the angrier I got. You can't treat people like you do and get away with it, Jordan." Her green eyes took on a shimmer.

"I handled everything badly. I'm sorry."

"The evening I went to the hospital, I had no idea why I went or what I'd say. I do know I was plenty mad, though. The second I walked into her room, she lit into me. Treated me like trash, same as you, but at least she had a reason. Then I saw your boys, the whole family all knitted back together, with me on the outside, nose against the glass. I hated all of you. It was my chance to hurt you back, and I took it."

She surprised and impressed him. No point in a person having power if they refused to use it.

"Before I even got to my car, I was horrified at myself. That poor woman hadn't done spit to me. I kept wanting to go back, or call her, and apologize. Figured if I waited a little longer, she might understand better, but then..." She grabbed a paper napkin from a holder in the middle of the table and held it to her eyes.

"Amanda, don't. None of us saw it coming."

"Never good putting too much wine into too small a brain," she said, inspecting the napkin. "That's no excuse, I know, but that's what happened, and I'm asking you to forgive me." Those lustrous emerald eyes held his, waiting for his answer.

"Seeing you at the wake," he said, his gaze following the slow swirl of the spoon in his coffee, "and then all the calls. I thought maybe you were trying to get us together again."

"Why on earth would I push myself on a man who

told me he doesn't want me? Never loved me."

"What if I did love you?"

"Well, sir," she said, eyebrows raised, "then I am one lucky so and so, because you sure had a cruel way of showing it."

"You scared me. We were headed someplace impossible."

"Jordan, this coffee is just awful." She grimaced and pushed the cup away. "And you're right about impossible. With you out of my life, I've had some good thinking time, and you know what?" Her wide-eyed pause told him she would wait for his response.

He shrugged.

"We had nothing, you and me. Cheating and lies are a foundation built on sand." She smiled. "I do remember a bit from my summer Bible camps."

"What cheating and lying? Diane knew."

"No, sir. When a man and woman can't be seen in public, something's slap-dead wrong."

He sipped his coffee. "Tastes fine to me. And, by the way, you don't have to go anywhere. I'm resigning, and you'd certainly be retained by my replacement."

"Wow." Forehead wrinkled, she flicked her gaze between him and the table. "You think that's smart? Being busy might be the best tonic for a while. You love being a judge."

"Now, if you *really* want a foundation built on sand." He coughed and took a sip of coffee. One mistaken confession to her was enough. Five million to that "Canadian" Foundation had no chance of being uncovered unless he was stupid enough to blab again. "I'm serious," he said, reaching toward the napkin holder, "you should stay on." He held the napkin to his mouth and continued to clear his throat.

"Too many memories."

"Some good, I hope."

"Sugar, until you dumped me, I woke up every day itching to get to that office. Wasn't just the snatches of loving, either. I felt like I was doing important work with an important person. We were a team."

"Amanda, my wife was dying. I had two options. Committing to her was the less terrible."

"All we had to do was wait. Told you I'd wait. But no, you had to hurt me, try to make me feel like dirt, which I am not."

"I'm sorry."

"And you can stay sorry. I'm a passionate woman, Jordan. I don't deny it, and I'm not ashamed. It pleased me to please you, but you twisted that into me being unworthy. I don't know why men do that. Well you know what?" she said, jabbing a finger. "Day after tomorrow, I'm getting me a new life, one without a sad-ass fool like you in it." She folded her arms, widened her eyes, and fell back into the chair.

"That's your apology?"

She popped upright in the seat. "Weren't you listening?"

"I'm teasing," he said, smiling, "and of course I accept." Too much of his life had already been lost to vendetta. "You couldn't have known what she'd do, particularly to Kevin. Nobody could. Now, can I tell you something?"

"Oh, boy. Guess I asked for this." She squirmed into the seat back and gripped the edges of the chair. "Go ahead."

"I loved you. Still do."

Her expression fell blank. "Don't lie to save my feelings, Jordan. You can't hurt me anymore."

"Not a lie."

"I asked you to say it, and you wouldn't."

"Amanda, once someone says that, they owe the other person something. There wasn't a next step for us."

"Course there was." She held up a finger, stood, and sidled toward the refrigerator. "This is rude, I know, but I can't drink this swamp water. Okay if I get myself some juice, or pop, or something?"

He nodded. She did it so effortlessly. It could be like this. Short angers, quickly forgotten. "Please don't go," he said, watching her search a lower shelf in the fridge.

"Dang, nothing but root beer. I hate root beer. Wait, what's behind this?"

He'd lost so much. Why would it be wrong?

"You got nothing in there," she said, shutting the door. "Do you take every meal in a restaurant?" Her finger swirled at the cabinets. "Glasses?"

"In front of you." The problem would be Wyatt. There'd never be a truce between those two. He'd lose the only family he had left. And she deserved a fuller life. No aging lover who sometimes needed a pill first. A chance for children, although he wasn't seeing an upside to that at the moment.

Tumbler in hand, she paused at the ice dispenser in the refrigerator door. "This is stupid. I'm gonna go." She returned the glass to the cabinet, pointed to her purse, and headed for it. "I promised to be quick, but you know me and my big mouth. You've been gracious, Jordan. Thank you."

"Would you like to see the house? Last chance. I'm selling it." That idea had never entered his mind, but the instant he said it, he realized that's what he had to do.

"No. I'm gonna go." She picked up her purse.

"Won't take long." He tugged at the handbag. "Amanda, we've enjoyed so much good wine together, let me at least show you my collection. C'mon. Two minutes." She let him take the purse and set it on the table. "After you," he said, pointing at the archway to the butler's pantry. "I'll be curious to see if you remember any. Next door on the right." He stepped around her, opened the door to the wine room, and waved her inside. "Climate control," he said to her suspicious expression after he closed the door behind them. "Let's start easy." He slid a bottle from the nearest rack, dusted it, and handed her a Justin Isosceles.

She smiled at the label. "Friday after Thanksgiving, last year."

"I don't think so. Pretty sure I brought Opus One that night."

"That was Christmas, sugar." She pinched the platinum chain disappearing below the straight neckline of her blouse. "This was hung on the neck of the bottle," she said, dangling a diamond pendant. "It was Opus One."

"I defer." Replacing the Justin, he wondered how many wine memories with Diane he might have gotten wrong, too. He sidestepped along a rack deeper in the room. "Let's dooo, ah." He slipped out another bottle and presented the Opus One label. "I'll pour us a glass, and we'll let it breathe while we tour."

"Jordan, no." She backed toward the door. "You're

not doing this to me again. I won't let you."

"Amanda, I just want to enjoy a glass of wine with you and brag about a house I hate more than you could ever know."

She shook her head, groped a hand behind her, and turned the doorknob. "You still think I'm stupid. It's insulting. Like I don't know what's happened every other time we shared a glass of wine. Well, what happened was we'd do something that made you disappear, and left me feeling bad about myself. I'm done with that." She backed out of the wine room and into the butler's pantry.

"Don't go." He followed her out, the bottle of wine still in his hand. "Please."

"No, sir," she said, finger wagging in front of her face. "There's something, I dunno, broken in you, or sick maybe, and it's contagious. What I did to Diane? That was never me, not until you. No one's ever made me feel bad about myself before you."

"Amanda," he said, holding a hand out to her, "please stay. We'll just talk. We'll enjoy a glass of wine and talk. Like friends."

She faced away from him and held up her palm. "Jordan, I came here to do something, and I have. Please stop following me. I know the way out." Her clicking shoes paused in the kitchen and got quieter during her march down the long hallway. He heard the front door open, closed his eyes, and braced for the slam. Nothing. She was either still in the foyer, or closed the door so quietly he didn't hear it. He hurried into the kitchen but halted at the table.

The diamond pendant sat in a tangle where her purse had been.

Chapter 44

Frank didn't remember coming inside the stand's cold storage room after attacking Wyatt. Sitting on a stack of cartons, he became aware of Angie hugging his face to her pillowy breasts, stroking and kissing his hair. "It's all right," she repeated in whispers. He pulled her closer and shuddered from leftover adrenaline. Reminded him of his younger, brawling days. Two arrests and a shaky probation before God sent Angie. Now, like then, she anchored him, saved him.

"Hello?" a man's deep voice called from the display area of the stand.

Angie froze. "Omigod, that's Judge Carpenter." She covered Frank's ears. "Coming," she hollered and pushed out of the embrace. "Beth, are you okay to go out there?"

"No," she said, her voice high and scratchy.

"Monica?"

"No way." She was crying, too.

"Okay," Angie said. "I'll be right back."

"Babe, wait." He stood, dug a red and white bandana from a back pocket, and swirled a finger under his nose. "You got some blood." The trail of brownish red from each nostril meant he must have smacked her in the scuffle. Of all that had just happened, hurting her bothered him the most.

She licked the hanky, swabbed her upper lip, and

handed it back. "Better?"

He nodded. "I'm so sorry, Angie."

Knuckles rapped on the door. "Angie, it's Jordan Carpenter. Is Wyatt in there?"

"Be right out." She cupped her hands around Frank's neck and shook it gently. "You okay now? No more of that stuff?" Her head tilted toward the rear door.

He nodded and bounced a finger at each daughter. "Stay here."

"Whoa." Angie pulled his elbow. "What are you gonna say? Think about this a little."

"It'll come," he said, opening the door.

"Hello, Frank," the judge said, extending his hand. "I didn't expect to see—"

"Did you know?" He ignored the open hand.

"I beg your pardon?"

Angie tugged at the back of Frank's bib overalls. "Honey, let's do this in here. Girls, out. Beth, you take the register."

"Did you know Wyatt ran down my girls?"

"Oh, God." The judge's shoulders slumped. He craned his neck to check behind Frank as the girls ducked by. "Is he in there?"

"He left. Answer my question."

Judge Carpenter's eyes closed. "Why couldn't he...? Yes, I knew."

"Get in here." Frank backed into the room, his hand still on the knob.

"It's not his fault," the judge said after Frank closed the door. "He wanted to go to the police, but his mother and I stopped him."

"Oh yeah?" Frank said, inching toward the judge.

"Did you make him drive off? He left my girls bleeding in the street. Not his fault? You make me want to puke. You and your whole, lying, goddamn family."

"Frank." Brow wrinkled, Angie bobbed her chin toward the judge's pained face.

"Oh, right," he said, picturing two caskets.

"Look, I understand," the judge said. "We all know there's no good excuse. He made a mistake. He's a good person who made a mistake. Torrie's haunted him since that night. That's why he's here. Do you think he wants to be a farmer? He's trying to make things right."

"What's wrong with farming?" Frank said, leaning closer until Angie wedged between them.

Judge Carpenter raised his open hands. "All I'm trying to do is remind you about what I think you see in him, why we wanted to protect him. Think about it. Nobody caught him. He confessed."

Frank stared, head nodding. "And what about our Torrie?"

"I'll pay for everything."

"I don't mean money!" His rush bumped into Angie and made the judge hop backward. "What's wrong with you?" He gripped Angie's shoulders, but she spread her stance, refusing to be shoved aside. The fright he saw in her eyes was for him, not for Carpenter or herself. Twice in the last few minutes she was ready to take someone else's beating to protect him. Shaking, tears building, he let go of her and spun away from the danger.

Her fingers stroked his back. "Judge, I think what my husband means is, Torrie gets no justice? The criminal deserves more consideration than the victim? Am I right, Frank?"

He nodded, still not calm enough to risk seeing the man's face.

"Folks," Jordan said, "you misunderstood. I didn't mean you could be bought, but there must be expenses because of Wyatt's mistake. At the very least we have to pay those. If he had stopped, our insurance would have paid. You wouldn't have said 'no' to that."

Frank faced the judge, who surprised him by holding his stare. "Carpenter, if my wife wasn't here right now, you'd be in a world of hurt."

"Have the police taken my son?"

He shook his head. "I haven't called them, yet."

"Why not?"

"I dunno. Feels weak or something, like letting someone else fight our battle."

"Angie," the judge said, "you mentioned justice. That was my wife's struggle. She couldn't see how Wyatt being arrested would fix anything. His life ruined, and for what? And Frank, yes, maybe I should have come to you sooner, but how do I do that without putting Wyatt in the noose? He doesn't belong in prison. You have to see that."

"I don't have to see a goddamn thing. How do I know he wasn't drunk? Or high?"

"He wasn't."

"How do you know?" His hands balled into fists. "Because you say so? Who the hell are you, anyway?" He itched to fire a quick combination into the judge's face. Batter him so bad he needed a tube in his head and a speech therapist.

Angie's crossed forearms pressed against his chest.

He stomped away from her and locked his fingers behind his neck to stop them from curling into weapons. Pacing near the back door, along with some deep breaths, helped the rage to settle out a bit.

"So," the judge said, breaking the quiet, "where does this go now?"

"Not sure." He continued pacing. "Gotta think, maybe talk it over with the family."

"Torrie, especially," Angie said.

He waggled a finger at Carpenter. "Gimme your number."

The judge dug a gold, monogrammed business card holder from his front pocket. "Call the cell number," he said, handing one to him. "Will it be today?"

"It'll be when I'm good and ready."

"Regardless of your decision," Judge Carpenter said, "I won't withdraw the offer to help Torrie, no matter what that entails." He pulled the door open. "I'll wait to hear from you." Long, graceful strides carried him through the aisles of the stand and across the gravel parking lot. Without looking back once, he drove away.

"He's right about one thing," Angie said. "The kid showed guts confessing like that."

"Took his beating like a man, too."

"He really is a good kid, Frank. Don't you think?"

"Babe, how does that matter? How do we let it go without getting dirty, too? What does that say to the girls?"

Hugging his arm, she laid her cheek on his shoulder, and shrugged. "Forgiveness maybe? Life's not always so simple? I dunno. It'll be interesting to hear what they say."

"What are you talking about?"

"You said the family was going to talk it over."

"No. Parents teach right from wrong. They don't

ask."

"You want to turn him in. I can tell."

"If right was easy, Angie, there'd never be any wrong." He pointed to a car turning into the lot. "You got a customer, and I got things to do."

"Poor kid. All that's happened, and now this."

"All he had to do was stop." On his way to the exit, he hugged and kissed Monica, then Beth, exchanging a "love you" with each. Beth's sad, confused face made him hold her for a few extra seconds. First peek out of her shell, and her first disappointment. She'd survive.

A mile or so from the fields, Frank stopped at a red light, the only vehicle in sight. Elbow out the window, he closed his eyes and exhaled peacefully for the first time in weeks. Their lives were moving forward again. Not like before the accident, but mostly for the good, maybe even for the better. Today, Beth and Monica stood against him, jumped into the ass-kicking and helped stop it. He'd been the infant throwing a tantrum, and they were the grownups. Torrie might not know it yet, but she was in the same spot as him. In charge her whole life, but now she was the baby. The younger girls would never knuckle under like before, to him or to her. If he and Torrie didn't like it, too bad. Might as well get mad at the sun for setting.

He parked at the end of the row where he'd left the tractor. Reluctant to complete the day's last detail, he let unhurried steps carry him through the afternoon sunshine, through the sounds and smells that were part of his daily reward, past the head-high tassels and harvest-ready cobs. Hoisting himself onto the tractor's chassis, he pushed a boot against an earth-caked tire and flopped behind the wheel. Hunched forward in the cracked leather seat, he pulled out his phone and the judge's calling card. *If right was easy, there'd never be any wrong.* He punched in the number. While the phone rang, his misty gaze roamed their little plot and its not-so-perfect rows of fragile life.

Chapter 45

Moseley still had two hours to kill before meeting with Judge Carpenter. Hands in his pockets, he stood at his front window. Watching the weedy parking lot and chain-link corral surrounding the dumpsters consumed about ten seconds. He pulled out his cell phone, flopped into the recliner, and called Connie Dalton's cell.

"Moseley, what's up? Having a good day, old timer?"

Her enthusiasm helped his attitude more than his AA meetings. "Great day."

"Did you go at lunchtime?"

He had not. The sponsor she'd arranged for him warned him to stay humble, but he couldn't shake feeling superior to every one of those coffee-swilling, cigarette-sucking flameouts. "That's some tough group. I thought the evening meetings would get the hard core."

"Nah, most of them have jobs. Lots of high-function types. So, what are you doing to stay busy? Riding?"

"I'm thinking of giving that up." He hadn't told her he sold the Harley. Telling her would have sounded like what it was, desperation.

"Aw, what happened? Got a new girlfriend who's afraid you'll fall and get a booboo?"

"Too old for both."

"Bullshit. Half the guys I ride with are over fifty."

"I notice you didn't challenge the woman part."

"Whatever."

"So," he said, "how's the Califano investigation going?"

"Deader than the Pope's nuts. I'm not even spending much time on it anymore."

"Connie, what if—"

"Wait. 'Connie'?" She laughed. "Connie? Holy crap. Does that mean you're Lenny now?"

He didn't realize he'd said it. "Um, sure. What's your day look like tomorrow?"

The way she said "Why?" oozed with suspicion.

"No promises, but I may have something for you on that case."

"Lenny—wow, that felt weird—you're not on the job any more. If you have something, turn it over."

"Yeah, absolutely."

"So? Do you have something?"

"What's your shift tomorrow?"

"Do you *have* something?"

"No. Okay?"

"Why don't I believe you?"

"Because good detectives don't believe anybody."

"What the hell is happening? Did you just call me a good detective?"

"The best. Miss Marple with D cups." He didn't get the laugh he expected.

"Moseley, don't do that. I don't like it."

"Do what?" That sounded stupid-cute, even to him.

"Just treat me like a friend, okay?"

He'd picked up nothing encouraging yet, but maybe if they had some time together when he wasn't being a total asshole, she'd start to like him a little. "Is that something we could talk about over a nice dinner?"

"Awkward," she said after a short pause.

"You're taken?"

"Lenny, I am, and I have to go. Have fun at the meeting tonight. I'm really proud of you."

He was the second to hang up. It made sense she had someone. Pretty, sexy, funny. Just as well, based on his history with women. His focus had to be on staying sober right now, anyway. Dreams about chasing her would just have been "projecting," as they called it in AA, and they warned him that's where most drunks derailed. Then again, Connie knew the AA drill and might have been protecting him until he got stronger. It didn't matter. He had other fish to fry, and Judge Carpenter was going into the pan tonight.

Chapter 46

In the billiard room, Jordan sat on the front edge of his desk, rapt by the blaze in the fireplace. Voluptuous, shimmying flames. Comforting, decorative, destructive. Vivaldi's *Four Seasons* floated in perfect balance from a dozen speakers, loud enough that his ears and skin absorbed the harmonies. He cradled a glass of '96 Romanee-Conti burgundy to his chest, near enough that the bouquet pleasured his nose, jacked up his impatience. Three hours in the decanter had opened it beautifully. Lips to the cool crystal, he spilled a teasing portion onto his tongue, swished and chewed until the flavors faded. He'd prepped two bottles, so his next sip was more generous. Warmth spread. A magnificent wine.

Nose hovering above the glass, he studied the fire and hearth. Just the idea of "hearth" evoked family, his dead and fractured family. Kevin visited first, arms wide, smiling, heartbreaking. As always since the murder, all imaginings of his unfortunate son began and ended with disbelief. His next sip conjured Diane. For years, he'd never enjoyed a fine vintage alone without missing her, but now that ache had been paired with an appalling exhilaration.

The door from the basement into the kitchen closed. "Dad?" Wyatt shouted.

Wine glass under his nose, Jordan shuffled to the

doorway. "Billiard room," reverberated in the two-story foyer. Still inhaling the fruity aromas, he resumed his position in front of the fire.

"What are you doing?" Wyatt said from outside the room. "It's like eighty outside."

Gazing at the fire, Jordan grabbed a remote from the desk, pointed it over his shoulder, and lowered the music. "Mr. Califano called."

"I left you a message, too. Guess you didn't pick it up yet. Dad, why is the fire on?"

"Isn't it spectacular?"

"What did Mr. Califano say?"

He blew out a slow breath. "They're going to the police. Well, they were. I got him to agree we'd turn ourselves in tomorrow."

"I don't care."

"Marty Bender is coming here tomorrow at ten. He'll go with us to the precinct."

"Dad, I don't care."

"Stop saying that!" Only the value of the wine stopped him from hurling the glass at Wyatt. "I know you see this as some grand opportunity to be heroic and noble, but you're just being stupid."

"Nothing matters, does it? Must be awful to be you."

He snorted a laugh and swirled the wine under his nose. "By the way, Detective Moseley's coming here tonight."

"You said tomorrow."

"Not to arrest us. Seems he's retired since his visit here. He called and said he knows your car's in the ravine and needs to talk to me about it. I can't see him as an extortionist, but it certainly has that odor. If so, he's going to be disappointed." He drained his glass and headed for the decanters on the bar. "This wine is amazing. Would you like a taste?"

"No."

"I have no idea what you drink with your friends, but it won't be anything like this." He lifted a duck-shaped decanter by the handle on its back. "You're sure?"

"I don't drink."

"You're kidding. Never?"

"Never."

"Not one drop, ever?" he said, pouring a second glassful from the duck's beak.

"What's so hard to understand about 'never'?"

Maybe Diane wasn't completely gone. "Where have you been?" he said after returning to the desk. He eased into the leather chair and leaned back, clunked his feet onto the dusty top. "It's almost seven-thirty. I left the Califano's store a little after three. They told me you'd already gone."

"Why'd you go there?" Wyatt edged a few steps into the room.

"I hope wherever you were, you got something to eat. We have nothing."

"Did they tell you I said it was me?"

Eyes closed, he nodded. "Mr. Califano was furious with me. Implied that only his wife's presence prevented considerable mayhem against my person."

"Don't believe that. She couldn't stop him from kicking my butt pretty good."

He popped his legs off the desk and sat upright. "Califano hit you?" he said, pushing to his feet and setting the glass on the desk. "Are you marked anywhere?"

Wyatt hauled his T-shirt to his neck and angled away so Jordan could see the damage. "Maybe here." Welts and brown blood pinpointed splinters, large and small, poking into and under the skin. "Can you pull some of them out?"

"He hit you with a board?"

"Shoved me into some crates. Itches more than hurts."

"Ho, baby," Jordan said, chuckling and rubbing his palms together. "That's assault. If Frank Califano wants to press the issue, he can join us in the holding pen."

"No!" Wyatt jumped away from him and yanked his shirt back into place. "It's over." His lips pulled down at the corners and trembled. "Why can't we just do what's right?"

"Idiot." He knocked knuckles on the top of his head. "There's no such thing as 'right.' Variables, circumstances," he said, hands rolling in and out of tangles, "they complicate everything, smear those dark lines you think exist. That's why there are juries. Guilty's a verdict, not a moral absolute."

"You're gonna blackmail Mr. Califano?"

"I prefer to think of it as negotiating from strength."

Head shaking, Wyatt backed toward the door. "I feel sorry for you." His sandals flapped down the hallway and into the kitchen.

"Don't you go anywhere," Jordan called to him.

The door to the basement slammed. Feet bumped down the stairs. The door into the garage banged shut. When the overhead hummed and grumbled, Jordan hurried to the kitchen, arriving at the windows in time to see Wyatt back his rental Volvo into the turnaround and speed toward the bridge.

In front of the fire again, refill in hand, he tried to relapse into the evening's pre-Wyatt tranquility, but the radiant heat no longer warmed. It made him perspire. High notes from Vivaldi's violins became screeches. All magical elements in the aroma and flavor of his Romanee-Conti still existed, but the pleasure had been extracted. Twilight deepened into evening. Crystal goblet asleep on his chest, he permitted his mind to bumble through a repeating swirl of legal wranglings, media glee, old faces, and lost opportunities.

His comfortable melancholy ended when headlights glared through a front-facing window and darted along the walls. The nervous lights calmed to a weak glow near the front circle. Detective Moseley, no doubt. He stretched for a remote on the desk and clicked off the fire. Glass in hand, he rocked out of the chair. A car door thunked as he trudged into the foyer. He flipped on the porch light and opened the front door without waiting for the bell.

Moseley, unsmiling, clasped the outstretched hand. "Evening, Your Honor."

"Welcome, and since we're both retired now, no more formalities. Call me Jordan. May I call you Len?"

"I prefer Moseley."

He led the detective into the billiard room and pointed to some barstools. "You're in for a treat, Moseley. Have a seat." Circling behind the bar, he topped off the glass Wyatt had refused. A small amount splattered onto the bar when he misjudged the end of the pour. "Damn, there's a hundred bucks shot."

"This place really is unbelievable," Moseley said,

his gaze sweeping the room as he straddled a backless stool and sat. "And no wine for me."

"It's not just wine. It's the finest wine ever made." He slid the stemware toward Moseley. "I'd say you're looking at about two thousand dollars right there."

"God almighty, no booze is worth that. And I'm in AA now," he said, pushing the glass back with two fingers. "So, all the same with you, I'll take the cash."

"Jumping right into it, I see." Eyes closed, he swirled the glass under his nose, sipped, and ran the wine over his teeth and tongue before swallowing.

"Judge, could you maybe hold off on the grape juice until we're done?"

"It's Jordan. Do you play pool, Moseley? Let's go." He rolled an arm as he headed for a wall-mounted rack of cues. "One game of eight ball before the dirty business. Would you prefer different music?"

"You could turn it down a little," Moseley said, trailing close behind. "And why is it so hot in here?"

"Oh, you have to see this. Grab two," he said, pointing to the cues and veering toward the remote on the desk.

"Judge, could we—"

"I told you, it's Jordan." He squinted at buttons on the remote. "Prepare to be amazed," he said, his arm drifting as he aimed. Flames whooshed from the pyramid of ceramic logs. "Isn't that majestic?"

"Maybe we should try this again tomorrow. Earlier."

"Tomorrow?" The blaze vanished, remote clattered onto the desk. "Not sure I'd wait if I were you. Inmates usually aren't very talkative."

"Hold it." Moseley spun from his march to the

foyer and approached the desk. "Have you already been arrested?"

"How about this? If you can beat me at eight ball, I'll fill you in. If not...?" He mimed a tip of the hat.

"What the hell. Shouldn't be hard in your condition. I'll even let you break."

He grabbed one of the cues Moseley had laid on the pool table. "Tell me something," he said, grinding chalk onto the cue's tip, showering blue dust onto his hand and the floor, "did you enjoy your work?"

"Solving puzzles, yes." Moseley squatted at the end of the table and banged balls into the rack. "All the rest was bullshit. You?"

"Not a day." One eye closed, he drew the stick back but whiffed the shot. "That was practice." Next attempt clipped the edge of the cue ball and knocked the tip off. "Fuck!" He snapped the stick over his knee and threw the pieces at the fireplace. "We'll share yours," he said, beckoning with his fingers. "Last try."

Brow creased and head shaking, Moseley handed over his cue. "How can someone end up with all this if they hate their work?"

Another miss-hit sent the cue ball on a spinning crawl down the green felt and into a corner pocket.

"Have you ever played before?" Moseley said, tossing and catching the white ball on his way to the top of the table.

"I was quite good. Thirty...my God, forty years ago." He swept a finger around the bar area until he zeroed in on his glass. "Ah, my aiming tonic."

Moseley's break shot sounded like a pistol report. Balls careened around the table, three finding pockets. "Really," he said, surveying the table, "how could you hate work this rewarding."

Jordan laughed. "Interesting word choice. How much do you know about shareholder class-action lawsuits?"

"Bupkis."

"Disgusting business, trust me. MBA's incensed at being outfoxed by other MBA's. Millions, hundreds of millions confiscated from wealthy companies for the benefit of even wealthier investors. Once I understood the public was predisposed to hate corporations, the rest was child's play. Find a company with a plunging stock price, locate a few shareholders willing to sue, and wait for a gargantuan check."

"Can't be that simple," Moseley said, chalking his cue. "Somebody had to do something wrong." He sank the eleven ball.

"You'd think, wouldn't you? But no, not always. Facts can be burdensome for juries."

"Amen, brother." Moseley leaned on the stick and eyed the table.

"Is it my turn?" Jordan said, reaching for the cue.

"No." He frowned and swiped chalk across the cue tip, checked his options from a variety of spots around the table. "So, if it's the rich against the rich, why would juries pick sides?"

"Ah, therein lies the secret. You see, much as the common people have been made to hate corporations, they hate insurance companies the most. Once a jury learns insurance could cover the award, it's game, set, match. Speaking of that, would you please hit something?"

"Don't rush me." Moseley spiraled a finger around the room while he squinted at the remaining balls. "I'll tell you, if I could get this doing what you did, I'd never stop. Why did you?"

"One morning, I finally admitted I was shaving a parasite. Left my firm," he said, snapping his fingers, "just like that. Well, almost that fast."

"Of course you kept the money." Moseley waved the back of his hand. "You're in my way. Bank the thirteen," he said, tapping the cue on a corner pocket.

"Everyone keeps the money."

"What about being a judge?" Moseley made no move to continue playing. "How can you hate that?"

"Let's just say it's not possible to cleanse oneself with more dirt."

"Meaning?"

"I'm not playing anymore." All Jordan wanted was to close his eyes and sleep. "You win."

Moseley laid the cue on the table. "In that case, let's sit at the bar and have us that chat about the Volvo."

"I've been curious all day," he said, eager to sit, "under what authority are you asking? You're off the force."

"Remember my partner, Connie Dalton?"

"Impressive female." He sat, sniffed the top of the glass, and let his lids fall. "My wife gave her a hard time. But then, she had a gift." He blinked and straightened. "And what about your partner?"

"See, I knew the car was down there," Moseley said, his hand flapping toward the ravine. "It is, isn't it?"

"Your partner?"

Moseley smiled. "For reasons I'm not going into, I never told her about the car. Then, even though I'd been mostly a jerk to her, she did me a big-time favor, maybe saved my life. So what I'm thinking is, if you call her and tell her you want to turn yourself in, she gets the collar, and I get something off my conscience. Whadaya say?"

"Good God," he said, laughing toward the ceiling, "New Jersey's suffering an epidemic of high purpose. I thought this was a shakedown."

"Yeah, I could see where you might, and I'd be lying if I said it hadn't crossed my mind, but I'm not like you."

He felt like snapping a fist into Moseley's face. "What the hell does that mean?"

"Buddy," Moseley said, patting his own chest with both hands, "I got only one thing left to lose, and that's not happening. Not for you or anyone."

The phone on the bar rang. "Thought I'd unhooked that damn thing," he said, stretching for the handset. Caller I.D. showed *unknown*. "This'll be quick," he said, certain that a reporter was on the line. "What?" he shouted into the mouthpiece.

"Dad, I'm in Flemington, at the police station."

His head tingled. "You didn't."

"I told them everything. This is my one call."

"Aw, son." He covered his eyes. "Why couldn't you wait until tomorrow? There's a protocol."

"Somehow you'd make it come out bad."

"All right, at least do this for me. Please stop talking until I get there. It should be within the hour. Will you do that? Please?"

"Nothing else I can tell them."

"Then leave it at that. Don't answer more questions and don't sign anything. I'll be there soon as I can.

Please promise me you'll do as I ask."

"I promise."

"Thank you. Put one of the officers on." He shook his head at Moseley's questioning stare. "Yes," he said, his gaze dropping to the bar, "with whom am I speaking...? Officer Wilbur, this is Judge Jordan Carpenter, Wyatt's father. I'll be there within the hour with our attorney, Martin Bender. I'd appreciate it if you'd keep my son out of the population until we arrive...Thank you." He hung up and dropped his forehead onto folded arms.

"Was he the driver?"

"You have to leave now."

"Don't get in your car, Judge. I'll drive you."

"My attorney will swing by for me. You know the way out."

Moseley's stool scraped along the wide plank floor. "Judge, one question. Why? With your money and connections, nothing bad was going to happen."

"I'm not sure that's true anymore, but answer this. Have you never done something brainless because of a woman?" Without lifting his head, he raised a palm. "Goodnight, Moseley."

Chapter 47

Officer Wilbur left the precinct's interview room to get Wyatt a Coke. First time he'd been alone since he turned himself in. A sick kind of scared grabbed his stomach, made a distant memory out of feeling heroic. Too late now, but his father was probably right. Waiting until tomorrow to surrender with a lawyer would have been smarter, except if he waited, he'd still be the chicken-shit son of that loser.

Anger felt good. With jail coming, he needed more of it. Get angry and stay that way, become everything he wasn't. But for how long? A year? More? For the millionth time, he pictured the girls scattered on the road, heard Tanner and Billy screaming for him to leave. Then the tug on his belt, and the shock of finding himself behind the wheel, driving away. All he had to do that night was stay, and he'd be at home now, not wondering how to look bad-ass as he passed barred doors and cat-calls.

Officer Wilbur opened the door and handed him a can of Coke. A woman in street clothes slipped in behind the officer. "Hello, Wyatt," she said. "Remember me? Detective Dalton?"

"From the house. Sure."

"We're OK, Chuck. Please close the door behind you. So," she said once they were alone, "is it comfortable in here?" She twisted an empty chair next to him and sat with her knees facing him. "Not too warm or cold?"

"I'm good."

"OK then." She hopped the chair a little closer. "This may feel a little abrupt, Wyatt, but the rules are very strict, so I have to get some housekeeping out of the way first. Officer Wilbur tells me you've been read your rights and understand them. Is that right?"

He nodded. The room seemed a lot smaller.

"And you've been charged with leaving the scene of an accident, assault with a vehicle, failing to report an accident including injuries, obstruction of justice, tampering with evidence, and reckless driving. Is that right?"

"Sounds right." He was impressed she said all that without referring to any papers.

Hands clasped on her knees, she leaned toward him. "Wyatt, I want to thank you for coming in here and telling the truth. I'm sure it's been terrible for you to carry that weight, especially with all the other sadness in your life right now. You did a brave thing."

He nodded, but avoided eye contact.

"I'm serious, Wyatt. Anyone can make a mistake, but not everyone has the courage to admit it. Be proud of yourself."

Gaze still on his hands, he nodded again.

"OK, here's what we do next." A pad and two pencils sat in the middle of the table. She slid them toward him. "I know you've already told Officer Wilbur that your car hit the Califano girls, and you were driving, so, what I'd like you to do for me is write down all the details you remember, and then sign the bottom. Okay? And don't forget to say what you did with the car." When he kept his forearms flat on the table and laced his fingers together, she pushed the pad closer. "Wyatt, this is how it's done. You write everything down, get to read it to make sure it's right, then you sign it."

"I told my dad I'd wait for him and my lawyer," he said, glancing at her.

"Well, you certainly have that right."

Her light brown eyes grabbed him, searched his face. They got inside, like there'd be no point in hiding anything from her. She seemed nice, and he wanted to keep sharing, but he'd already admitted everything. That was enough for now. He'd stay quiet like he promised.

"Wyatt, you've already confessed. I'm just asking you to write that down, plus what you did with the car."

"I'm going to wait." When her attention darted to a mirror on the far wall, he realized they were being watched. "Who's back there?" he said, bobbing his head at the glass.

She stood and headed for the door. "Would you like a cup of ice for that Coke?"

He shook his head. *Bet they're taping me.* Secret eyeballs studying him was weird. Flipping the bird or picking his nose crossed his mind, but only for a second. The tape might be used at his trial. Stuff like that might make it look like he wasn't sorry. But what did sorry look like?

Long after he'd finished the Coke, a knuckle rapped on the door. Detective Dalton stuck her face in. "It seems your friend, Billy, has gone backpacking in France, but we just brought Tanner in. I'm going to be with him for a while. Do you think there's anything he'll tell me different from what you've said?"

"If he does, it won't be the truth." Billy must have told his parents. They'd probably keep him away until nobody cared anymore. If any of them deserved a break, it was Billy.

"Just wanted to make sure. Oh, and your father called. He and your lawyer will be here soon. You still okay? Anything you need?"

"Nothing, thanks." To help pass the time, he tapped his index finger on the table to a beat he guessed was one second each. At the count of one thousand-seven hundred-fifty-four, a knock hit the door. Officer Wilbur entered, followed by his father and a man who must have been Mr. Bender. His father had changed into a button-down white shirt and pinstriped suit pants, but his stubbly face and bleary eyes still made him look like a street bum. Standing, Wyatt let his father hug him, but he didn't hug back. He and his lawyer shook hands.

Mr. Bender, kinky gray hair and built like a linebacker, shoved a paper at Officer Wilbur. "This is an order releasing my client into his father's custody, immediately."

"Hasn't even been an arraignment, counselor," Officer Wilbur said, unfolding the paper. "Must be nice to be a judge's son." He flipped a glance at Wyatt before scanning the document. "This isn't my call. Wait here."

The instant Officer Wilbur closed the door, Mr. Bender shoved out his palm. "No talking. They record everything."

"Are you all right?" his father said, hooking a hand around Wyatt's neck and giving it a little shake. The man looked a hundred years old and ready to bawl, might even be drunk.

"Dad, I should've confessed a long—"

"Kid, are you deaf?" Eyes wide, jaw hanging, Mr. Bender faced his father and shrugged.

"Back off, Marty. Anything he says in your presence is attorney-client privilege. You know that."

"Judge, I don't tell you how to do your job. No talking."

He sat while his father and lawyer paced the room in silence.

Detective Dalton knocked and entered. "Gentlemen, nothing I can do about this," she said, fanning the air with the court order. "Captain says this has to go through the D.A.'s office, and that doesn't open until nine tomorrow. He's ours for tonight, I'm afraid."

"That's crap," Mr. Bender said. "Take me to him."

She shrugged. "Follow me."

"We'll get you out of here," his father said when they were alone. "You're going to sleep at home tonight. Promise."

"Dad, are you deaf? No talking." His father's reaction seemed the same as when they were on the phone an hour earlier, more sad than mad, but he couldn't feel sorry for him. Home. No such thing anymore. He was never going "home" again. It would be sick to spend another minute under that roof. By still living there, his father showed how little he cared about any of them. The bastard probably couldn't wait to screw Amanda in his dead wife's bed. Leave slut smell where his wife's shampoo and skin lotion still lingered.

"Wyatt, use your head."

"Go back to your house, Dad." No way he could

ever forgive his father. He may have loved and admired him once, but no more. "I don't want to know you, and I don't want your lawyer."

Teeth showed through his father's thinned lips. "I get it," he said. "You're good. I'm bad. Congratulations. But the hero part is over. Time to cut your losses. There's a process. Mr. Bender and I know what we're doing."

"Have a nice life, Dad." He dropped into a chair, covered his ears, and closed his eyes. Had to block out the slippery line of bullshit that was coming. The guy had made a fortune convincing people that wrong was right, but he wasn't going to fall for it. Humming in a loud voice helped tune out the noise, and then it stopped. Pressure in the room changed when the door slammed.

Calm and nervous grabbed him at the same time. The future had begun. Like his mother reminded him on the morning she died, he wasn't a prisoner to what either parent was, or what they'd done. He would be the new Carpenter, not the next. As witness to so many examples of how not to live, his choices going forward would be clear and simple. Bad things might be ahead for a while, but they'd be part of a caterpillar/butterfly thing. He admitted being afraid. Part of it was the dark alley kind, but there was another not-so-bad kind. Probably the kind immigrants felt once they were safely on the boat.

Chapter 48

Marty Bender stomped down the precinct corridor toward Jordan. "Stupid asshole won't budge." He stopped and pointed to the closed door of the interview room. "Why are you out here? Don't tell me one of them is in there with Wyatt. Who the hell—"

Jordan knocked the lawyer's hand away from the knob. "Let's go."

"Go? What are you talking about?" He rattled the folded court order in front of his face. "I went to a lot of trouble for this. They can't ignore it."

"Take me home."

Bender poked a thumb back over his shoulder. "They're just afraid of the media. Old boy cronies, special treatment for a rich kid, that kind of bullshit. They want *you* to call the D.A. so they have some cover. Do it. Five minutes and Wyatt's in the car with us." He looked puzzled when Jordan shook his head. "What," Bender said, reaching into his suit jacket, "you want me to call?"

"I said let's go." He pointed toward the exit and started for it.

"Mind telling me what the hell we're doing?" The bulky attorney trotted to catch up. "You make me leave a dinner party, track down a fucking judge, then pick you up. For what?"

"Marty." He paused and tipped his face to the

ceiling. "No talking."

He spent the ride home fighting off sleep and staring through the rain-sprinkled windshield. Before each sweep of the wipers, oncoming headlights and overhead street lamps animated the drizzle into bursts of sparkles, a diversion so hypnotic he was disappointed when the car stopped in front of his house.

"You got anyone in there, Judge?" Bender said, pushing the shift lever into *Park*. "You look terrible."

"Thanks for everything tonight, Marty." He shook the lawyer's hand. "Send your bill here, to the house."

"I'm out? I'm not defending Wyatt?"

"It appears his plans don't include either of us." He didn't know why he'd stayed silent about his own legal situation, but he had no interest in going through it at the moment. "I do have another client for you," he said, one foot out of the car, referring to himself. "I'll call you tomorrow."

"I should put you on commission. Sure you're okay?"

He nodded.

Bender handed him a card. "I don't know if you have this one. Cell number's in the lower right."

"Thanks again," he said, slipping the card into his pristine white shirt pocket.

Inside the house, he stood in the dark foyer. His last night there should feel meaningful somehow, but the best he could come up with was more of the '96 Romanee-Conti. Eyes still adjusting to the dimness, he shuffled into the billiard room. At the bar he located the half-empty decanter and a crystal glass. He spilled in a generous pour, swirled and sniffed. It hadn't turned. If the impossible happened, and his connections failed to keep him out of prison, good wine might be what he would miss most.

Glass in hand, he set off on a roam of the first floor. Like a museum visitor, he hugged the perimeter, slowing to examine objects, many of which he had no memory of seeing before. He hesitated before entering his office, a room he hadn't been in since Diane killed herself and Kevin.

Without turning on a light, he clicked the door behind him and crossed the empty space where his desk had been. Quiet rain wiggled down the window glass, the same window Diane had demanded being near during her convalescence. She'd tried to explain her fascination with the view to the ravine, and the reassuring, victor-less war between light and dark, but that was the same day Wyatt confessed, and only moments after she'd told him about her cancer. Nobody would have been interested in her mystical ramblings given those circumstances. He tented a hand over his eyes and leaned against the window glass. Even with rain muddling his view, the ravine was a darker dark than the night. He studied and waited. She'd said it was a daytime thing, but the night had light, and the earth never slowed. He should have been able to sense something.

Impatient for a clearer picture, he set his glass on the sill and hurried through the house and the garage. Outside, he slowed and shortened his stride. Fine, warm rain coated him as he approached the railing. He stepped over and inched along the cliff's edge, stopping directly above where the Volvo would sleep for one more night. Unable to detect any hint of the car, his gaze returned to the shapeless shadows in the vista.

She'd drawn enough inspiration from it to do the unthinkable. While he waited for something, anything, his clothes grew heavier. Chill spread. Mist collected into droplets in his hair, trickled through his brows, across his lashes, and along the sides of his nose. His shoes scuffed forward. Pebbles pinged and bumbled down the face of the ravine, taking some seconds before they fell silent.

"No," he whispered. Head shaking, he stood tall. She'd done her last thing to him. He slid one foot away from the rim, then the other. Jumping off would have been a witless follow-on to her drama. A false implication of his guilt and regret. And the fall might not have killed him. He could have become a cripple, a quadriplegic, subject to a degrading maintenance.

He scraped backward until his legs bumped the fence. Trembling hands clamped onto the rail as he hoisted himself over. Safely on the driveway, he froze. A pair of headlights sniffed their way up the driveway, weaving but always closer. They trained on him, the blinding glare growing larger until it stopped only feet away. Engine died. Lights stayed on. Driver's door opened.

"Thought I saw someone down here," Moseley said. "Judge, what the hell are you doing?"

This detective no longer had authority to arrest him. Surging relief revived him. "I could ask the same," he said, lurching toward the garage on stiff legs. "I thought we were done." A shudder rattled through him.

"How long you been out here?" Moseley said. "You're shaking like a starving dog." The detective's loping strides caught up with him at the side door of the garage. "OK if I come in?"

"I'm tired, Moseley," he said, stamping water onto the garage floor. "I'm going to bed."

"Detective Dalton called me, Judge. She said your son kicked you in the nuts pretty good tonight. She said that with all you've been through lately, well, maybe you could use a friend."

"We're friends?"

"She said 'a friend'. She doesn't know I'm here."

"So why are you?"

"She gave me the whole rundown of her interview with Wyatt, but nothing about where the car is, so I knew he hadn't told her."

"If he didn't, I'm certainly not. That is, assuming I even know."

"It's over, Judge. They brought in another kid, Tanner somebody. Says he has information. He's holding out for a deal."

Jordan smiled. "Poorly played, Tanner." There was nothing to leverage, unless the weasel believed he could dangle a corrupt federal judge.

"Why did you say that?"

"Good night, Moseley."

"Judge, the way I see it, you got maybe an hour before you're covered in shit. Me? I'd take the high road." He handed him a business card. "Connie's cell number is on the back. Cut her a break."

"Connie," Jordan said, nodding and slipping the card next to Marty Bender's in his soggy shirt pocket. "I see. Partners in other ways, as well?"

"I wish." Moseley smiled down at the painted concrete floor. "Probably got a better chance of seeing the Easter Bunny. Nah, she's a terrific person who was good to me when I didn't deserve it. Can't think of a better way to say thanks." Hand on the knob of the side door, he fired an index finger at Jordan. "Do the right thing, Judge. It feels good."

Chapter 49

Jordan waited until the sound of Moseley's car trailed off. During the short slog to the elevator, he pinched the two business cards from his shirt pocket and studied them. That maggot, Tanner, had fouled the timetable royally, so Moseley was probably right, the best tactic would be to call Detective Dalton, but Jordan knew he couldn't. Quivering, he paced the little elevator throughout the glacial ride. At the first floor, he wobbled through the wine room and into the billiard room on stiff legs, his arms stretching forward into the near darkness.

He bumped into the desk and patted for the remote. One click popped the fire to life and pulled him close to the flames. Bender's card found a spot on the mantel, but he spun Moseley's into the blaze. Trembling fingers unbuttoned his shirt while he watched the card dance on the thermals, settle onto a ceramic log, and shrivel into a black feather.

His sopping shirt sizzled and steamed on the logs. Slacks, underwear, and socks followed. Naked, he tottered in a slow circle. Warmth drew the rattling chill from his limbs. During each rotation, he squinted into dark corners, hoping to locate an evocative sound, something beyond the fire's roar.

The day's accumulated weight buckled his knees. Rather than topple into the flames, he dropped to his hands and knees on the warm hearth. Pain in his joints demanded he lie down. Avoiding the puddle of drips, he settled onto his side, close enough yet far enough from the blaze. The fire's draft chilled his back. He rolled over. Colder still, so he faced forward again. A hot shower and warm bed waited upstairs, but he had neither the ability to stand nor the will to leave the warmth he already had. Powerless, he surrendered to sobbing, embraced it.

The doorbell startled him. "That was no hour," he said, swiping wetness from his eyes and face.

"Judge Carpenter," a woman hollered. A fist pounded on the door. "Police. Open up."

Detective Dalton's voice. He inched closer to the flames, eyes squeezed shut.

"It's Moseley, Judge. I know you're in there. I can see you still have that fireplace going." More pounding. "C'mon. Don't make us break it down."

Moseley shouldn't have been there. Wrong voices were everywhere. He tucked his knees to his chest and covered his ears against the rising babble. "You're not winning," he said, tears dropping faster.

"Coming in, Judge," Detective Dalton shouted. "Stand clear." Something chewed and splintered the front door. It crashed into the entry.

Air rushed against him faster. He cupped muffling hands over his mouth.

"It's me, Judge," Moseley said from somewhere nearby. Hinges creaked. "Dalton, call for an ambulance."

He shuddered when a hand gripped his shoulder.

"They're on their way," Detective Dalton said. "Chuck and I got this, Lenny. You better take off now.

And thanks."

One last stab at innocence. "Moseley," he said, his prized baritone reduced to a squeal, "she had no right."

"Judge, she has a warrant."

Someone killed the fire.

Discussion Topics:

1. Do you think there's ever a valid reason for suicide?
2. Do you think Jordan was at all justified in his belief that Diane was out to get him?
3. Do you think Diane was wounded or evil?
4. What would you do to protect a child? Can you understand Diane's reasoning?
5. What were the contrasts between the Carpenter and Califano families?
6. Should Wyatt have allowed his father's guidance after surrendering?
7. Is failing to make a decision a decision?
8. Was the ending satisfying?
9. After finishing the book, did the title make sense?

A word about the author...

Rick Maloy attended Villanova and Fairleigh Dickinson Universities, graduating with a BS in Business Management. He committed to full-time writing after selling his NYC financial services business in 2004. His stories have won and placed in the Florida First Coast Writers' short fiction contests. Other stories have appeared in numerous e-zines until he turned his focus to novels. *Evenings and Mournings* is his second release.

Rick and his first-and-only wife, Ann Marie, live in Ponte Vedra Beach, Florida. He can be reached at: rick@rickmaloy.com.

Made in the USA
Lexington, KY
12 February 2018